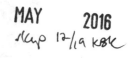

APOCALYPSE Z  DARK DAYS

APOCALYPSE Z SERIES

THE BEGINNING OF THE END

THE WRATH OF THE JUST
(FORTHCOMING)

APOCALYPSE Z
DARK DAYS

MANEL LOUREIRO

TRANSLATED BY PAMELA CARMELL

amazon crossing

The characters and events portrayed in this book are fictitious. Any similarity to real persons, living or dead, is coincidental and not intended by the author.

Text copyright © 2010 by Manel Loureiro
English translation copyright © 2013 by Pamela Carmell

Apocalypse Z: Dark Days was first published in Spain by Dolmen as *Los Días Oscuros*. Translated from Spanish by Pamela Carmell. Published in English by AmazonCrossing in 2013.

Published by AmazonCrossing

www.apub.com

P.O. Box 400818
Las Vegas, NV 89140

ISBN-13: 9781477809310
ISBN-10: 1477809317
Library of Congress Control Number: 2013909115

For Maribel,
who didn't live to see it,
but who would have loved it
the most

Their slain also shall be cast out, and their stink
shall come up out of their carcasses, and the mountains
shall be melted with their blood.

—*Isaiah 34:3*

SOMEWHERE OVER
THE WESTERN SAHARA

A little lizard sat motionless for hours on a sun-baked rock in a bleak corner of the Sahara desert. His sides expanded and contracted as he breathed in air as hot as a blast from hell. He flicked out his rough tongue, testing the air, biding his time till nightfall when he could go hunting.

Suddenly, the lizard detected a sound too low to be heard by human ears. He cowered under the rock in case some strange, fearsome predator was making that noise.

After a few seconds, the sound overhead crescendoed from a slight hum to a deafening rattle. The sound grew fainter and fainter, and then was gone.

The little lizard cautiously poked his head out and blinked his gummy eyes in the fierce midday light. For an instant, he stared up into the ruthlessly bright blue sky as the Sahara shimmered in the heat.

If he'd stuck his head out thirty seconds sooner, he'd have glimpsed something completely out of place in that corner of the world: a huge, yellow and white Sokol helicopter, with the faded logo of the AUTONOMOUS GOVERNMENT OF GALICIA painted on one side and a cargo net, filled with fuel drums, hanging from its underbelly. The pilot, a small guy in his forties, with a bushy, blond mustache, had a tired but determined look on his face; some fingers were missing from his right hand. In the copilot's seat was a tall, thin man in his thirties with a scraggly beard

1

and sharp features. His profoundly weary eyes stared blankly at the un-folding desert landscape, his mind very far away, as he slowly pet a large Persian cat asleep on his lap. Rounding out the odd group were an older woman and a teenaged girl sitting in the passengers' seats.

The thin man would've told anyone who'd listen that he'd had an uneventful life as a small-town lawyer in northern Spain, dividing his time among work, family, and friends. The death of his young wife just a year before the Apocalypse had left a huge, painful hole in his heart and turned his life into a relentless cycle of pain and routine. Until the Apocalypse nearly a year ago, when everything went to hell.

Everything.

At first, he didn't pay much attention to the brief, conflicting re-ports in the press about a jihadist faction that had the brilliant idea to attack a Russian army base in Dagestan, a remote former Soviet repub-lic; take hostages; and steal either chemical or conventional weapons to sell on the black market.

What those attackers didn't know was that research into biological weapons had been carried out at that base. Some of the world's most virulent strains of viruses were sleeping peacefully in test tubes there. To be fair, the jihadists weren't really to blame. That base was a half-forgotten detritus of the old Soviet empire; Western intelligence agencies didn't even know it existed. Compared to what came next, the break-in was small potatoes.

Depending on how you look at it, the attack was successful—or a horrible failure. The jihadists successfully took over the base, but they accidentally released a viral strain that should never have been created. Less than forty-eight hours after the attack, all the terrorists were dead. Or kind of dead.

The worst part was that that virus was now free. And nothing and no one could stop it from spreading like wildfire.

At first, no one knew anything about it. In the old, over-confident Europe, as well as in America and Asia, life went on calmly and peace-fully. During those first seventy-two hours, something could've been done to get the pandemic under control. However, Dagestan was a very small, very poor country; its government didn't have the resources to stop the virus. The virus was already past the incubation phase.

By then it was too late.

No one, not even our Spanish lawyer, became worried until a few days later. The first news of a rare hemorrhagic fever sweeping the Caucasus Mountains was just background noise in the newspapers and on TV, drowned out by the final picks for the European soccer championship and the latest political scandal.

Almost no one paid attention to that virus, so it just kept spreading. A few days passed before anyone realized that something was terribly wrong. Large areas of Dagestan were dark and silent, as if there wasn't a single living soul left. The government of that tiny republic took a closer look. Terrified by what it saw, it called upon Moscow for help. The Russians were so horrified by the situation, they immediately closed their borders with Dagestan—and with every country on its border. Too late to do any good.

The news started filtering out to the rest of the world, sounding at first like confusing nonsense. Then a series of conflicting reports from the Russian government, the CDC in Atlanta, and several other organizations claimed it was an outbreak of Ebola or smallpox or West Nile virus or the Marburg virus that first broke out in Germany in the sixties—or none of the above. Outrageous rumors, blown out of proportion, started to circulate. The shadow of darkness leapt from Dagestan to neighboring countries, as refugees fled "it." Whatever "it" was. Putin's government declared a news blackout in an effort to get the situation under control, suppressing freedom of the press within the Russian Federation, then finally broke down and requested emergency aid from the international community.

But, once again, it was too late.

By that time our lawyer and most of humanity were waiting in suspense for updates on what was happening in that corner of the world. It was no longer back-page news; reports were splashed across every front page. Despite heavy censorship, images leaked out, showing lines of refugees stretching as far as the eye could see and columns of soldiers just as long. The most observant commentators remarked that it was strange for the army to be battling the epidemic, but they were in the minority. Most people just paid attention to the official report. Finally, international aid teams were deployed to help control the epidemic. Fifteen days before, they'd have had a chance for success.

But not any longer.

A few days later, the epidemic went global when aid teams returned home, taking with them members of their group who'd been injured by those things. Although no one realized it, the pandemic was now definitely out of control. The logical thing would have been to "eliminate" anyone infected, since governments were beginning to understand what they were facing, but political interests and public opinion overrode common sense.

The last chance to control the pandemic evaporated and the virus began its deadly march, turning the pandemic into an Apocalypse.

At that point, our Spanish lawyer was as terrified as the rest of the world. Reports of the pandemic raged nonstop on newspapers, TV, radio, and the Internet. He watched helplessly as the virus slowly gained ground, day by day. Soon there was no news from Dagestan. Russia went dark a few days later. Then Poland, Finland, Turkey, Iran, and on and on throughout every country in the world. Most European countries sealed off their borders and declared martial law but the virus spread like an oil spill across the planet. In an unprecedented move, the European Union unanimously agreed to form a single office of crisis management that continued to keep a tight grip on information and doled out the news in dribs and drabs. But reports kept turning up on the Internet. There were almost as many theories and unsettling rumors of the walking dead as websites, claiming it was an alien invasion, the Antichrist, genetic experiments, or monsters from the Underworld.

But everyone agreed on one thing: Whatever it was, it was very contagious and deadly. Anyone who got infected spread the disease.

That crisis, which had been described briefly in the news just two weeks before, finally reached Spain. The point was driven home to our lawyer the day he saw King Juan Carlos on TV declaring martial law, dressed in his military uniform the way he did during the attempted coup d'état in 1981.

Then, of all the misguided plans those governments came up with, they picked the worst. In keeping with overriding medical logic—isolate the healthy from the sick—they decided to concentrate the healthy population into enclosures around the country called Safe Havens, huge sections of town, surrounded by security forces. By then everyone understood that contact with an infected person ended very badly.

What our lawyer chose to do next turned out to be the best move. He didn't want to go to a Safe Haven; it sounded suspiciously like the Warsaw ghetto. When the army's evacuation team swept through his neighborhood, he hid in his house. Everyone else left, but he chose to stay behind. Alone. But not for long.

In a matter of days, the world began to crumble. Electricity and communication systems began to fail as crews didn't show up for work or simply disappeared. Soon TV channels worldwide emitted only pre-recorded shows interrupted by news briefs that hysterically ordered everyone to gather in the Safe Havens. By then, censorship was completely breaking down. Officials acknowledged that infected people somehow came back to life after they died and became extremely aggressive toward the living. It was like something out of a B-movie and would've been laughable, if it weren't true. And if the entire world hadn't fallen apart in a matter of days.

That little monster accidentally freed from its test tube twenty days before finally showed its true face.

What happened in forty-eight hours was hard to explain. Infrastructure was falling apart everywhere; the electrical grid was failing all over the world and no one had a global vision. Safe Havens proved to be death traps; the noise and activity of the humans congregated there drew the Undead like a magnet. When hordes of Undead besieged those Safe Havens, panic broke out and those centers fell, overrun by the monsters. Most of the refugees were changed into Undead. The official message on the few surviving TV channels changed dramatically: Stay away from the Safe Havens.

But once again, that message came too late. The situation was beyond anyone's control.

Our lawyer, isolated at home, in a deserted neighborhood, with only his Persian cat named Lucullus for company, watched in amazement. When the Internet finally shut down, he braced for the worst.

And it came quickly. Less than forty-eight hours later, the first Undead wandered down his quiet, suburban street in northern Spain. He was trapped in his own home. Over the next few days, he watched the relentless parade of Undead in terror from his window.

A few days later he decided to head for the Safe Haven in Vigo, the closest major city. He was desperate to see other humans, plus he was running out of food and water. He had two choices: Try to dodge the Undead to get some place safe, or die of starvation at home. Despite the warnings, a Safe Haven became his only option.

So he headed off on a perilous journey and for several days his life was in constant jeopardy. He drove through destroyed villages to the Port of Pontevedra, veering around car wrecks no one had cleared away. From there, he sailed for Vigo in an abandoned sailboat. When he finally reached the Vigo Safe Haven, his last hope collapsed—it was in ruins. No one was alive there and thousands of Undead wandered aimlessly.

He was seriously considering suicide when he spotted a rusty old freighter, the *Zaren Kibish*, anchored in the harbor, with a ragtag crew of survivors huddled onboard. Its captain recounted the horrors of the last hours of the Vigo Safe Haven and how it fell, like so many places around the world, from hunger and disease and the assault by the Undead.

Once again, fortune smiled on our lawyer. Aboard the *Zaren Kibish*, he met one of the few survivors of the Vigo Safe Haven, a Ukrainian guy named Viktor "Prit" Pritchenko. He was a short guy in his forties, with a huge, blond mustache and ice-blue eyes. He turned out to be one of the Eastern European helicopter pilots the Spanish government had hired every summer to fight forest fires. Another solitary man trapped far from home and family. Pritchenko decided to befriend our lawyer.

After several terrifying weeks facing the Undead and the *Zaren Kibish*'s despotic, mentally unstable captain, they finally devised a plan. They would try to reach the Ukrainian's Sokol helicopter that was parked at the forest ranger base camp a few miles from the port. From there, they'd fly to the Canary Islands. Because those islands were so isolated, they were one of the few places in the world that had escaped the pandemic. According to the last news reports, remnants of the Spanish government and a few survivors had gathered there.

The only problem was they had to evade the deranged ship's captain and his armed crew, who were obsessed with their plans to save their own hides, plans in which Prit and the lawyer were just pawns to be sacrificed. After a risky journey across the ravaged city of Vigo, they finally escaped with high hopes.

But one last test of their courage remained.

In an abandoned car dealership where they'd taken shelter for the night, Pritchenko suffered a freak accident while handling a small explosive device, causing second-degree burns and the loss of several fingers. In the past, that wouldn't have been a life-threatening accident, but in those difficult days, it was. With his friend on the verge of dying, the lawyer scoured Vigo for a hospital. He knew he wouldn't find a doctor and most likely any hospital would be infested with Undead, but he had to find the medicine his friend needed.

He didn't figure on getting lost in the bowels of a huge, abandoned hospital, surrounded by Undead, its dark corridors, halls, and stairs a death trap.

Just when the situation seemed hopeless, Lucia came to their rescue. Seventeen, tall, slender, with long black hair and deep green eyes, she was the last person they'd expected to find in that cavernous building. Finding her in that grisly nightmare was so incongruous, our heroes thought they were hallucinating. When the girl told her story, they realized she was also a terrified survivor that fate had mercifully set down there.

During the migration to Safe Havens, Lucia had gotten separated from her family. She'd wandered around the area, trying to locate her missing parents, and had ended up there. Like thousands of people adrift in that confusion, she didn't find her loved ones, but she stayed on as an aide to the exhausted doctors stubbornly trying to keep the hospital up and running.

When masses of Undead converged on the building, Lucia retreated to the safety of the vast basement of the hospital. It was well provisioned and watertight; its doors were heavily reinforced. Her only company was Sister Cecilia, a nun with training as a nurse, who volunteered to stay at the hospital until the end. They'd been holed up in the basement ever since, waiting for rescue teams that never came.

When Lucia heard gunfire and human voices ricocheting through the halls, she left the safety of their shelter to investigate. She was equally surprised to come across the lawyer and the pilot. Instead of a battle-hardened rescue team, she found a pair of dirty, hungry, lost refugees, one of them gravely injured, both on the verge of emotional collapse. She sprang into action like a much older, wiser woman, dragging the two survivors and their orange cat to the basement, where Sister Cecilia, the only living nurse for hundreds of miles, tended to the Ukrainian's wounds. After weeks of terror, the lawyer and his friend had finally found a true safe haven.

The next few months passed like a dream. Comfortably holed up in that basement, fortified with electrical generators and enough food for hundreds of people, the four survivors found some peace and respite in that underground existence, hoping to find a way back to the outside world.

But another surprise forced them to leave their cozy den and revive their plan to fly to the Canary Islands. A powerful summer thunderstorm started a fire a few miles from the hospital. With no one to fight the blaze, it burned out of control, across that deserted landscape of flammable debris and dry brush, right up to the hospital doors. The four survivors escaped that firestorm with barely enough time to grab their gear.

Two days later, they topped off the helicopter's fuel tanks, stored drums of fuel in a cargo net hung from the chopper's belly, and headed for the Canary Islands, where they thought they'd find vestiges of humanity. They had just one goal. To survive.

1

"Prit! Prit! Can you hear me?" I asked. "You crazy Ukrainian," I cursed under my breath. The damn intercom had cut out for the third time since we took off from Vigo. I grabbed a bracket on the wall as the heavy helicopter hit another pocket of hot air and lurched. Unfazed, Prit steered through it at top speed. Though Prit couldn't hear me through the intercom, I could hear him happily humming his dreadful rendition of James Brown's "I Feel Good."

I set Lucullus in his carrier. I envied the way that orange ball of fur could fall asleep, oblivious to the roar of the engines. How the hell could he stand it? Even muffled by our helmets, the noise was driving me crazy after five days straight. Cats can adapt to anything, I guess.

I peered behind me into the passenger cabin. Sister Cecilia was belted in tight, praying in a monotone voice as she slowly fingered her rosary. In her spotless habit and huge red helmet, the little nun was quite a sight, marred only by her slightly green face and her worried look every time the helicopter hit some turbulence. Flying didn't sit well with the nun, but she'd been stoic, not complaining once.

Lucia was sound asleep, stretched out in the front seat, a vision even in frayed shorts and a tight, oil-stained T-shirt (she'd gotten dirty helping Prit at our last stop). I brushed a lock of hair out of her eyes, trying not to wake her.

I sighed. My feelings for that girl created a big problem and I didn't know how to resolve it. Over the last five days, Lucia and I had been stuck together like glue. I couldn't deny that I was deeply attracted to her olive skin, long legs, her curves, and cat eyes, but I was trying to keep my cool. For starters, it wasn't the time or place for an affair. And then there was the age difference. She was a seventeen-year-old kid and I was a thirty-year-old man. A thirteen-year difference was no small thing.

Lucia moved in her sleep and muttered something I couldn't make out. The look of pleasure on her face made me swallow. I needed some air.

I inched down the narrow corridor connecting the cargo bay with the cockpit and dropped into the seat beside Pritchenko. The Ukrainian turned, flashed a big smile, and handed me his thermos. I took the thermos and knocked back a long drink. Tears filled my eyes and I coughed, trying to catch my breath. That coffee was about fifty percent vodka.

"Coffee with a kick." The Ukrainian snatched the thermos out of my hands and chugged half its contents. He didn't even blink. Then he pounded on his chest and belched loudly. "Much better for flying." He passed the thermos back to me. "Yes sir. Much better." He smacked his lips, satisfied. A big smile spread across his face. "In Chechnya, my squadron drank our vodka straight . . . but it was colder there," he said with a laugh.

I shook my head. Prit was a lost cause. Inside the hot cockpit, the Ukrainian was shirtless, drenched with sweat. He was wearing worn fatigues, a huge black cowboy hat he'd found in a bar, and green mirrored sunglasses. His imposing mustache was the only part of his face I could actually see. He reminded me of a character in *Apocalypse Now*.

There was no doubt that Prit was an impressive pilot. In Vigo, he managed to get that chopper into the air, even though it was loaded down with tons of fuel in its tank and several more in drums hanging under its belly.

Images of that trip played over and over in my mind. Every day, we grasped the true scope of the Apocalypse. And what we saw convinced us that human civilization had gone to hell.

The first few hours were the worst. As we'd headed south along the coast of Portugal just a few hundred feet in the air, we gazed slack-jawed at the widespread chaos and desolation.

The light caught our attention first. The air was unusually clear, almost transparent since factories had been closed for months and no cars were polluting it. If it weren't for the smell of rotting flesh and trash all around, you'd have thought you were in an untouched wilderness from five thousand years ago. One look at the stiffs walking around everywhere shattered that illusion.

The highways were completely impassable. The twisted remains of cars dotted the pavement every few miles, and monstrous pileups often blocked the road entirely. We even saw a couple of collapsed viaducts and highways completely covered by landslides. An especially steep stretch of the highway that linked Oporto to Lisbon had become a wild, raging stream several miles long. Water from a broken dam flowed freely, creating little peaks of foam as it careened against reefs made from the remains of cars.

Nature was slowly reclaiming her terrain. Proud human constructions, wondrous feats of engineering, were slowly being devoured by weeds, water, earth, and whatever else God put in their way.

A crackling in the helmet's intercom yanked me out of my daydream and back to the Sahara. The fucking radio had decided to work again.

"The fuel tank is almost empty." Prit's voice sounded metallic in my ears. "I'm going to take a pass over this area. Look for a good place to land."

And keep your eyes open, I told myself. *We don't want any more fucking problems, not when we're so close.*

The other pit stops had gone reasonably well, but we couldn't be too careful. I had to remember what happened the day before.

2

In a God-forsaken place between Portugal and Extremadura, a desolate region in western Spain, Prit landed the helicopter in a parking lot next to a roadside diner. The entire expanse of cement was empty except for a rusty Volkswagen SUV and a Fiat hatchback with four flat tires. The restaurant looked abandoned and lonely, its neon sign covered by a year's worth of dust.

As it landed, the Sokol kicked up a huge cloud of dust and sand. Before it could settle, Prit and I jumped out of the chopper, pistols in hand, our hearts in our throats, peering desperately through that ragged cloud for Undead staggering around the area.

After we made sure the parking lot was deserted, my heart quit racing. When the Sokol's engines were turned off, a deathly silence spread over the parking lot. There wasn't a single sound, not even birds chirping. The roar of the helicopter must've frightened them all off. Or maybe there were no fucking birds left in the area.

For a moment, I got the uneasy feeling we were the last people left on the face of the earth. Just then Lucullus got spooked and let out a strange meow that woke me out of my trance.

Pritchenko and Lucia ran over to the helicopter's transport net, unhooked it, and folded it back, revealing the yellow drums filled with jet fuel. Pushing aside the empties, the Ukrainian rolled a full drum up to the helicopter. With a flick of his wrist, he popped the cap open and inserted a rubber hose, connected the other end to the Sokol's tank, and let the fuel flow into the bird.

During the few minutes it took to fill the tank, we were extremely vulnerable. With the chopper on the ground, its cargo net open and highly flammable liquid pumping into its tank, a fast takeoff was out of the question. If any Undead had shown up, we'd have been screwed. After making sure nothing was moving in the area, I motioned to Prit that I was going to grab a cigarette. All I found while scrounging around in the cabin were a couple of squashed, damp Camels. That pissed me off. We'd taken plenty of supplies and medicine from the hospital, but we were running really low on smokes.

I gazed over at the restaurant at the far end of the parking lot: dubious. It was a dive, but I'd have bet a million euros there was a cigarette machine by the door. The place looked deserted, so I decided to check it out.

Before I headed for the restaurant, I turned to tell everyone I was going. Prit and Lucia had their backs to me and were in a heated debate about how to stack the empty drums in the net. Sister Cecilia was taking a quick nap, glad for a break from those terrifying heights and to be back on terra firma. Lucullus was indifferent to me, as he groomed himself, oblivious to the world. I shrugged. I'd only be gone a minute.

The door was locked, so I looked around for another way in. Flower pots filled with wilted plants were lined up in front. A sun-bleached sign for ice cream lay on the ground next to a tattered umbrella, a dust-encrusted table, and a couple of plastic chairs. Tossed in the far corner, collecting dirt, was a denim jacket so faded its color was unrecognizable. The door wouldn't budge. I had better luck with one of the old wood-frame windows that opened into the kitchen. The passage of time and the heat generated by the grill had warped it, leaving it open a few inches at the top. I drew out my knife and stuck the blade in the gap to jimmy it open. After a minute or two, the latch broke with a dull *crack*. The window rose silently, leaving enough room for me to climb into the cool, shady interior.

I stealthily made my way into the kitchen, peering into the darkness. The change from bright light to shadows left me blinded for a few seconds. To make matters worse, the rotten smell took my breath away. I covered my nose with my sleeve. My eyes teared up and bile rose in my throat.

As I got accustomed to the half-light, I could make out details in the kitchen. The smell was coming from a huge, industrial freezer standing wide open. Hundreds of pounds of pork and beef had been rotting in there for months. On the counter, thousands of maggots swarmed over what had once been pork ribs and were even crawling on the handle of the knife lying beside the meat. Next to that, a pile of rotten tomatoes waited for someone to slice them for a salad that would never be served. On the stove was a scorched pan; the smoke it gave off as it burned had left a large ring on the ceiling. The gas jet remained open, but the gas had long since run out. It was a miracle the place hadn't burned to the ground.

Judging from the scene, the folks in that greasy spoon had fled in panic, not stopping to do the most basic things. I knew exactly what had frightened them so much.

I eased the kitchen door open. A dozen tables covered with rotting food were arranged around the dining room. It looked like a still life in chiaroscuro some great artist had painted. A purse hung from the back of a chair, abandoned by its owner as she fled.

I looked around the charmless room till I spotted a cigarette vending machine next to the bar. A calendar, forever open to February, was stuck to the mirror, surrounded by bottles of cognac, photos of Real Madrid and team flags. I slipped behind the bar and rummaged through drawers crammed with receipts till I found a bunch of keys. I smiled, pleased to find that one of those keys opened the cigarette machine.

From outside came the muffled sound of metal cans clanking together, signaling that Prit and Lucia were closing up the cargo net and were ready to take off. I panicked as I pictured them taking off without me, leaving me in that dirty, forgotten corner, far from the hand of God. That was a ridiculous idea, completely unfounded, but to a mind with so little rest, it seemed plausible. I rushed around, stuffing as many packs as I could into my backpack, spilling cigarettes onto the floor. I even grabbed the cheap brands. Who knew where I'd find the next supply?

I was about to leave when I decided I'd better finally answer the call of nature. After flying for seven hours without a break, my bladder was about to explode. Prit bragged that he could piss into a bottle as he was flying. No doubt he could, but the idea of peeing in front of a nun and a seventeen-year-old hottie just didn't sit well with me, so I'd held it. Until then.

I slung my rifle across my back and unzipped my pants on the way to the john to save time. As I stood at the urinal, I felt a huge sense of relief.

Just as I was zipping up, I saw a hand reflected in the chrome urinal. Behind that hand, an arm, then the rest of the woman. She was enormous, around two hundred pounds. What was left of her curly hair was in fat ringlets. Someone—or something—had eaten half her face and ripped her arms out of their sockets. I spotted a half-devoured arm lying in a pool of dried blood on the bathroom floor. The arm I'd seen coming through the door was attached to her shoulder by just a couple of tendons; it swayed wildly as she lurched from side to side.

Before I could turn around, the monster jumped on me and flattened me against the wall. I felt her breath on my neck and heard her teeth clanking against the barrel of the rifle on my back. Fortunately she didn't have any arms, otherwise she'd have stopped me cold. I fought off her first onslaught, but the situation was still dire. Bracing my hands on the wall, I pushed back but the thing's teeth had a firm grip on my rifle. Just then, my feet slipped out from under me.

We hit the ground and rolled. I wriggled free of her dead weight and started crawling to the door. I watched in horror as she ferociously chomped down on one of my boots. With my other foot, I flailed around wildly, kicking her in the gaping red hole that had once been her face.

I didn't want to die. Not there in the filthy bathroom of that God-forsaken roadhouse, dragging myself along the ground with my pants unzipped.

With both hands I grabbed one of the spears I always carried in the sheath strapped to my leg (my spear gun was back in the helicopter). I raised it over my head and plunged it into the center of that creature's skull. With a soft squish, the spear's steel tip slid into her head till it reached bone, where it stuck.

Holy Christ! The whole thing was over in a flash—fifteen seconds, tops.

I inched up the wall and got to my feet, never taking my eyes off that Undead thing. As always after a fight like that, my stomach was in knots, and I broke out in a cold sweat. I tried to light a cigarette, but my hands were trembling so much, I couldn't flick the wheel of the lighter, so I gave up.

I staggered out of the bathroom, with the bitter taste of vomit in my mouth, feeling the adrenaline coursing through me. I'd never get used to killing one of those creatures. I felt sick every time, even though I knew they weren't alive. Every time my life was in danger, terror paralyzed me. And every night, for so many months, horrible nightmares were my bed companions.

I wasn't the only one. Lucia tossed and turned at night, fleeing the nightmares that hounded her. Prit would wake up suddenly with a crazed look in his eyes. He'd stare blankly into space for hours, then knock back the better part of a bottle of vodka. When I woke up in the middle of the night, I must've had the same expression on my face. No one had gotten more than five hours of sleep for months.

I finally managed to light a cigarette and bolted out the door. I squinted in the sunlight, disoriented for a moment. I turned toward the Sokol, whose huge blades were slowly tracing large circles in the air. From the copilot window, Lucia was scrutinizing me, as Pritchenko checked all the fluids before taking off.

I dragged my feet through the dust as I walked back to the helicopter. Lucia watched me with a piercing gaze. She must've guessed what had happened. I was exhausted and emotionally drained. That little episode was a summary of what my life had become—a nightmare that never let up.

3

"Come in! *Dabai! Dabai!* Do you read me?" Prit's voice rang out over the intercom amid crackles and pops. I was so lost in thought I hadn't heard him. I shook my head to push the nightmares out of my mind and focused on the Sokol as it shot like an arrow across the Sahara.

"Talk to me, Prit!" I yelled into the microphone over the howl of the engines, as the helicopter traced a wide spiral above the ground.

"That might be a good place to land."

I looked where he was pointing. We were flying over a miserable little town that clung to the Atlantic shore, where the sands of the Sahara sank under the cold ocean. There were about twenty houses and a whitewashed mosque ringed by fields of stunted crops. Half a dozen long, sun-bleached fishing boats rested on the beach. A dusty road ran north and south through town and disappeared in the distance.

At the southern end of the town was a large open space, about five hundred feet from the nearest houses, surrounded by a dilapidated wood fence and thorny bushes. Probably a goat pen once, but there was no sign of any goats. A perfect place to land.

With a long, graceful pirouette, Prit brought the chopper down, until we were hovering about twenty feet above the goat pen. The fuel drums clanked against each other as the cargo net settled on the ground. With a light flick of the controls, the Ukrainian landed the helicopter alongside the net. In just a few seconds, the Sokol was back on land, kicking up a sandstorm and blowing down the wood fence.

When the sand settled, we calmly scoped out the space around us. The silence was broken only by the wind filtering between the adobe houses. Instantly, we felt the sweltering heat. It must've been over 110 degrees. The air was dense, thick like hot soup; just drawing a breath was an effort. Even in the best of times, that bleak town at the barren edge of the desert wouldn't have been a pleasant place to live. Now uninhabited and in ruins, it looked ominous.

On high alert, Prit and I ventured out of the enclosure to take a look around and stretch our legs after hours and hours of flying. The town's main road was in horrible shape; huge potholes had swallowed up chunks of pavement and were then covered over with sand. No one had set foot on it in months.

We headed into town cautiously, picking our way down the middle of the road. That town was very close to where the Polisario Liberation Front had fought to end Spanish colonial rule in northern Africa. Many of the roadside ditches in the area were strewn with land mines set by the Polisario or the Moroccan army. Getting blown to bits by a land mine so close to the Canary Islands would've really sucked.

One of the first houses we came to had a strong smell, like spoiled milk. It wasn't the usual smell of rotting flesh. The softer, sour, even spicy smell confused us.

With a nod, we quietly cocked our rifles. We took a deep breath and darted around the corner, aiming wildly in every direction.

The Ukrainian looked completely bewildered. "What the hell is that?"

"No fucking idea, Prit." I lowered my gun and scratched my head. "I'm just glad I wasn't here when it happened."

Stretched on the ground at the end of the narrow alley in front of us were about two dozen bodies that looked like so many others we'd seen. The difference was these bodies hadn't decomposed. The scorching heat and the extremely dry desert air had mummified them. Their tattered clothing barely covered their skeletal limbs that the sun had scorched a dark mahogany. What skin remained was stretched as tight as a drum.

Cautiously, we eased up to the bodies. They reminded me of the mummies in the Egyptian Museum in Cairo. When I kicked the nearest one, the sound was like a piece of firewood. They were completely dehydrated.

Almost all the bodies were mutilated and had numerous wounds, such as gunshots to the head, along with dried blood on their clothes. After months of living among the Undead, we knew what those beings had been before someone offed them.

Prit bent down and picked up a shiny copper casing lying on the ground. He took a quick look and said, "5.56 NATO. Probably from a rifle like the one slung across your back." He didn't need to say another word.

The Moroccan army still used the old 7.62 x 51mm CETME that the Spanish military sold them by the thousands when it upgraded in the nineties. That meant that the regular Moroccan army hadn't done that. But who had—and when?

Suddenly a deep growl came from the pile of corpses. Prit and I jumped as if we'd been poked with a cattle prod. We heard the growl again, deep and raspy, but nothing moved in that motionless heap of human remains.

I nervously released the safety on my HK and shot Prit a puzzled look. The Ukrainian licked his dry lips, hesitated, then inched up to the mound as if it were an atomic bomb.

We heard that growl a third time. It was coming from a body sitting on the ground against a wall, legs outstretched, arms by his sides, and his head resting on his chest. The guy was riddled with bullet holes. Tainted blood stained the wall behind him, tracing the path his body had taken as it slid down. Both knees had been destroyed by gunshots; a couple of dried-up tendons were all that held one leg to his body.

I whistled softly. I couldn't believe my eyes. That Undead guy had had the bad luck to survive the gunshots. None of them were to the head so they'd only crippled him. Abandoned in that alley for months, drying in the desert sun, he'd been unable to move and unable to die.

I leaned in for a closer look. His limbs were completely dehydrated and rigid; his flesh was slowly turning to jerky or wood. That son of a bitch couldn't move a muscle, but there was still a glimmer in his withered eyeballs. For the first time, I felt sorry for one of those things. I couldn't imagine the hell of inhabiting that piece of wood. I doubted he knew what he was, but deep down in that dried-out skull dwelled a furious, raving mad being, trapped in there forever. With that discovery, we relaxed a little. Any Undead in the area more than a few weeks old would be in the same sorry state, dry as esparto grass and unable to move.

How ironic, I thought bitterly. The most uninhabitable places on earth—the deserts—were the only places humans would be safe. But the fact that they were uninhabitable ruled them out as the place for humans to settle.

Prit was staring at the beast. I could tell some deep thought was crossing his mind.

"Prit, what's up, man?" When I put a hand on his shoulder, the Ukrainian flinched.

"I was thinking . . ." He licked his lips, hesitating. "If extreme heat can do this to those things, then the cold can freeze them. You follow me?"

"I don't know where you're going with this, Prit, but I don't think . . ."

"Winter in Germany is hard, very hard." His eyes shone with excitement. "My wife and son were in Dusseldorf, where winter temperatures hover around ten degrees below freezing. If all the Undead froze, maybe my family is okay!" The Ukrainian was so excited he was nearly jumping up and down. "Maybe we should go there!"

I looked at my friend with dismay. He still clung to the hope that his family was alive. "Prit, I think you're confused," I said gently, trying not to hurt his feelings. "Extreme heat and extreme cold aren't the same. I doubt those Undead would freeze to death, as long as they keep moving. Maybe in places where the temperature is fifty or sixty degrees below freezing, but human life is nearly impossible there, too."

"But . . . I don't understand why . . ." Anxiety contorted my friend's face.

"Prit, think for a minute. The condition these bastards are in is the result of dehydration, not temperature," I explained, pointing to the Undead at our feet. "The human body is largely made up of water; very high temperatures dry up all that moisture. No matter how cold it gets up north, there'll always be enough moisture in the air to keep those bastards going."

The letdown in Pritchenko's eyes told me he understood what I'd said. The chances that his family was still alive in Germany were slim. *Like my family's chances*, I thought bitterly. We were the Last of the Mohicans. We moved away slowly, but not before Prit, out of hate or pity, jabbed his knife into the Undead guy's eye. The creature's grunts stopped immediately.

Exploring the rest of the town yielded no surprises. Whoever exterminated all the Undead had cleaned out the place. We found nothing useful: no food to replace our rapidly dwindling supplies, no fuel, no weapons, and no water. The village had a deep well, shaded by a shed, situated in front of the mosque. The villagers had used a motorized pump to draw up the water, but there was no trace of that motor. The looters had taken it. All they'd left behind were the bolts that had attached it to the floor of the shed.

The adobe walls of the houses had cracked in the sweltering desert heat. Strong winds had carried off some of the roofs. In a couple of years, if no one intervened, the desert would swallow up that town. It would disappear, as if it had never existed.

The sun was setting over the ocean, turning the sky a spectacular red and bringing the temperature down. We didn't find any Undead lurking in any of the houses, so we decided to set up camp in the mosque, the only building with carpets on the floor, and spend the night there.

That night, sitting on the beach, cigarette in hand, under a starry sky, I relaxed for the first time in months. That was when it hit me . . . I'd made it—I was still alive. For the first time since I started that trip, I broke down and cried.

4

THE CANARY ISLANDS

"Holy Mother of God! We're saved!" Sister Cecilia's voice warbled with excitement, as the hazy outline of Lanzarote loomed on the horizon. We'd reached the easternmost island of the archipelago.

I shot the little nun a surprised look. At the sight of land she'd come out of her trance and shrieked excitedly in those cramped quarters. Lucia kissed Prit and me and hugged us so tight, she nearly choked us.

We all had a right to rejoice. Our goal was in sight.

We'd taken off from Africa a couple of hours before and had covered the distance faster than we'd estimated, thanks to a tailwind. Now, Lanzarote shimmered in the sun like a mirage in the middle of that turquoise sea. It was the most beautiful sight I'd seen in months.

Prit nonchalantly announced that we'd touch down in about twenty minutes. "And twenty minutes after that, I'll be drinking a nice cold beer. Better yet, a whole keg with a pocketful of Canary Island cigars." Behind me, Lucia rattled on to Sister Cecilia about getting clothes that weren't three sizes too big. "Something feminine that shows off my figure." Even Lucullus got caught up in the excitement. He zipped around from one end of the cabin to the other, forcing us to put him back in his carrier amid yowls of protest. I was just relieved we'd made the nearly three-thousand-mile trip with no mishaps. Given the circumstances, that was no small feat.

I started fiddling with the radio, looking for a frequency so I could contact the island and identify ourselves. The last thing I wanted was some nervous finger to pull a trigger. We were new to the area and had to proceed with caution.

The concerned look on my face silenced the rejoicing in the cabin. No matter how much I turned the dial, I only got static. My gut froze into an icy knot. If the radio didn't pick up any broadcast, it could mean one of only two things: Either the island was maintaining radio silence . . . or there was no one there who could operate that radio.

I felt sick. If the epidemic had reached the islands, our chances of survival plummeted. We were three thousand miles from Europe, flying over an island in the middle of the Atlantic, and the last of our fuel was running out. We couldn't turn back or go somewhere else. We'd bet everything on the Canary Islands . . . and it looked like we'd lost.

In the silence, I could feel three pairs of eyes boring into my neck, as the helicopter covered the last nautical miles between us and land. In a few minutes we'd have what Prit called "dry feet."

What the hell was I going to tell them? What the hell were we supposed to do?

"There's no signal, is there?" Sister Cecilia broke the heavy silence, with a note of fatalism in her voice.

"No, Sister. I don't think there's anyone down there." The Lanzarote coastline was flying past under our feet.

"That can't be! That just can't be!" Lucia shook her head. "Let me try." She pushed me aside and grabbed my headphones.

I watched with fascination as Lucia's slim fingers turned the dials with the delicacy and precision of a goldsmith, stopping at every little crackle or hiss, searching for a spot where a human hand might be behind the signal. I realized I'd let my nerves get the better of me and had handled the radio too roughly, compared with Lucia's delicate touch. Suddenly her face lit up and my heart raced wildly.

"Here's something!" She exclaimed, nearly frantic as she ripped off the headphones. "Listen to this!" Prit flipped a lever that connected the radio to the cabin, his eyes glued to the terrain stretching before him.

"Tenerife North Airport GCXO. Automatic emergency warning . . . headers twelve-thirty free, main runway clear . . . contact tower on channel thirty-six, do not land without authorization. Repeat, do not land without authorization. Report directly to the quarantine area. Tenerife North Airport GCXO, automatic emergency warning . . . headers twelve-thirty free." The message was repeated twice more in Spanish, then it replayed in English.

"What does that mean?" Lucia asked. "What're they talking about?"

"Tenerife North Airport." Prit muttered under his breath. "Los Rodeos."

I nodded. Tenerife North Airport was one of two airports on the island of Tenerife, along with Reina Sofia Airport at the southern end. The automatic signal indicated that someone had survived the epidemic. The part about a "quarantine area" convinced me of that. That was the good news.

The bad news was that we still had to get there. A quick glance at the fuel gauge made it clear we wouldn't make it. A red light started flashing on the control panel and a shrill alarm went off. Prit pulled a small lever and the flashing light stopped; a steady orange light replaced it. We all looked over at the Ukrainian, confused.

"I just switched over to the reserve tank. We've got enough juice to fly for another fifteen minutes. After that . . ."

"What then?" I muttered.

"Lanzarote Airport's radio signal is still broadcasting, but that doesn't mean much. It's powered by solar batteries, so the signal could replay for months. It doesn't mean we'll find anyone there."

A heavy silence fell. We had no other choice.

I thought for a few seconds. "We're here, so head for Lanzarote Airport in Arrecife. It's our only option."

The Ukrainian nodded and tilted the heavy Sokol to the left, following the signal.

5

For six or seven minutes, we skimmed the rooftops in Arrecife. Before the epidemic it was a city of about fifty thousand, but we didn't spot anyone on the streets.

It looked about like all the other cities we'd seen along our relentless journey, except for one thing: There were no signs of fighting, no pileups of abandoned cars, no buildings burned to the ground, or any other sign of the Apocalypse. The public gardens, although in ruins and wild, didn't look like a jungle like other parks had after being abandoned for over a year. The streets were dirty, but there were no large piles of trash and debris and no papers fluttering around. The city looked like it was asleep, like any early Sunday morning. I almost expected to see a delivery truck filled with newspapers drive around a corner.

"There!" Lucia yelled. "On that plaza, in between those two green buses!"

Everyone looked where she was pointing. I swallowed hard. Just then two men stepped out of one of those buses. One was dressed in the uniform of the Spanish Legion. The other looked like an important dignitary in his forties, wearing a suit and tie, his hair tousled. They walked along as if they were two friends, chatting, oblivious to the roar of the Sokol overhead. Perfectly normal, except that the civilian was missing half his face and the legionnaire's chest was crusted with blood.

They were Undead.

The epidemic had landed on that plaza.

I punched one of the helicopter's struts as Prit let out a stream of Russian cuss words. Stunned, Lucia watched those two guys through her binoculars, unable to believe her eyes. Sister Cecilia had resumed praying to her rosary in a monotonous, broken voice. The old nun's face radiated a strange peace. She was well aware we had a few hours of life left—at best—and she was settling her accounts, preparing to greet God . . . which would be soon, if we didn't come up with a plan.

"Something's wrong with this picture. The city is devastated, sure, but there're no signs of struggle!" I shouted over the noise of the rotors. "Take a good look! There are very few Undead on the streets, a few dozen at most!"

"He's right!" Prit was shouting, too. "The city looks like it was emptied out in an orderly fashion! I'd bet my last bottle of vodka those Undead down there came from somewhere else, after the city was evacuated!"

"That would explain why there're so few of them. It doesn't explain where everyone went or why they evacuated the city."

"Or where those Undead came from," Lucia added, grimly.

We were lost in our thoughts as the helicopter covered the last few miles to the airport. When I cocked my rifle, everyone flinched. Questions about what we'd find there raced through my mind. Though I was sweating hard, a shiver ran down my back. Before we arrived at the airport, I headed to the back of the cabin and struggled into my worn, patched wetsuit (some of the repairs looked like scars, mementos of past incidents), with a lot of grunts and contortions. By the time I'd gotten it on, the Sokol's shadow was gliding down the runway at Lanzarote Airport.

"Look at that!" Prit said, pointing to the control tower. "There must've been some kind of dust up there!"

The control tower was demolished, scorched by smoke and flames. Piles of rubble and broken glass lay at its feet. The gaping holes in the windows at the top looked like cavities. The tower looked like it had been burned intentionally, not by a wildfire. The rest of the terminal gleamed in the midday sun, unscathed. Four small planes were slowly falling apart where they'd been abandoned. They were emblazoned with the name BINTER, the airline that had once linked all the islands.

At the end of the runway, a huge 747 lay on its side, its nose buried in a mountain of sand. It was painted white with the words TALA AIR-WAYS written across the fuselage and tail in huge, red, block letters. I had no idea where that company was licensed. The colors could've been European, or Asian. Probably a charter airline. Lanzarote's runway was clearly too short for that mastodon of the air to land, so when it touched down, it couldn't stop and had skidded on its side off the runway. But I saw no wreckage anywhere. The scene was scrupulously tidy, as if after that plane's spectacular landing, someone had collected all the debris and cleaned up the area. As the Sokol flew its last lap, running on fumes, I could tell that parts of the plane, such as the flaps, had been carefully removed.

"Cannibalized," Prit said softly over the intercom.

"Whadda you mean?"

"Cannibalized. In Chechnya, we had problems getting parts and supplies sometimes, especially when the Mujahideen learned how to use anti-aircraft missiles. To keep at least some of our planes in the air, we salvaged parts from damaged planes and used them in the planes we could fly." He paused. "Cannibalized," the Ukrainian said softly, as he focused on setting the Sokol down next to the airport's fuel tanks.

A couple of minutes later, the helicopter landed smoothly. The hum of propellers trailed off when Prit shut down the engines. I immediately jumped out and ran toward one of the fuel trucks I'd seen from the air. As I got close to it, I felt my heart clench like a fist. That truck had been "cannibalized" too. All four wheels were gone and it rested on concrete blocks. Its hood was wide open, revealing a gaping hole where the motor had been. I knew right away that the gas tank would be as dry as the Sahara Desert.

I turned to Prit, but he and Lucia were running toward a small metal fence that surrounded what looked like a fuel pump. The Ukrainian shook the gate that was fastened with a simple padlock. He took a couple of steps back, got a running start, and let fly a powerful kick that destroyed the lock with a loud crunch. The gate hung off its hinges at an odd angle, leaving a gap just big enough for Lucia to slip through like an eel.

The Ukrainian shouted out rapid-fire commands as he struggled to connect a hose to the mouth of the fuel pump. "Press that lever. No, the other way! You've gotta push the button to purge the system. Not that one, the one next to it!"

I ran up to them to help but stopped short. A couple of wobbly figures, silhouetted in the distance, were making their way out of the terminal building. Behind them, dozens more sprang out of several doors, all focused on the three survivors, oblivious to the approaching danger as they struggled to connect a hose.

"We've got company!" I yelled at the top of my lungs.

I'd heard that phrase in dozens of Hollywood movies. When the heroes said it in the heat of battle, it sounded confident, manly and strong, but to my ears, it sounded like the shrill screech of a terrified eunuch.

Lucia and Prit looked up, startled, and stepped up their efforts to start the pump. I set one knee down on the blazing hot ground and shifted my rifle off my shoulder.

I calculated the chances we'd make it out of this. I'm no math whiz, but I quickly realized there was no way we could fill the Sokol's tank before that crowd reached us. For a moment I thought I'd piss myself.

What the hell. It was as good a day as any to die. At least we'd go down swinging.

My hands were sticky with sweat. Behind me I heard Prit and Lucia struggling to start up the pump manually since there was no electricity to run the motor. The nun had joined them, willing, as always, to lend a hand, but there was so little space inside the fence and she just got in the way. I understood perfectly why she was there. I wouldn't want to be alone as those harbingers of death closed in.

I had my own problems. The Undead wobbled unswervingly down the runway toward us, dragging their feet. We were about fifteen hundred feet from the terminal, a considerable distance for those creatures to cover, so we had a little time. But it wasn't enough to get the fuel pump running and load the fuel into the Sokol's tank.

There were thirty bullets in the HK's magazine and I had two more magazines clipped to my belt. I made mental calculations again and realized it was impossible for me to stop that Unhuman tide. Or even slow it down.

I had less than a hundred bullets against more than two hundred creatures. If that weren't bad enough, I'd only fired the weapon a couple of times. A few days ago, in a field, the Ukrainian had given me a crash course. I wasn't a great shot to begin with, even worse at that distance. I'd mostly taken the Undead out in hand-to-hand combat with a considerable amount of luck.

"What the fuck're you doing?" Lucia yelled. "Shoot! God dammit! Shoot!" That girl could swear like a truck driver, especially when she was scared.

"Please! Stop them!" Sister Cecilia's voice joined in, panicked.

Stop them. Are you fucking kidding me? Why don't I just waltz over there and invite them to get a beer at the airport bar? Or go to the beach, get a tan, and play volleyball!

Panic was creeping through me, cold and secretive. Time seemed to stand still. I couldn't think clearly. Despite my friends' cries, I stayed there on one knee, stiff as a board, in the middle of the runway. Suddenly, one of the Undead, a tall, middle-aged guy wearing shorts and a faded T-shirt, bumped into his neighbor and fell flat on his face. One of his flip-flops was long gone and his bare foot was completely destroyed from being dragged on the ground. At that moment, I saw every detail in sharp focus: the white bone sticking out of the guy's foot; the sun shining in the distance; the delicate scent of decay blowing in on the wind; blades of grass shyly poking up through a crack in the pavement next to my knee . . .

"SHOOT!" Prit roared, red in the face, the veins in his neck about to explode, as he pumped the lever like a man possessed.

That shook me out of my trance. I lined up the sight the way the Ukrainian taught me, adjusted it to its maximum magnification, and aimed at the crowd, letting my mind go totally blank.

Through the sight, I saw that sea of monstrous faces as clearly as if they were right in front of me. Men, women, children, young and old, high class and low class, all with a sinister glow in their eyes. Those dead eyes filled me with dread and raised the hair on the back of my neck. On a dive years ago, I saw that same dark, detached look up close—in the eyes of a gray shark.

My first shot was high; it wasn't even close to the Undead I was aiming at. The next several shots were on target, and four bodies lay limp on the runway. In that lapse of time, the Undead had advanced another hundred feet and were closing in. Seized with panic, I realized I could only bring down a handful of them, at most, before they were on top of us. Unconsciously I began to pray while I was shooting.

A cough came from the hose connected to the pump, then a series of clangs echoed from under the ground, and finally the pungent smell of benzene filled the air. The tank was open. A jet of fuel leaped from the mouth of the hose lying on the ground and stained the runway.

Pritchenko let out a wild cry of joy, while Lucia happily patted his back, but then his cry quickly died in his throat. In seconds, the jet of fuel went from a strong stream to a trickle and then nothing.

"That can't be," he muttered. "That just can't be!"

"Lucia!" I heard him shout, as I replaced the magazine in my rifle. "Tell me what the pressure gauge says when I press this lever! Ready?" The Undead were within five hundred feet.

"Anytime, Prit!" Lucia yelled.

When the Ukrainian pressed a lever, a shrill whistle rang out as air that smelled of fuel wafted out of the pump.

"What does the dial say?" screamed Prit. "Tell me what it says!"

"Mark nine hundred!" Lucia answered, as scared and confused as the rest of us.

The Undead had advanced another fifty feet. More than a dozen bodies dotted the runway now. They were close, very close.

"Shit!" the Ukrainian shouted, punching the valve. "Shit," he said over and over as he furiously threw a wrench into the Undead crowd.

I stared for a moment. Pritchenko's eyes were flooded with tears and his expression was one of utter desolation.

"The tank's empty. Just air inside. It's empty."

"It's over," I whispered.

"It's over," Prit repeated, a deep sadness in his voice, his arms limp at the sides.

All the color drained from Lucia's face, as she fell back against the fence. Prit looked at the two women, then down at the HK in my hands. *Don't let them suffer the indignity of being Undead*, his eyes said.

He didn't have to say a word. I knew what I had to do. We wouldn't let that crowd take us alive. I hoped I'd have the guts to finish the job and that my hand wouldn't shake when my turn came.

I turned to Lucia. She was white as a sheet and trembling like a leaf but she had a determined look in her eyes.

She stared into my eyes and nodded. She knew what came next. I read "I love you" on her lips. "Me too," I said. My soul was torn in two by what was going to happen. I shuddered. Tears ran down my cheeks and I couldn't see clearly.

I raised the gun and aimed at Lucia. A few seconds later, we heard a rattling coming down the runway. Lucia had closed her eyes and braced herself for the impact of the bullets. When nothing happened, she opened her eyes and saw my astonished expression and Pritchenko's and Sister Cecilia's spellbound faces.

That rattle was not a firearm. It was a helicopter, approaching fast.

6

"There!" the Ukrainian shouted, pointing to a tiny dot on the horizon that was growing larger by the minute. "Headed right for us!"

To say that hope was reborn in us was putting it mildly. But the helicopter was still a couple of minutes away and the Undead were closing in. They were less than three hundred feet away. That didn't give us enough time.

"Head for the control tower!" shouted the Ukrainian. "Run! God dammit! Run!"

"Wait," I said as I jammed the last magazine in the HK. The first Undead were now within a hundred feet of us. "I can't leave Lucullus!"

My poor cat, frightened by the gunfire, meowed plaintively in his carrier back in the helicopter's cabin. I handed my rifle to Pritchenko and raced back to the helicopter, loading the spear gun slung on my back as I ran. I had only six spears left, but that was better than nothing.

I dashed inside the helicopter, bashing my shin against the steel post. I grabbed Lucullus's carrier and groped around for the other HK we'd stashed behind the backpacks. Finally, my fingers touched the cold metal of the gun barrel. I swept aside the pile of our belongings, racking my brain for where we'd stashed the ammunition. Then I flashed to the image of Sister Cecilia and Lucia carrying a large chest—they'd packed it under the rest of our gear, behind the medicine boxes.

I started tossing bundles aside, but abandoned the effort after a quick glance out the cabin window. A group of about eight Undead was less than thirty feet from the helicopter. If they cornered me in that tight space, I was a goner.

Not looking back, I jumped out of the helicopter, cursing a blue streak. Just then, the rattle of the other helicopter's rotors almost drowned out Prit's muffled shots. With astonishing sangfroid, he retreated slowly to the control tower, covering Sister Cecilia and Lucia, who were running ahead. As cool as 007, the Ukrainian held the gun to his eye as he slowly walked backward. From time to time, he stopped, calmly aimed at the oncoming tide, and fired. Almost all of his shots left an Undead in a heap on the pavement, but the Undead were less than twenty feet away and he was running extremely low on ammunition.

I backed away from the Sokol, not taking my eye off the eight Undead surrounding the helicopter. Lucullus let out an enraged yowl, alerting me just in time. I turned and nearly bumped into four Undead. They must've come around the back of the helicopter and now cut off my path to the control tower. Switching Lucullus's carrier to my left hand, I aimed the spear gun at the Undead closest to me and pulled the trigger. The spear entered the base of his neck and angled upward with a soft *choop*. He collapsed and flailed around on the ground as if he were having an epileptic fit. I lowered the spear gun and reloaded quickly, then turned to the other three Undead, who were almost within arm's reach.

For a split second, I stared in amazement—two of those beasts were Moroccan soldiers. I could tell from their uniforms, but they were just as fucking Undead as the rest. The other was a teenage girl, in shorts and a yellow bikini top that had slipped off, exposing one of her breasts. That would have been a nice sight if it weren't for the hole in her belly that was teeming with maggots.

The Moroccans advanced toward me, shoulder to shoulder, their arms outstretched. *Desperate times call for desperate measures.* I crouched down like an American football player, let out a yell that would've made a Comanche proud, and rammed them. That sudden movement took the Undead by surprise and they fell like bowling pins. However, my momentum caused me to stumble and I landed at the girl's feet. She eagerly lunged for my throat.

Without thinking, I raised my left arm and slammed Lucullus's carrier into her face. The carrier and the girl's jaw shattered with a hideous crunch. I leapt to my feet but felt one of the Moroccan's hands fumbling to grip my leg. Again, I said a prayer of thanks for my wetsuit. If I'd been wearing anything else, the bastard would've gotten a firm grip on me and I wouldn't have had a chance, since the other eight were almost on top of us.

When I got back on my feet, I saw with dread that Lucullus was standing on the runway, stunned by the impact, looking first at me, then at the Undead as they struggled to their feet.

"Go on, Lucullus," I said, as I cocked the HK. "Run!"

I don't know if cats understand what their owners say, but they do have a strong survival instinct. Because of my shouting (or more likely, because of those creatures hunting us), Lucullus took off like a shot toward Lucia, who was silhouetted in the distance against the control tower.

I didn't hang around to study the scene. I ran for my life!

7

Jaime wasn't a bad kid. Midtwenties, tall, well built. He had a lot of friends, a girlfriend, a job, and a car. He played on a handball team and spent the weekends in the country, like everyone else. He'd grown a beard and let his hair grow long, which didn't look good on him, but he liked it, along with the tribal tattoo he'd gotten a few years ago. A regular guy.

The only problem was, Jaime didn't remember any of that. At the moment, Jaime was staggering around like dozens of other creatures, in the blazing sunlight that washed over the runway at Lanzarote Airport. He was one of Them now.

Jaime was an Undead.

Jaime's mind, or what humans call reasoning, had shut down almost a year before when he'd become an Undead. If a doctor could've looked at his brain with a CT scan, he'd have been astonished to find that all the activity was taking place in the so-called "reptilian brain," the most primitive part. In that hypothetical scanner, Jaime's reptilian brain would be glowing with vivid colors, inundated by an abnormal amount of activity. The rest of the brain would be cloaked in darkness, like a city during a power outage.

Jaime didn't remember how he'd gotten to the airport or where he'd come from or where he was going. His tattered clothes suggested he'd been in that state for several months. Nasty burns on his right arm indicated that, at some point, he'd gotten too close to a fire. Those burns would've been extremely painful if he were still human. But Jaime didn't feel anything, not even the huge gash in his right thigh, which caused him to limp, where an Undead had bitten him. That bite had been his ticket to Avernus, the entrance to the underworld—hell.

Although Jaime couldn't talk or reason, he could still feel basic emotions: hunger, excitement, and anger. A wave of anger mixed with desire and a ferocious appetite washed over him every time a living being crossed his path. Especially if it was human.

They were the tastiest prey. They ran around, screaming every time they saw Jaime or his companions in that nightmare. Some managed to escape. Some shattered an Undead's head into a thousand pieces with the metal and fire instruments they held in their hands. But they were the exception. Most didn't stand a chance.

Jaime had no idea how many humans he'd hunted since he'd become an Undead. He didn't know that lodged in each lung was a bullet that should've caused respiratory failure. He didn't know his appearance terrified humans—his long wind-blown hair, his shorts and Hawaiian shirt stiff with blood (some of it his, some of it human), his skin riddled with burst veins, and especially his lost, hate-filled glare.

Jaime didn't know who was walking beside him; he probably wasn't even aware they were there. All he knew was that he'd been wandering aimlessly inside that building when a sound from the sky had drawn him outside like iron filings to a magnet. Now, there were a handful of humans just ahead of him, running away, like they always did. Every cell in his body moaned with the desire to feel that warm, living, pulsing flesh, to grab it, bite it, chew it, feel that warm blood flowing into his mouth . . .

That was what gave meaning to his life—or rather, his non-life.

Jaime could see at least four people. Two of them looked more fragile (Jaime didn't remember the difference between man and woman). They were almost at the foot of the tall building. Another one was dodging a group of Undead, with a small, furry, orange animal jumping wildly around his legs. The last human, a little guy, with a bushy, blond mustache and cold blue eyes, walked backward slowly, never taking his eyes off Jaime's group. From time to time he lifted that metal thing to his face and a flame came out of the end of it with a bang. Jaime's dead brain didn't know what that flame was but he feared it.

Every time there was a burst of that flame, something whizzed past Jaime's head with a painfully loud buzz, followed by a crack. Then splinters of bone and blood went flying, and one of the Undead fell to the ground but didn't get back up. But that didn't matter to him. Nothing mattered. He just wanted to get his hands on those beings and feel their living warmth.

The two smaller humans had reached the gates at the foot of the tower and were trying to clear away the debris blocking them. They were soon joined by the man with the little orange animal. The smaller man was just a few steps from Jaime's group. He'd already picked up that man's pungent, warm, alive, human smell.

Again, the small man raised that piece of metal, but this time there was no flash, just a click. For a moment the man stared at the metal thing; then he threw it with a furious shout at Jaime's group and ran like hell for the tower.

The humans at the foot of the tower formed sounds with their mouths, something that Jaime and the other Undead could no longer do. Jaime didn't understand those sounds, but they fueled his hunting instincts even more. The whole group of Undead picked up their pace.

When his group reached the tower, it was sealed off by a heavy metal door. Under normal circumstances, a door like that would've been an insurmountable obstacle for Jaime and his companions, but this one had been breached by an explosion from inside and didn't fit snugly in the door frame.

Succumbing to his anger, Jaime beat on the metal door with all his strength. The crowd of Undead around him had the same goal and had nearly flattened him against the door. A single idea ran around and around in his brain, like a warped bicycle wheel: gotta get to them . . . gotta get to them . . . gotta get to them . . .

The warped door didn't hold up long as the crowd pressed in against it. With a gut-wrenching screech, the door gave way and crashed to the ground. The path was clear.

Since he was in front, Jaime was one of the first to rush up the stairs that led to the top of the tower. He knew those humans were up there. He could feel them.

The feet of dozens of Undead echoed in the stairwell as they climbed in a mad rush, toward their prize. On the next step, Jaime nearly fell flat on his face when he collided with one of the humans. It was a guy in puzzlingly slippery clothes. He'd planted himself at the bottom of the next *flight of stairs and aimed a strange set of sticks at him. The former Jaime would have recognized it as a spear gun.*

That spear gun fired with a hiss. Jaime felt a piece of metal pierce the bone in his forehead and sink deep into his brain. Neither he nor his rival knew that when the tip of the spear reached his cerebellum, Jaime would feel pain for the first time in months. The pain spread through his body in waves, fueling his anger. He extended his arms toward that human, but he couldn't take a step. He saw the ground rising fast but didn't register that he was falling until his head hit the concrete landing.

He could see the guy cast a scared look at the crowd pursuing him then retreat to the upper floor. He could still detect the feet of the other Undead passing by, oblivious to him as they continued after their prey. But soon the world began to fade as darkness slowly flooded every corner of Jaime's mind. After a moment, the unquenchable fury he'd felt all those months receded the way the ocean retreats from the shore.

In the last millisecond of his existence, Jaime once again knew who he was. Before his life was extinguished forever, he finally felt a sense of relief.

And peace.

8

The tower was cool and dark inside, a welcome change from the suffocating heat on the runway. When I reached the double doors where Sister Cecilia and Lucia waited, I stopped to catch my breath. My lungs had felt like they would burst as I raced a thousand feet stuffed into a wetsuit like a sausage. All those sedentary months in the basement of Meixoeiro Hospital had taken a toll. Lucullus, meanwhile, was hopping all around me, clearly glad to be out of his jail cell.

I watched Prit advance slowly down the runway, his back to me, his eyes glued to the Undead closing in on him. Every few seconds, he stopped, took careful aim, and fired with amazing success. Bodies of the Undead dotted the runway like a string of pearls, as pools of their blood dried in the sun. But each time he stopped to shoot, he gave up a few feet of ground and the remaining horde was gaining on him.

Suddenly, Prit's face creased with worry—he was out of ammunition. Enraged, he flung his HK at the Undead and took off as fast as his bowed legs could carry him.

I turned to the nun and Lucia, who were struggling to reset the metal doors that an explosion had ripped from their frame.

"Come on," I cried. "We gotta get that door in place or we're screwed!"

"Stop talking, Mr. Lawyer, and give us a fucking hand!" snapped Lucia.

Chastened, I lifted one of the warped doors and brushed off the debris covering it. I was sweating buckets, cursing under my breath, as I struggled to set the door in its frame and shore it up. Lucia and Sister Cecilia were urging Prit on at the top of their lungs, as he ran down the runway as if the devil were on his tail. You could probably hear their damn screams all over the island. When the monsters heard all that yelling, they moved faster despite their wobbly gate.

Pritchenko finally reached us and shot through the gap between the two doors as if he were a mortar round, crashing into a pile of rubble behind us.

"You hurt, Prit?" I shouted, as I braced the door with a concrete girder.

"Just my pride," said the Ukrainian, laconic as ever. He brushed the dust off his pants and grabbed my HK off the ground. "Think it'll hold?" he asked skeptically, as he studied the barricade holding up the doors.

"Doubt it. Not with that crowd pushing against them. But they'll buy us some time," I said, as I shoved the last beam in place.

We could barely hear each other over the roar of the helicopter as it circled the tower. I could see its crew taking stock of the scene below them. For a moment, I wondered what the pilot was thinking as he looked down on that multitude pressing against the tower and the Sokol abandoned at the far end of the runway.

"Head for the top of the tower!" Prit cried, as I loaded my spear gun.

The first few Undead had reached the doors and were pounding wildly on them. A mad jumble of moans exploded out of their throats. The chilling memory of that claustrophobic day cooped up in a dark crawl space in that store in Vigo came racing back. My hands started to shake and I was helpless to stop them.

Sister Cecilia and Lucia, with Lucullus in her arms, labored up the stairs behind Prit. From time to time he had to clear away a pile of rubble blocking the stairwell. The debris crashed to the floor below, where we'd just been standing, raising such huge dust clouds I could barely make out where the doors were.

I crouched down on the first flight of stairs, coughing uncontrollably from all the dust, and waited, looking down at the doors every time that roaring mass pushed especially hard. There was absolutely nothing I could do. That barricade wouldn't hold for long.

I started up the stairs in the dark, till I came to the third floor landing, where I had to sit down and catch my breath. A huge bang, like an explosion, startled me. The groans of the Undead got twice as loud. The doors had fallen.

They were inside.

Their halting steps echoed on the metal stairs. I swallowed hard and waited. My sweaty hands gripped my spear gun even tighter as I leaned against the railing.

The first Undead suddenly appeared on the staircase, silhouetted in the light from a small window. He was a young guy, in his twenties, with long hair and a beard. His clothes were in tatters and he had two gaping bullet holes in his chest. A huge gash on his right leg made him limp but didn't stop him from climbing the stairs. His face and clothes were covered in dried blood; his dead eyes glowed with hate. Cement dust had settled on his body, making him look even more diabolical.

A terrible sneer spread across his face when he saw me. As he took a few halting steps toward me, I took a deep breath and aimed the spear at his head. At less than five feet, I couldn't miss. With a squishy *chuff*, the spear cleanly pierced his forehead, planting itself deep into that hellish creature's brain.

He looked confused for a second and then crashed onto the concrete landing. I didn't hang around to admire the landscape; I turned and ran to the top of the tower. The helicopter rumbled right above our heads.

A charred skull smiled down at me at the top of the last flight of stairs. With a shiver, I jumped over it and headed for the ladder to the trapdoor that opened onto the roof.

As I climbed up, I heard the Undead stream into the cupola of the tower. Prit grabbed the back of my wetsuit and pulled me up. Sister Cecilia quickly drew the ladder up behind me. I gasped when I looked back down through the trapdoor. Dozens of rabid Undead were crowded around below, trying to reach us.

I'd made it by a hair.

Relieved, I looked over at Pritchenko but his shocked expression made me turn around. I peered at the helicopter hovering overhead and was stunned by what I saw. And yet, there it was, right in front of my eyes: the helicopter, painted in camouflage, had tilted when they threw us a ladder. On the door, in big, bold letters were the words ARGENTINA AIR FORCE.

9

An army helicopter from Argentina.

In the Canary Islands.

Moroccan soldiers, Argentine helicopters . . . What the hell was going on? I hoped someone at the top of that ladder had the answer.

A gloved hand at the end of an arm in a drab olive uniform helped me into the cabin. When we were all on board, the helicopter flew off, circling the runway at full speed. I lay on the floor, panting, feeling the nausea that washed over me every time I had a brush with death. I sat up and tried to collect myself. I didn't want the first impression that a bunch of strangers had was me throwing up out the chopper's door.

I turned to smile at the man with the gloved hand. He was tall and thin, in his thirties, wearing a flight suit, his face partially covered by a helmet and mirrored goggles. The guy spoke before I could get a word out.

"Up against the bulkhead, please," said the voice, polite but firm with a distinct Argentine accent.

"Hello, my name is—" I stuck my hand out to my savior but stopped short when the guy pointed the barrel of his rifle at my stomach.

"Sir, up against the bulkhead . . . NOW!"

I raised my hands and, with my eyes glued to the rifle, moved to the aft bulkhead, where the rest of my "family" was lined up. Lucia looked terrified. Sister Cecilia wore an expression the Christians must've had when they faced the lions in Roman times. Stripped of his rifle, Prit shot fire from his eyes; his whole body boiled with rage. Given the slightest provocation, he'd break someone's neck. I knew my friend was capable of that and more, so I put a hand on his shoulder to calm him down.

"Easy, pal," I whispered. "Don't do anything stupid. Let's see what's going on here."

I turned and faced the front. The cabin of this helicopter was a lot smaller than the Sokol's, so we were just three feet from our new traveling companions, a man and a woman, both dressed in fatigues. Up front, the pilot and copilot had their hands full controlling the helicopter, which was shaking violently, caught in a stream of hot air. The copilot was talking to someone over the radio. I couldn't hear what he was saying on account of the noise coming from the rotor, but the musical rhythm in his voice left no doubt he was from Buenos Aires.

Argentines, like the helicopter. But their flight suits had the Spanish Air Force insignia embroidered on the right sleeve. When the woman leaned over and said something to the man, her accent was unmistakably Catalan, from northern Spain.

"Sorry for the reception!" she shouted over the noise. "But rules are rules. Nothing personal, but until you pass the quarantine, we have to follow protocol." She paused for a second and then looked at us curiously. "Are you Froilists?"

"Froilists?" I asked, bewildered. "What's that?

With a wave of her hand, she said, "You'll find out soon . . . if you live that long."

That didn't sound very promising.

"Where're you from?" asked the tall Argentine. Although the conversation seemed relaxed, he didn't take his eye off us, especially Pritchenko. The finger resting on the trigger of his rifle said *Don't do anything stupid*. This guy knew what he was doing.

"Pontevedra . . . I mean Vigo, in Galicia," said Lucia.

"You're from the Peninsula?" Clearly he didn't believe us.

"Yeah! So?" His smartass tone had pissed me off. "We flew to the Canaries along the African coast. Then one last jump to Lanzarote, where we ran out of fuel and now . . . you guys . . ." I left my words hanging in the air.

I shot our interrogators a challenging look. It was their turn. They looked at each other and relaxed a bit.

"Hey! Take it easy!" The Argentine said, more to Pritchenko than to me. "We don't know who you are or where you come from or if you're telling the truth. The most important thing is we don't know if you're infected or not. Until we know for sure, we have to take precautions, okay?" I finally got it. This was one of the last outposts of survivors; of course they'd take every precaution and quarantine us. Our saviors didn't know if we were infected with the virus that created the Undead. With a shiver, I realized that if they had the slightest doubt, all the welcome we'd get was some lead to the head.

"You're serious . . . you're from Galicia?" The Catalan girl turned to Lucia, with the same doubt in her voice.

"Of course we are!" Lucia exploded. "I flew over two thousand miles in that fucking Russian blender, crossed the Peninsula and the Sahara desert. I've had it up to here! Got it? I want a hot meal, a long shower, and I want to sleep for three days in a real bed! So don't ask me if I'm serious, because I don't feel like fucking around! Okay?" The pressure was too much. She broke down and sobbed.

I threw an arm around her shoulders and pulled her close, stroking her hair. For all her tough-girl posturing, she was just a seventeen-year-old kid, robbed of her entire world. She had every right to explode.

"Where're we headed?" I asked.

"Tenerife," the Argentine guy replied, calmer. "One of the last safe places on the face of the earth." He looked deep into my eyes. "We're going home."

1 0

The searing midday sun glinted off the Atlantic Ocean in a million flashes of silver. The silence was broken only by the cries from flocks of gannets and the clatter of the helicopter flying low. The salt-laden wind whistled through the open side doors and tore through our hair.

"How're things in Tenerife?" I asked loudly, to be heard in the cabin.

"Sorry. Can't say," said the tall Argentine tersely. "Until the authorities make a ruling on you, the less you know, the better."

The petite, thirty-something woman with the Catalan accent chimed in, "Even if you pass the quarantine, immigration services'll have to approve you. It's not up to us."

"Immigration Services? What're you talking about? I'm a Spanish citizen. So are the two ladies. And Prit's papers are in order. We don't need permission to be on European soil . . . at least we didn't used to."

The woman's intelligent eyes glistened and she shook her head. I was puzzled to see her pull on latex gloves. "Things have changed a lot since the Apocalypse. The situation is very complicated. Rules, regulations, and laws from before have gone out the window. The Canary Islands are no paradise—they're the Wild West." There was a thick silence in the helicopter as her words sank in. "But we're always thrilled to come across humans in the midst of all this shit," she said with a broad, sincere smile, as she stuck out her latex-clad hand. "My name's Paula Maria, but everyone calls me Pauli!" she exclaimed in a lively voice. "Welcome back to civilization!"

"Thank you, Pauli." I shook her friendly but prudently gloved hand. "This is Lucia. In the corner is Sister Cecilia, and the charming guy with the dashing mustache is Viktor Pritchenko, from the Ukraine."

"Well, the scowling guy next to me is Marcelo. As you've probably guessed from his accent, he's *Porteño*, from Buenos Aires." She gave the guy a friendly nudge with her rifle.

Marcelo gave a quick nod, his grim expression unchanged. He was as stern as Pauli was congenial. They made a very odd couple.

"What's the procedure?" Pritchenko spoke for the first time.

"It's a no-brainer," Marcelo said with a dismissive shrug. "We leave you on the quarantine ship. Once medical tests verify you're clean, immigration officers will take care of all the paperwork. Quick and easy."

"Marcelo makes it sound so cold-hearted, but we can't be too careful," intervened Pauli. "I imagine Alicia will oversee your case."

"Alicia?" All those names were making my head spin after being cut off from the world for so long.

"Commander Alicia Pons is the head of transit and immigration services in Tenerife."

"Oh! The Commander! To what do we owe the honor?"

"Very simple," Marcelo replied. "If your story is true, you're the first living beings to make it here from Europe in over eight months."

A heavy silence filled the cabin, broken only by the occasional crackle of the radio. The silhouette of Mount Teide appeared on the horizon. We'd reached Tenerife.

We were returning to civilization.

Whatever *that* was.

The conversation died out. We were mentally and physically exhausted after what we'd been through over the last several hours. Most of our new *countrymen* weren't very talkative either. Pauli babbled nonstop but Marcelo glared at us, mute and deeply suspicious. A glum silence soon spread through the tense atmosphere in the cabin.

In a matter of minutes, we were flying over land: the island of Tenerife. The crew on the helicopter said it was totally free of Undead, but after fighting those monsters for so long, I found that hard to digest.

The first buildings on the outskirts of Santa Cruz de Tenerife came into view. The sun was sinking slowly, casting the first shadows of night. The air had cooled considerably; heavy yellow clouds were forming in the distance. The drone of a half dozen conversations over the radio broke the silence in the cabin. Most were military transmissions, but chatter occasionally came over the airwaves, too.

Suddenly, over the loud speakers came a catchy song that had been popular about a year before. The radio operator must've liked it, since he let it play for a while before switching over to a military frequency for landing instructions.

"What's wrong?" Lucia asked, alarmed, grabbing my arm.

"With me? Nothing. Why?"

"You can't fool me." She took my head in her hands. "You're crying."

Embarrassed, I wiped my hand across my eyes. Fat tears were rolling down my cheeks, leaving long streaks in the cement dust that still covered my face.

"It's nothing. It's just that that song . . ." My voice broke.

"Makes you think of someone, right? That happens to me a lot." Lucia's face darkened. "We all lost loved ones."

I slipped my arm around her shoulder and pulled her close. I stroked her hair, inhaling its sweet scent.

"That's not it. For the first time in nearly a year, I'm listening to music. I'd forgotten what that was like."

Prit broke in. "You're right. I hadn't realized that until just now. A year without music. That's strange . . . really strange," he murmured to himself.

And it's a good sign, I thought. *Here's a place where a radio station can broadcast music, any kind of music, a place that isn't plagued with those monsters, where people live normal lives, where they want some entertainment. A good place, all things considered.*

Just then, I detected movement on the ground below. My hand instinctively reached for the sheath strapped to my leg. Then I remembered they'd confiscated my spears when I got onboard.

I peered into the fading light and tried to make out the scene below. A group of about fifteen people was walking slowly up a hilly, winding road. That was all I saw since the helicopter was flying at full speed. I did notice that they were all armed.

As we rounded one last hill, the port of Tenerife appeared before us. The helicopter flew swiftly over city streets, where thousands of people were going about their daily lives. Ecstatic, we crowded around the helicopter doors, gazing down at a scene that was rare in the world now.

"Look, Prit! People! People as far as the eye can see!"

The Ukrainian laughed loudly and a smile spread across his face beneath his immense mustache. "We did it! We did it!" A childlike joy lit up his face as his eyes darted from one place to another.

Sister Cecilia laughed like a little girl, giving thanks to God and to a long list of saints. Lucia pointed out everything, trying to absorb the images forever.

After a few minutes, we had left that urban sprawl behind. My anxious eyes refused to relinquish that image of vitality, which fell away too soon.

The helicopter flew back over the ocean, to the far end of the dock, where a number of large ships crowded the harbor. Anchored a considerable distance away was a ship painted a dull navy-gray. The strange structure in the front ended abruptly and its stern resembled a small landing strip. It looked like some nitwit navy engineer had left half of the ship back at the shipyard.

The L-51 painted in huge white letters on the side identified it as part of the Spanish fleet. We were going to land on one of the strangest ships that ever sailed. Up until a few months ago, it had been an amphibious assault ship. As we flew over the ship's stern, I read the name on the hull and smiled at the bitter irony. After nearly a year dancing with death for thousands of miles, I was back home.

The ship was named *Galicia*.

1 2

By the time we landed on the *Galicia*'s deck, the sky had turned blood red. Marcelo pointed to the sliding door and motioned for us to climb out. Suddenly, the atmosphere grew tense. The Argentine made a show of drawing his side arm in case of trouble. Even jovial Pauli was all business, with a serious look on her face. The large revolver she was holding looked like a cannon in her small hands. If she fired that gun, the recoil would probably propel her backward. Both the pilot and copilot were also armed with handguns. They'd turned around and faced the cabin, convincing us to leave the relative safety of the helicopter and jump onto the deck.

A warm wind filled with the scent of fertile land reached our noses when we set foot on the *Galicia*'s deck. Two small choppers with bulbous glass covers also sat on the landing pad—reconnaissance helicopters, I guessed. I glanced up at the ship's mast. I could just make out the Spanish flag flying overhead in the half-dark of twilight. A flag I didn't recognize fluttered in the breeze below the national flag. It was dark blue with the shield of Spain in the center, but above the shield was a crown sitting atop a wall instead of just the crown. Most of the other ships flew the same combination of flags.

I scratched my head, trying to understand, but soon I had more important things to think about. A dozen people clad in hazmat suits filed out a door at the base of the superstructure. Polarized visors covered their faces so I couldn't make out their gender or age. From their height and gait, I concluded that most were men, and three or four were women. As they got closer, I automatically stepped closer to Prit, who instinctively covered my back.

"I don't like this one bit, man," the Ukrainian hissed, his eyes glued to the group.

"If things get ugly, let's all jump overboard, agreed? You grab the nun and I'll grab Lucia and the cat."

"Lucullus won't be too thrilled about swimming to shore. Me, either," Prit shuddered. "I hate swimming when I can't see the bottom."

"Better saltwater than lead, Prit."

"For now let's play it cool." The Ukrainian's soldier-like gaze swept the area, coldly assessing our situation. "We're too high up. They'd fry us before we hit the water. Look up there."

I looked where he pointed with his eyes. Dressed in combat fatigues were a couple of sailors, stationed behind a heavy machine gun on a ledge about twenty feet high with a clear view of the entire runway. They'd know if we sneezed.

Lucia listened with a terrified look in her eyes. I sighed, downhearted. We had no choice but to accept what those people planned to do with us.

The first of the team in hazmat suits had reached us. I couldn't see his eyes, but I guessed he was examining every member of my "family," including Lucullus, who was squirming in Lucia's arms. He studied us for a really long time. After all, we were a very colorful, almost shocking group.

Out of the corner of my eye, I saw Pauli, Marcelo, and the two helicopter pilots head into the ship. Clad only in shorts and T-shirts, they crammed their flight suits into toxic waste disposal bags. This was just routine procedure to them.

"Don't worry, Peninsula guys," said Pauli as she walked by. "We'll see you when you get out of quarantine!" With a cheerful wave, she disappeared through the door, followed by the sour-faced Marcelo.

Great. Now what?

"Welcome to Tenerife. I'm Dr. Jorge Alonso." The filter in his suit distorted his voice. He seemed to be in charge. "Please stay calm. If you cooperate and follow instructions, everything'll go as smooth as silk. This is a mandatory medical procedure, so relax and let us do our job.

The sooner we finish, the sooner you'll get out of quarantine. Let's make this easy, okay?" His voice was conciliatory, but firm, as he pointed to the door the helicopter crew had passed through.

I nodded, too stunned to speak.

The corridors of the ship were painted regulation navy gray; dozens of pipes and cables crisscrossed the ceiling. We passed several doors that were locked tight. One of the doors had a porthole; three or four sailors had crowded around on the other side of the glass to get a look at the "survivors from the Peninsula." I didn't know what to think . . . Were we that bizarre? That could be good or bad. Very bad.

We stopped where two hallways intersected. Dr. Alonso took the lead again.

"Men here, women over there, please."

"Wait," I said. "We'd like to stick together. We came here together and we want—"

"I don't care what you want or don't want, sir," he cut me off. "Rules are rules. Men down this hall, women and children down that hall. Please cooperate."

"Hey, be reasonable," I answered, summoning up my inner negotiator. "This is new to us, so if you wouldn't mind, we'd rather—"

This time a tall guy, also in a hazmat suit, spoke up. "Look, friend. This isn't a debate. It's not even a discussion. Do what we say. End of story. Got it? If you don't like it, I hope you know how to swim, because Africa's a long way from here. So don't fuck around and do what Dr. Alonso says. Men on the right, women on the left! LET'S GO!" he roared, brandishing an electric prod.

I raised my hands and headed down the hall on the right. After giving that guy a killer look, Prit joined me. I wouldn't want to be in that guy's shoes if he ever crossed Pritchenko's path in a dark alley.

Sister Cecilia and Lucia went down the aisle to the left. Suddenly, Lucia broke away and planted herself next to me, setting Lucullus in my arms.

"Take him." She gave me a quick kiss. "I haven't forgotten what you said in Lanzarote."

"Stay calm. It'll be okay." My voice broke. "Watch out for her, Sister!" I called after them as they walked down the hall. "Be careful! See you soon!"

"Don't worry, my son! We're in God's hands!"

No, we're in these people's hands, Sister, I thought. *And that might not be such a good thing.*

"Where're you taking them? What're you going to do with us?" Pritchenko was pissed off.

Dr. Alonso shrugged. His soft, sweet voice gave me chills. "Like I said, my friend. To quarantine. Now, if you don't mind, through that door, please."

1 3

Basilio Irisarri was an alcoholic. When he went on one of his many benders, his shipmates would have to drag him back to the ship. Basilio didn't know it but that detail saved his life.

Basilio was an old-school sailor: simple, direct, and crude. He first shipped out when he was seventeen. He became experienced and capable, having spent time on many ships, mostly as boatswain, in charge of maintenance. He was promoted to chief petty officer a few times, but his surly, belligerent personality coupled with his binge drinking always dragged him down. He was forty-five, tall, and carried a growing spare tire around his waist. His arms looked like pistons, and the knuckles on his huge hands were battered from fighting in ports all over the world.

A year and a half before, Basilio joined the crew of the *Marqués de la Ensenada*, an oil tanker in the Spanish navy, anchored in Cartagena, Colombia. Six hours after going ashore, Basilio and a couple of shipmates had gotten plastered and had wrecked a bar, broken a chair over a pimp's head, and picked a fight with several Colombian police officers. MPs arrested them and sent them back to their ship, where they were locked up in their quarters.

Basilio spent the next forty-eight hours in the throes of a terrible hangover, but he heard a lot of voices screaming and sailors running around up top. Through the narrow porthole in his cabin, he watched Cartagena's military port quickly become an anthill.

Many ships, packed with people, hastily weighed anchor and jammed the mouth of the port trying to get out. On land, thousands of people, mostly civilians, tried to reach anything afloat, no matter the cost. The authorities had planned to evacuate the city by sea, but clearly the situation had overwhelmed them. There were too many people and too few ships. Out his tiny porthole, Basilio watched the Colombian military scurry around, trying to bring order to the chaos, but the terrified crowd was out of control.

Basilio didn't read newspapers, and he hadn't listened to the radio or watched TV for days, so he had no idea that in the days leading up to the Apocalypse, chaos was rampant all over the world. At first, with all the gunshots and explosions throughout the city, he thought there'd been a civil war or revolution in Colombia. But the frantic activity of the soldiers convinced him it was something else.

Anchored next to the *Marqués de la Ensenada* were an American destroyer and a French frigate. Large detachments of their crews (except the sick or those locked up like Basilio) had gone ashore to join the overwhelmed Colombians in trying to control the panicked crowd. In horror, Basilio witnessed an avalanche of thousands of people sweep over those American soldiers and French sailors, as if they were toys, in their rush to the sea.

The shores had quickly become a hive of thousands of men, women, and children splashing and punching one another, trying to keep from drowning or being crushed by people falling on top of them. The water was churned up by thousands of arms and legs. People were knocked senseless when they stuck their heads up for air in the midst of that morass.

Someone panicked and started firing wildly into the crowd. Soon hundreds of people were exchanging shots, desperate to board the ships remaining in the harbor. Columns of black smoke rose across the city. Law and order was breaking down and nobody could stop it.

Basilio's mouth was as dry as the desert. He rubbed his eyes, hoping that that hellacious scene was just a hallucination brought on by the DTs, but he knew it was painfully real. He turned away from the porthole, unable to watch anymore, but he couldn't tune out the screams of thousands of people drowning a few feet away. The pounding and clawing of people futilely trying to climb the ship's smooth sides were like blows to his head. Yet Basilio didn't shed any tears. He was safe. *Every man for himself,* he thought.

Six hours later, one of the lieutenants on the ship opened the cell door. His uniform was soaking wet and torn. Blood poured from a huge gash in his head. Of all the crew that had gone ashore, he and a sergeant were the only survivors. Over seven hundred people, mostly civilians, were crammed into every corner on that tanker. Only four members of the original crew, including Basilio, had survived the chaos.

Loaded down with refugees, the *Marqués de la Ensenada* began a harrowing journey back home. It lacked enough food, water, and medicine for that many people. Its crew barely knew how to steer the ship. A violent hurricane nearly sent the ship to the bottom. When it finally reached the port of Santa Cruz de Tenerife in the Canary Islands, more than a hundred people had died along the way. Twenty with "suspicious wounds" had been executed on board. There were still fifteen cases of infection onboard, which forced everyone to spend a month floating in the port in quarantine.

Enduring a month without a drop of alcohol was torture for Basilio.

Basilio had lived in Tenerife ever since. He'd even enlisted in the navy. The world had changed in a year, but his propensity to get into trouble hadn't. A drunken spree that ended in a massive brawl five months before had gotten him assigned to a disciplinary post—guard duty on the quarantine ship. It was the worst fate a guy could have, cut off from the city, surrounded by people who might be infected. His drinking problem had landed him in what to him was the closest thing to hell in Tenerife. He cursed that shitty post every day.

Basilio was stationed at the sentry post in the corridor that led to the isolation cells. It was small and spartanly furnished with just two chairs, a wooden table, and a rack that held a half-dozen shiny, black automatic rifles.

His hands trembling, Basilio poured a big glass of the local rum out of a bottle he'd hidden under the ammo box. He had to think of something fast. He knew he was fucked and he wasn't going to get off easy. It was that fucking nun's fault, that fucking nun from hell. Why'd she have to stick her nose where it didn't belong? No, that fucking group from the

Peninsula was to blame. They'd been trouble from the start. Who'd have thought anyone would still be alive there?

A few months after the Apocalypse, very few survivors made it to Tenerife; even fewer survived quarantine. His duties aboard the *Galicia* were unpleasant but not very demanding. Occasionally, small groups from northern Africa all the way to the Sahara desert made it to the Canary Islands on any boat they could get their hands on. Basilio despised those people. They were just damned African scum, most on death's door who didn't have the good sense to die at home. It baffled him why the authorities took those people in when supplies were alarmingly low. Basilio would've sent them all back to Africa with lead in their skulls, but those fucking faggots in the government didn't know how to take charge of the situation like real men.

Basilio spit on the floor in disgust. Those Africans presented a problem, but also some distraction, especially the women. Most of them didn't speak Spanish, English, or anything like it, just Arabic or one of those African dialects even God didn't understand. But that gave the sailors an advantage. On more than one occasion, Basilio and a couple of guards had had some fun with those girls in a back room they jokingly called "Paradise."

Of course, none of the medical staff, commanders, or civilian authorities knew about Basilio and his cronies' little secret. They'd have been in serious trouble if anyone ever found out. Martial law was still in force and rape was punishable by death. But since those downtrodden African girls didn't speak Spanish, they couldn't complain. Besides, most of them had suffered so much along the way that being raped one more time didn't matter much. They'd made it to the only safe place in two thousand miles, so they almost all kept quiet. Any woman who made trouble, well . . . Basilio smirked and knocked back half the rum in his glass. She wouldn't be the first to have her file pulled and put in the "likely infected" pile. Just one step away from becoming fish food.

But this group was different. They were Europeans, and that changed everything. If that weren't enough, they'd flown over from the mainland! Somehow, they'd survived for over a year, surrounded by Undead. The authorities had taken a real interest in them. Alicia Pons herself had taken on their case.

Fuck, Basilio, you're in a shitload of trouble! he thought, pouring himself another drink. *When she finds out about this, you're a dead man. That Pons bitch'll cut your balls off and feed 'em to you with hot sauce.* He slammed his fist on the table, as he racked his brain for a way out.

They were a strange group. First there was the fucking lawyer with the cat. He hadn't stopped bellyaching since day one, demanding to speak to the person in charge. When they tried to put down his fucking cat, he raised such hell the doctors gave in. He broke the doctor's arm in two places! Alicia Pons decided the cat could live, the most unbelievable decision so far. Basilio couldn't see how that paper-pushing asshole had survived. He just couldn't picture the guy shooting a gun.

The Ukrainian guy was another story. That guy was dangerous. He was short, blond, about forty with a huge yellow mustache. He was missing a couple of fingers on his right hand; he must've lost them in a fight. The guy was very quiet, calm, but he watched you . . . oh, damn, the way his pale eyes bore into the back of your neck gave you the creeps, as if he were thinking over how he could hurt you faster. (Basilio had no idea how right he was.)

The young girl was a fucking hottie. Nice body, with curves that made your head spin and that face . . . blessed Christ, she'd make a cloistered monk's blood boil. And there she was, within arm's reach.

During the first weeks, Basilio played it safe. He made some raunchy comments as he made his rounds, but he hadn't touched her. However, that morning, when he took the girl and the nun to their medical exams, he'd let his hand graze the girl's breasts. He was very drunk and not fully aware of what he was doing. He'd done that with the African girls but they were so cowed they'd let him get away with it. But this girl exploded and slapped his face.

Basilio knew from experience that alcohol and anger didn't mix; it was a lethal cocktail he'd never conquered. Before he knew it, a red veil formed over his eyes, and his temples started to throb. No woman laid a hand on him, especially in front of his men. He slammed his fist into the bitch's temple and she collapsed on the ground like a rag doll. He raised his baton over his head to teach that bitch a lesson. Suddenly the fucking nun stepped in the middle and, incredibly, she slapped him too.

Then he lost it.

Basilio beat his head against the wall, thinking how stupid he'd been. When he finally came to his senses, the nun was lying unconscious on the floor, blood streaming from her cracked skull. He didn't know if he'd killed her. To make the fucking situation worse, it took place on the last day of quarantine, just hours before they were to be released. At that very moment, Commander Pons was heading to the *Galicia* to process their papers and bring them on land. The nun was in the infirmary, more dead than alive. The other guards had scattered, looking for a place to hide until the storm passed.

In forty minutes, Basilio Irisarri was going to be in deep shit unless he came up with something—fast.

1 4

Day after day for a month, as I lay on my bunk, I stared up at the shape on the ceiling made by peeling paint. Sighing, I stroked the beard I'd had for weeks; it reminded me how much time had passed. At first they gave me a razor and shaving cream, but, after the day I fought to keep Lucullus, they'd taken away everything sharp or pointed. I must've looked like a homeless guy or nut job in those ridiculous green hospital pajamas.

My big furry cat sprang off the ground and made an elegant landing—right on my crotch. Wincing, I grabbed Lucullus around his fat belly and set him on the bunk next to me. He purred as I scratched behind his ears.

In the beginning, I yelled my head off, demanding to speak to the person in charge. I threatened, begged, pleaded—all in vain. When my voice gave out, I collapsed against the wall of my six-foot-square cell. There were no windows and not much furniture, just some bunk beds, a small bench bolted to the wall, a sink (but no running water), and a toilet that was missing its lid. The walls were thick steel plates welded to the floor and ceiling. A vent in the middle of the ceiling looked like it had been added later. I had the feeling there were rooms like it on all sides, above and below me. They'd transformed the *Galicia*'s huge cargo bay into a hive of cells to accommodate all the refugees.

I recalled a documentary I saw about that ship. The *Galicia*'s hold could be completely flooded with seawater through a huge gate located in the stern. Landing craft had been housed there. I shuddered when I realized that what I'd thought was an air vent on the ceiling was for letting water into the cell if necessary.

Whoever had designed that quarantine facility had planned for everything, including a riot. With a flick of a switch, whoever was in charge could drown everyone in that hold. Fast, easy—and discreet. That thought dissuaded me from raising any more hell. From the silence, I guessed that the vessel was practically empty. My friends and I were probably the *Galicia's* only guests.

A tray of food was passed through a slot in the door three times a day. The food was tasteless but varied. There was a lot of rice, beans, freeze-dried food and, to my surprise, fresh vegetables, such as lettuce, carrots, and potatoes. It'd been nearly a year since I'd had fresh vegetables. If it weren't for the vitamin C we took at Meixoeiro Hospital, we'd have become anemic or developed scurvy. I can't describe the joy I felt when I saw a fresh tomato on the tray. That little tomato tasted better than any banquet I'd ever eaten. I'd closed my eyes and let its juice run down my throat.

I fantasized that none of this was happening and that when I opened my eyes I'd be at home stretched out on the couch with Lucullus, watching a game on TV. Sadly, of course, when I opened my eyes, all I saw was the fucking chipped ceiling.

Once a day, three doctors entered my cell and drew blood. They took my temperature, pulse, and blood pressure to verify I wasn't becoming an Undead. In the beginning, they were escorted by a couple of armed soldiers who stood guard in the hall (they didn't all fit in my tiny cell), but my submissive attitude soon gained their confidence and they conducted their checkup unescorted. Until two weeks ago.

That morning, three medical personnel wearing red ID armbands entered my cell. Before they started, one of them said they had to take my cat for "a clinical trial." Something in the guy's tone of voice threw up a red flag. After years of practicing law, I could tell when someone was lying. And this guy was a lousy liar.

My subconscious made the decision before I realized what I was doing. When Dr. Liar bent down to pick up Lucullus, who lay curled up at my feet, I pushed his neck down and slammed my knee against his nose.

Dr. Liar screamed in pain. Bright blood streamed from his broken nose and coated the inside of his Plexiglas mask. As he writhed on the floor, I jumped on the other two guys who just stood there, paralyzed with surprise.

I grabbed the tall guy's arm and yanked him toward me. Dr. Tall tripped over Dr. Liar, writhing on the floor, and crashed into the sink. As Dr. Liar struggled to his feet, I kicked him in the back and sent him flying into Dr. Tall. His left arm had gotten wedged between the toilet and the sink, so when Dr. Liar collided with him, his shoulder bent at an unnatural angle with a crunch that sounded like a compound fracture.

I turned to the third doctor, but he'd run into the corridor and sounded the alarm. Then it dawned on me what I'd done. I stood, frozen, in the middle of the cell. Groaning in pain, Liar and Tall stumbled out of the cell, leaning on each other. Someone closed the door and turned off the light. I was in complete darkness.

Trembling, I grabbed Lucullus and curled up in my bunk, staring at the door. I muttered to myself, *Now you're really fucked. Any minute, someone's going to open that door and then I'll be screwed. You might've signed your death warrant, you stupid ass. At least they didn't see me beg,* I thought, trying to cheer myself up. Pride is a ridiculous thing, but when you're in desperate straits and it's all you have left, it becomes your most valuable asset.

I crouched in the corner of my cell, tense as a lute string, expecting three or four goons to storm in at any moment and give me a much-deserved, world-class beating or a bullet in the head.

But nothing happened. Not for the next hour. Or the next day. Nothing.

The only change was that the medical exams stopped. Someone still shoved food through the slot every day. I'm sure they were studying me through the peephole in the door, but for two weeks, nobody came into my cell or talked to me. Being locked up in that tiny room, alone, drove me crazy. I'd read stories about prisoners who lost their minds serving life sentences in tiny cells in American maximum-security prisons. I wondered if that'd happen to me, too.

I was lost in those thoughts one morning, scratching the stubble on my chin, when suddenly I heard footsteps in the corridor and voices I couldn't identify. The footsteps stopped abruptly at my door. Then keys jingled loudly as someone turned the lock. I jumped out of bed, shoving Lucullus behind my back. *They've finally come for me.* I tensed every muscle in my body, ready for whatever came next.

A female figure with her hands on her hips was outlined by the half-light coming through the door. I squinted, trying to adjust to the light. When the figure took a step into my cell, I could see her perfectly. For a moment, we just looked at each other in silence. Then the woman spoke.

"I'm Commander Alicia Pons, head of the medical corps." Her voice was firm but gentle at the same time. "Your quarantine has ended, but not without some *problems.*" I heard amused sarcasm in her voice that quickly became serious again. "You're not the only member of this group who's been involved in an *incident.* Anyway, let me say that you all passed. I officially welcome you to the Tenerife Secure Zone."

We stepped out into the corridor. After a month locked up in that cubicle, my first steps were a little shaky. With Lucullus in one arm, I braced myself against the wall with the other to get my balance. Only one guard accompanied us; he didn't know how unnecessary he was. I was so weak I couldn't have run a hundred feet, let alone escape from the ship or swim to shore.

We came to a brightly lit room with large windows that looked out onto the flight deck. In the middle of the room, an army officer worked at a computer surrounded by several other machines, including a printer. It was the first computer I'd seen up and running for over a year. A friendly civilian took a couple of pictures, while a soldier politely took my fingerprints. I had the strange feeling that, after a year living as a fugitive in the Wild West, I was back in the system without the slightest idea what that system was.

"We'll have your documents ready in a few minutes, sir," said the soldier, typing quickly at the computer. "ID, access passes, ration card—everything you'll need to live in Tenerife. Meanwhile—"

"We'll talk," Alicia Pons broke in, "and bring each other up to date. How's that sound?"

"Great idea," I said, a bit sarcastically. "I'd love to know what the hell's going on around here."

"Follow me," said Pons. "In the next room, we can talk privately. Plus, I think they've prepared some refreshments. That'll help pass the time."

When we entered the next room, my eyes grew really wide. Neatly arranged on a table were trays of fresh fruit, sandwiches, fresh-baked bread, and a Spanish omelet. The heady aroma of steaming coffee filled the room. Back in Vigo, all I'd eaten was canned food, so that spread looked like it was from the fanciest restaurant in the world. It took all my will-power not to pounce on the table like a crazed Hun.

"Please have a seat. Help yourself," Alicia Pons said, as she filled a cup with strong, boiling-hot coffee. "You must be hungry. Take anything you want."

I thanked her then attacked the tray of sandwiches, while Ms. Pons sat back and studied me. I took that opportunity to steal a look at her, too. She was in her thirties, medium height, with auburn hair, slim, with delicate features. All in all, a good-looking woman. She was dressed in a navy uniform, but no hat; her thick hair was gathered in a bun at the nape of her neck. I spotted a gold wedding band as she unconsciously tapped a blue pen. She seemed fragile, but one look in her eyes told me that this woman was resolute and brave. All the soldiers, officers, and civilians treated her with the utmost respect. She clearly carried a lot of weight around there and knew how to command that respect.

"So . . ." she began, reading a paper on her desk. "One physician with a fractured septum, and one with a fractured arm and dislocated shoul-der. Care to explain what the devil was going through your head?"

"It was an accident," I said, my mouth half-full, as I grabbed an-other sandwich. "The arm, I mean. The nose, well . . . I didn't think I'd hit him that hard." I paused, a little embarrassed. Her bright, blue eyes drilled right through me.

"You and your friends have told us an amazing story," she said, leaf-ing through a stack of papers on her desk. "A Russian ship, an exploding briefcase, a refuge in a hospital, a city in flames, a two-thousand-mile helicopter flight . . . " She looked up and smiled. "Your life certainly hasn't been boring over the last few months."

"It's been pretty rough," I mumbled with my mouth full of sand-wich. My eyes flitted over all the dishes on the table.

"It's been rough for everyone," she replied, looking over more pa-pers. Among the mountain of files, I spotted several photographs of me, Prit, Lucia, Sister Cecilia, and even Lucullus. In one aerial shot, we were running down the runway at the Lanzarote Airport, a mob of Undead on our heels.

"Everyone here has a riveting story to tell. Some are funny; most are dramatic. Yours surpasses them all by a mile, believe me."

"Just trying to stay alive," I said, reaching for the coffee pot. "Like everyone else."

"Believe me, you folks did remarkably well. In fact, you're the first survivors from the Peninsula since Operation Judgment. That alone makes it even more amazing."

"Operation Judgment?"

"The evacuation of the remaining Safe Havens on the Peninsula, ten months ago." She looked at me strangely. "You don't know what's happened in that time?"

"I haven't bought any newspapers lately, Lieutenant Pons," I answered as I bit into an apple, letting its juice run down my chin. "Where I've been, there weren't any newsstands open."

"Captain."

"Excuse me?"

"It's Captain Pons, but most civilians call me Mrs. Pons. You were saying?"

"Well, *Captain* Pons, I haven't had access to any source of information for almost a year. I have no idea what's going on in the world, what the fuck's still standing and what's gone to hell. I don't know where I am, what my status is, where my friends are, who the hell you are or what you represent." I talked faster and faster, not letting her get a word in edgewise. "All I know is, for a year we've been traveling around a landscape right out of hell, full of Undead. When we finally reached a place where those things weren't wandering around everywhere, we were treated like criminals and locked up for a month. Now here I sit. I've been fingerprinted like a common criminal and you, *Captain*, haven't had the decency to clarify the situation . . . *sir*," I let fly all the anger bottled up inside me. "So no, I'm not up-to-date."

Alicia Pons froze. My outburst had taken her by surprise. Then she threw her head back and laughed uncontrollably. For a moment, her lack of respect pissed me off, but her laughter was such a breath of fresh air and so contagious, she finally got a smile out of me.

"I'm really, really sorry. Please forgive me," she said, her smile still shaky as she tried to regain her composure. "Our situation here is so complicated, sometimes I forget how ridiculous and drawn out the procedure is. I understand your anger, but please, relax. You're among friends. Believe me. Let's start again." She reached her hand across the table. "I'm Captain Alicia Pons, but you can call me Alicia."

"Nice to meet you, Alicia." I relaxed a bit. "You know my story. Would you mind telling me what the hell has happened in the world?"

"Of course," said Alicia, a more serious look on her face. "I warn you it's not a pleasant story. Far from it. The world you knew is gone and now we have . . . Well, wait till you've heard everything."

For a moment, I thought back, a little amused. Just a few months ago, I'd had a similar conversation on another boat with another "captain," a conversation that started me on a journey that took me to the brink of death. I hoped this conversation would take me to some place more pleasant.

"At first no one took it seriously." Alicia poured herself another cup of coffee. "During the first week, there wasn't any reliable information. Putin let himself be swept away by the predictable Russian paranoia and declared a total blackout on the matter. You probably remember that the news was full of . . . nothing. Governments around the world were in pretty much the same boat. No one knew a thing. The Russians had a stranglehold on information and Western governments knew more or less the same as CNN."

"How's that possible? There're satellites . . ."

"Satellites are only machines that take pictures. Humans 'look' at those pictures and interpret them. But before you can find something, you first have to know what you're looking for. Back then, no one was looking for Undead in satellite photos, since almost no one thought they existed. Don't forget that Dagestan was—*is*—a very remote place. Not much information was getting out at the time. Finally, eight days later, the U.S. government got a full report through a CIA source inside the Kremlin."

"Eight days? It took longer than that for things to get ugly. Why didn't someone do something in the meantime?"

"Simple. They didn't believe the report," she said staring into her coffee cup. "After 9-11 and the nonexistent weapons of mass destruction in Iraq, U.S. officials questioned the accuracy of CIA reports. So when someone reported that the dead were rising from their graves and attacking the living, it sounded like a bad B-movie. No one took it seriously. They wasted some very crucial weeks.

"But the Americans knew something was brewing. And not the Ebola or Marburg or West Nile viruses—or any of the excuses the Russians gave that first week. And that *something* was biological. It had the Kremlin scared shitless, so scared they finally allowed a team from the World Health Organization and the CDC into Dagestan. European governments, Japan, and Australia also sent medical teams to control what they thought was an epidemic—"

"I remember it well," I cut in. "Army medical battalions were supposed to collaborate with the Russians to control the situation."

"And in the process, snoop around and find out what the hell was going on." She shook her head, gazing into space. "Of all the bad decisions made back then, that was definitely the worst. Teams of hundreds of people converged upon the area just when the situation was critical. The infection was already out of control. Dagestan was a 'hot spot.' Thousands of Undead were swarming all over the place. Looking back, it's so obvious, but at the time we knew almost none of what we found out later."

Alicia Pons was silent for a moment, as she mindlessly rifled through the neat stack of papers in my file. Then she continued her story.

"Three or four days after the medical teams arrived, the situation became clear to everyone. Those medical teams quickly realized what they desperately needed in Dagestan was combat troops to kill those vermin. Unfortunately, they realized that after several doctors had been attacked by patients they'd thought were in shock."

"Undead," I ventured.

"Yes, that's right. Teams deployed to the area were ordered to return to their home countries as fast as they could. Of course, they took their wounded with them. The Japanese may have transported a few 'patients' back so they could study the virus."

"Good God," I whispered running my hands through my hair. "Those medical teams helped spread the chaos."

"Within forty-eight hours, a number of 'patients zero' turned up in virtually every corner of the world. Only isolated places like the Canary

Islands were free of infection. The few cases reported here were quickly dealt with. By then we had a pretty clear idea of what was happening. In all honesty, at first, no one knew what the hell the infection vector was. Unfortunately, it didn't take long to find out."

"How's that possible? Anyone with eyes could see the cause-and-effect relationship between being bitten by an Undead and becoming one of them! What were they thinking, taking infected people back to Europe, Asia, and America?"

"As I said, nobody in his right mind believed the strange account of the dead coming back to life. It was too crazy to be true, like all the other wild theories circulating in those days. That theory turned out to be true, but nobody knew that at the time. Let me show you something."

Coffee cup in hand, she rummaged through a black folder, took out some papers, and spread them out in front of me. They were pictures taken through a microscope, enlarged several thousand times. The first was of a strange cell culture. The cell walls were dotted with dozens of small volcano-shaped fissures. Part of the cellular material had been projected through those fissures and scattered every which way, while other areas looked charred, as if a tiny torch had scorched them.

She showed me another picture, enlarged to show the inside of those cells that were full, tiny dots. Some of the dots were projected through the same fissures in the cell wall and had impregnated other cells in the culture. In the last picture, enlarged the most, was a small, elongated, innocent-looking tube that was curved on the end. It reminded me of a shepherd's crook.

"Meet TSJ-Dagestan." With a flick of her wrist, Alicia spun the photo around till it came to rest in front of me. My gaze was riveted to that harmless-looking stick. How could that little bastard be responsible for taking the human race to the brink of extinction?

"Things started to get really interesting the second week. But before I go on, how about another cup of coffee? There's so much more to tell." The captain slowly filled her cup. I noticed she drank her coffee black.

"After two weeks, the situation was totally out of control." She took a sip, winced, and added some sugar. "Information was erratic, fragmented at best, or it just vanished. Many countries closed their borders. But by then that was useless. It was like closing the castle doors after the enemy has gotten in. No estimates are a hundred percent reliable, but we believe that seventy-two hours after the medical aid teams returned from Dagestan, the virus was already out of control."

"How's that possible? How could it've spread so fast?"

"Simple," Pons patiently replied. "The TSJ virus is a very clever son of a bitch. Whoever designed it had a vast knowledge of virology and knew how to enhance those features that would ensure its ability to spread. Experts say that the TSJ-Dagestan virus started out as a modified strain of the Ebola virus to which part of the genetic load from other viruses was added. According to experts at the CDC in Atlanta, it was the work of a true genius. What do you know about Ebola?"

"Ebola?" I felt like a school kid taking a test. "It's a hemorrhagic virus from Africa. There's no cure for it and there are several strains. The press mentioned it a lot in the weeks before the Apocalypse."

"The Ebola virus is a ruthless killer that's transmitted through contact with bodily fluids—blood, saliva, semen, or sweat—making it a highly contagious pathogen. Within a few days, the infected person develops a high fever and a terrible headache. Three or four days later, its victim starts bleeding from every orifice as Ebola transforms their internal organs into a puree of dead cells. The blood flowing out their eyes, mouth, ears and anus is actually their organs reduced to a river of putrefaction. Ninety percent of patients die in a matter of days. It's effective, fast, and lethal."

"Fuck," I breathed.

"But that effectiveness is its greatest weakness. Ebola is so lethal and so fast, it doesn't allow its host to travel any great distance before becoming seriously ill. It originated in the heart of the African jungle, where travel is extremely slow and difficult, so outbreaks of Ebola affected people in a radius of a few kilometers. Ebola is such a perfect assassin, it kills its victims before they have time to spread the infection to new hosts."

"Let me guess. TSJ doesn't have that weakness."

Alicia Pons smiled weakly. "Ebola is a common cold compared to TSJ. It's transmitted by contact with bodily fluids, like Ebola. Saliva and blood are perfect breeding grounds. Once in a host, it multiplies rapidly and settles in the internal organs, which it starts to devour, like Ebola. At that point, the host is doomed. Within five days, he or she will be dead, turned into something much worse. That's the moment little TSJ demonstrates the evil it's capable of. Unlike all other viruses, TSJ isn't content to disappear when its host dies. Through a process we're still trying to understand, TSJ is able to maintain the host's dead body in a state of suspended animation in which . . . " She burst into bitter laughter, but stopped when she saw the surprised look on my face. "Why am I telling you this? You know as well as I do what happens next!"

"I think so. But I watched an infected person become Undead in a matter of hours, not five days." The image of Shafiq, the Pakistani sailor from the *Zaren Kibish*, flooded my thoughts. He'd been attacked by one of those monsters during our escape through Vigo. Later that night, Prit and I watched him turn into an Undead as we huddled in the back of a small grocery store. So I knew firsthand how grisly the process was. That seemed like a lifetime ago, but it had been less than a year.

"He must've died from other causes. Most Undead reach that state in very little time. We estimate it takes between three and twenty minutes after an infected person dies for him to rise as an Undead."

"So . . ."

"So, around fifty percent of people attacked by an Undead die on the spot or within the next hour from the injuries inflicted by their attackers. Twenty minutes later, they rise as Undead, and the diabolical cycle continues when people are scratched by an infected person or come in contact with an infected person's body fluids. Splashed by someone's blood or saliva . . . a thousand different ways. All those aid workers and soldiers returned home, unaware they were already carrying the death sentence for all mankind. Back home, they kissed their husbands, wives, children; shared a drink with friends in a bar . . . and spread the disease. When cases started to emerge, there wasn't just one 'patient zero'—there were thousands all over the world. The pandemic was already up and running before anyone realized it." She ended in an ominous tone.

My head was spinning. I thought I knew how the virus was transmitted, but hearing an official confirmation of how virulent and easily spread that virus was was way too much to process. I'd been extremely careful every time I touched one of those things, but I could've unwittingly become an Undead during those chaotic weeks, just like tens of thousands of people. The pieces of that awful puzzle were starting to fit together.

"How long can the damn things last? Is there a vaccine?" My thoughts were racing.

Alicia Pons studied me for a few seconds, debating what to say next. Finally, she clasped her hands on the table and swallowed hard. "From what we know so far, those beings can last indefinitely. The natural process of putrefaction is arrested or slowed way down. They don't breathe, so their bodies aren't subjected to oxidation. Their metabolism is so low they don't seem to need nourishment. Those things could be—"

"Could be what?" An icy fist squeezed my heart. Deep down I knew the answer.

"Eternal," Pons said in a hollow voice. "Humanity may have to live with them forever, unless we exterminate them . . . or they exterminate us."

Her words echoed in my head like a gunshot. If I hadn't spent a year living on the razor's edge, constantly fighting those monsters, I'd have thought she was making it all up. I knew she wasn't exaggerating, yet it all sounded so unbelievable.

"This is so . . . crazy," is all I managed to say.

"Of course it is." Pons stood up and walked over to a refrigerator. "Talking about people rising from the dead and attacking the living is crazy. The fact that they don't need to eat, breathe, or sleep is also crazy. It's crazy that they don't decay or suffer any wear and tear—that they're still moving around even though they're dead as a damned doornail. No matter how unbelievable it all sounds, you know as well as I do, everything I've said is true."

Alicia's voice was muffled as she rummaged around in the refrigerator, clinking bottles together in her search. She scooped up a can of soda from the back of the refrigerator with a triumphant cheer. She stood up, turned around, and walked back to the table holding the can and a glass.

"Drink this," she said, as she opened the can with a snap and poured half of its contents into the glass. "It's always a shock to face events that reason and science say can't be possible—and yet there they are. The reaction worldwide is very similar. And right now, you don't look so good."

I gratefully accepted the soda Alicia held out to me. My mouth was horribly dry. After I'd gulped down half the can, I felt a little better. But my head was still spinning.

"I was splashed with the blood and guts of those beings more times than I like to think about, Alicia," I said hoarsely, trying to calm my nerves. "If TSJ is transmitted the way you say, why haven't I gotten infected?"

Alicia stared into the empty glass on the table, her mind far away.

"You know, you shouldn't have drunk that soda so fast. That stuff is getting scarce, even on the black market. I hear it's trading at astronomical rates. It may be a long time before you can afford to drink another."

Her sorrowful eyes came to rest on the half-empty can, then rose to my face again. "If you or your friends had been splashed with blood, saliva, lacrimal fluid, or nasal mucus from an infected being, you'd've turned into one of those things. By now you'd have had a fair amount of lead in your brain, my friend," she said, as she poured a little more soda. "That's what the quarantine is for, so we can be one hundred percent sure that new people aren't going to be a . . . *problem.*"

Alicia settled back into her chair. "Clearly that didn't happen to you all."

That explanation didn't reassure me. If I'd had an open cut when I'd been splashed or gotten some fluid in my eyes, my story would've ended right then and there. I'd have become part of the legion of the Undead.

"Once vectors of infection surfaced worldwide, the entire planet became a living hell in a matter of days. Health services collapsed first, when it became clear that the hundreds of infected patients in hospitals were beyond a cure. Those Undead transformed hospitals into slaughterhouses, death traps. By the time the army got involved, it was too late. We have no data from other countries, but we believe that seventy percent of the medical staff in Spain died in the first forty-eight hours after the initial outbreak."

"Seventy percent?"

"That's a conservative estimate. Judging by the number of doctors and nurses who survived and are currently on the islands, the number is probably much higher." Alicia's face darkened. "The same thing happened with the police, firefighters, and EMTs. Everyone who tried to help in the early hours of the chaos was exposed to TSJ."

The air conditioning droned as Alicia's words hung in the air. All the pieces of that dramatic tapestry began to fit into place.

"Once governments accepted that the world was falling down around them, the phones of various state departments rang off the hook. There was even a meeting of the European Union to address the issue."

"I remember. Their faces said it all."

"They finally got scared." Alicia's voice hardened. "However, even then they couldn't agree on a plan that might've saved the continent, maybe even the world. All they did was appoint a Joint Crisis Committee and declare a news blackout, then tuck their tails and run back to their own countries, shitting bricks. Most countries armed their borders, hoping to head off the Undead." She sipped her coffee and clicked her tongue. "But by then the Undead were in every country. Borders meant nothing to those deadly hunters."

"You mean it was like that all over the world?"

Alicia laughed mirthlessly. She looked at me in disbelief, wondering how I could be so clueless. "Of course not," she replied with a scowl. "It was worse."

"Worse? How could it've been *worse*?"

"Faster, stronger, with worse consequences. For example, in the United States there were more vectors of infection at one time than anywhere else in the world because the Americans sent more medical personnel and more military to Dagestan than any other country. In addition to that, U.S. troops in Iraqi Kurdistan who oversaw the enormous camps of Dagestan refugees got infected too. By the time the U.S. government woke up, the virus was out of control in over thirty cities across the country."

I whistled softly, picturing the virus spreading across a country the size of the United States.

"When reporters from CBS discovered what was going on, the network bypassed censorship and issued a special report. Immediately after the broadcast, panic spread throughout the country. Millions of people swamped airports and highways, struggling to get out of the cities. Families threw all their belongings in their cars and headed for rural towns where they thought they'd be safe. They didn't know that many of them already carried the virus, so it spread rapidly across the country. The U.S. government rushed to copy the European model of Safe Havens, but it was too late. Mass hysteria had taken over. The nation's institutions began to collapse as more and more officials didn't show up for work, either because they'd fled or they were dead."

With a chill, I pictured the horrific scene. The United States has an intricate network of highways and airports, so when thousands of infected people fled, they were like Trojan horses, spreading the TSJ virus to every corner of that huge country.

"We believe there are still a few Undead-free zones, especially in the middle of the country. Those areas held out thanks to vast distances, the deserts, the low population, and because gun ownership was widespread before the Apocalypse. We don't know what the living conditions are like in those regions, if anyone is in charge or if anarchy is widespread. From what little intel we have, the situation varies greatly from one area to the next. Some places are trying to rebuild some semblance of an organized society out of the ashes. In others it's the survival of the fittest. It can't be easy living out there."

"What about South America?"

"Well, it varies. Mexico was affected, almost to the level of Europe and the United States. Hundreds of thousands of Americans thought they'd be safe if they crossed the border. But all they did was spread the virus. Imagine the surreal situation facing astonished Mexican border guards when they discovered that their rich, proud neighbors to the north were now 'wetbacks.' They closed the borders, but it was too late. Thousands of panicked *Americanos* managed to sneak across the border. In large parts of Mexico, the locals went on a 'gringo hunt,' egged on by the Mexican press. Anyone who looked like a Yankee 'swallowed a pint of a lead,' as the saying goes. Shoot first, ask questions later. But within ten days, the Mexicans had their own problems to worry about. Something like that happened in Venezuela, only there—"

"I remember hearing something about a war between Chile and Bolivia," I chimed in.

"That's right. In the midst of all that chaos, the Chilean army crushed the poor Bolivian army and pressed deep into the southern part of that country. But the chaos in their own nation forced them to turn back. That, and the hordes of Argentine refugees crossing its borders."

"The Argentines?"

"In all that madness, the Argentines were dealt the most fucked-up blows," Alicia said in a mocking tone.

I smiled. As the conversation progressed, Alicia's language got more colorful. She seemed more comfortable talking to me and I felt the same.

"Buenos Aires was one of the largest urban centers in the Southern Hemisphere. Millions of people were packed into a relatively small area. As the rest of the world was falling apart, Buenos Aires didn't have a single case of infection. Not one. It was one of the few civilized places on the planet that was 'clean,' but no one took any preventive measures. A week later, when thousands of refugees flocked to the city, no one oversaw their arrival, checked their health, or set up a quarantine. Nothing, as surprising as that may seem. When cases of the epidemic turned up in an overcrowded urban area, nobody—absolutely nobody—bothered to take control. The Argentine military tried to imitate its neighbor, Chile, and overthrow the government, but the civilian government didn't go down easy. There were demonstrations, shootings, an aborted *coup in extremis* . . . As the world was disintegrating, the Argentines were stunned by the power struggle among their leaders. Finally someone got really scared, but it was too late. Members of the government absconded with all the money they could get their hands on and hopped on a plane headed for God-knows-where."

Alicia took out a pack of cigarettes and offered me one. I took it in silence and let her light it. Interestingly, she didn't light one for herself but put the pack back in her pocket. I was mesmerized by the way she flicked her lighter on and off as she talked.

"I don't know where those assholes went, but I hope those monsters got every one of them," she sighed, shaking her head. "Two weeks after that, the Embalse Nuclear Power Station, near the city of Cordoba, blew up, casting a radioactive cloud over the entire north. No one ordered the shutdown of the plant. Operators disappeared. No one stopped the system from failing. In a brutal example of negligence, every government official dropped the ball. We assume that the plant kept operating unattended until the uranium destabilized and set off a chain reaction that ended in nuclear explosion. All of northern Argentina and southern Brazil are now a radioactive wasteland, where life is impossible, except for the Undead. Of course, they're already dead!" she said, frowning.

"How can people do shit like that?"

"In Asia things were even worse. The Chinese lost their heads and tried to eradicate the disease from their main population centers with controlled nuclear explosions."

"NUCLEAR BOMBS?" I couldn't believe that was true, even though I'd heard about it when there were still TV newscasts.

"The value of human life is more relative in other cultures. What's inconceivable in the West makes perfect sense to a person from the East where the community matters most, not the individual. If you can save the community by eliminating tens of millions of individuals in one fell swoop, no matter if they're healthy or sick, you don't hesitate."

"And that was their strategy."

"That was their strategy," Alicia replied, nodding.

"Did it work?"

"Not one bit. Radiation can't kill someone who's already dead. Sure, they incinerated millions of Undead, along with millions of innocent people. Given that country's dense population, even if only a small percentage of Undead survived the explosion, that equates to *millions* surviving who then scattered in every direction from the razed cities." Her eyes bored into me. "Think about it."

"Absolute chaos . . . worldwide," I whispered.

"We aren't the worst. In Asia and the Middle East, human life is no longer possible. At least, life as we know it. As for Africa . . . the stories the few survivors have told us are shocking. Africa is hell on earth. We surmise there's almost no one living on the continent, except for small, isolated groups scattered throughout the rainforest or Tuareg nomads roaming the Sahara desert. Dozens of small-time kings and warlords filled the power vacuum when the governments collapsed. Disease, war, famine, and nature swept away anyone the Undead didn't get. Africa has regressed hundreds of years," she said with a frown. "The living are almost more dangerous than the Undead."

"We stopped in a fishing village on the coast of Morocco."

"You said in your statement it had been ravaged by 'fire and the sword,' as the saying goes. That's the pattern all across the continent. It's a fight to the death for resources *and* survival."

"Resources? Africa is probably the most fertile place on earth! It could easily provide food for the rest of humanity!"

Alicia laughed and looked at me as if she knew a huge secret but wasn't sure whether to tell me.

"We don't just need food. We're running desperately low on all the basics: medicine, fuel, clothing, ammunition, vehicles that run. Think about it: Every box of medicine our hospitals consume means one less box of medicine in the world. Every gallon of fuel our helicopters burn means that much less transportation by air. Every bullet we fire at those bastards takes us one step closer to defending ourselves with bows and arrows! No industry, no international trade, no technology, no tankers bringing fuel into ports. Think the world's a mess now? Wait a couple of years and you'll look back on this as the good old days. We are rushing headlong into a new Dark Ages. And as long as those creatures are out there, there's not a thing we can do about it!"

"But there must be something we can do . . . "

"If you've got a brilliant idea none of us has thought of, pal, lay it on the table right now," she replied, half mocking, half serious. "I guarantee you'll be the most popular guy on the islands."

"But I thought civilization on the islands still worked. I assumed this was the real Safe Haven where we could all continue our lives!"

Alicia looked at me for a moment, then she stood up and motioned for me to follow her. "Come with me. There's something I want to show you."

1 5

We went back on deck. Twilight glowed red on the horizon as a warm, sand-laden wind blew across the harbor, turning the air into hot, thick soup. Each breath felt like I was shoveling boiling air into my lungs. As soon as we left the cool air conditioning inside, we started to sweat. I wished I still had some of that soda.

Alicia walked to the gunwale and absentmindedly offered me another cigarette. I shook my head. I was light-headed and my mouth was as dry as the desert. After a month in that cell, I had an attack of vertigo as I walked down the *Galicia*'s long runway. In silence, we looked at the city that encircled the bay. Lights started to glow as darkness closed in. I was just about to ask about the fate of my friends, but before I could say anything, Alicia pointed to the port.

"See that ship? The biggest one, across from those tall buildings."

I looked where she was pointing. A massive ship painted bright blue, much larger than any other vessel in the harbor, bobbed lazily in the waves. It sat unusually high in the water, exposing a wide swath of its topside that would normally be underwater. That could only mean that the vessel had no cargo in its holds.

"That's the *Keiten Maru*, a Japanese supertanker. It used to belong to one of the largest conglomerates in Japan before the Apocalypse. That monster can transport one-hundred-and-fifteen thousand tons of crude oil. As all hell was breaking loose, it was returning from the North Sea loaded with Norwegian oil, bound for Japan. Before reaching the

Canaries, three crew members died of TSJ, including the first mate. Even as crew members were falling ill, the uninfected survivors managed to round up the Undead and lock them in a hold. But panic broke out, so they dropped anchor here. Then the world collapsed and the ship was stranded forever. Paradoxically, its misfortune was our salvation. Without the *Keiten Maru*, we wouldn't have had a chance." Alicia's pale eyes seemed to look right through me.

"Why's that? What linked that ship to the fight against the Undead?"

"That massive load of crude. We refined all that wonderful stuff into fuel," she said, pointing to the towers that dotted the horizon.

Of course! The Cepsa Refinery.

"When the system collapsed and the islands were cut off from the world, we had enough fuel for two weeks, tops. The *Keiten Maru* brought us an adequate fuel supply. But, despite strict rationing, we've been burning through the last of our supply for a month. At this rate, we'll use up the last liter in four or five weeks."

"That's bad, right?"

"Worse than bad. It's catastrophic. Without fuel we lose all our technological advantage. No more airplanes, helicopters, boats, or cars. We'd have to go back to the candle and the horse. We would almost surely starve to death."

"Why not sail over to Nigeria or Venezuela, connect a pump, and load more fuel?"

"It's not that easy. When the chaos spread, many oil-producing countries sealed their wells. With no staff to run them, they were time bombs. Corporations shut down all Venezuelan and Mexican wells, but in Nigeria, no precautions were taken. Aerial reconnaissance shows that many wells have exploded, creating large oil spills. As for the pipelines . . . after a year with no one to service them, they're just scrap metal."

She swallowed cigarette smoke and glanced at me over her shoulder.

"Even if the wells were in good condition, operating the way they did before the Apocalypse, it would be impossible to pump anything out of them without deploying a huge security team who'd face who knows how many thousands of Undead in order to protect the technicians . . . if we *had* any technicians. They'd have to repair oil rigs with materials we also don't have so they could pump crude through a pipeline that hasn't been serviced in over a year, to a ninety-thousand-ton ship we can't get to without the help of an experienced pilot who's familiar with those waters, and without an army of tugboats to position it in a pumping station we're not sure still exists. So, you see, it's not that easy."

"What about the Persian Gulf? It's farther away, but that huge ship could make it there easily. Besides, ships there are loaded at sea through hoses that . . ."

"Nothing's left in the Persian Gulf. Know who the Wahhabis are?"

I shook my head, bewildered. The situation looked bleaker and bleaker.

"They're an ultrareligious branch of Islam in the Gulf that advocates a literal interpretation of the Koran and Sharia Law. The Middle East was one of the first areas hit by TSJ, since it's so close to Dagestan. During the last weeks before worldwide collapse, the Wahhabis proclaimed that TSJ was God's punishment for mankind's greed and wickedness, and the only way to escape death and the horrible fate of the TSJ virus was through acts of purification. Money had corrupted mankind's soul, and returning to a primitive purity was the only way to save civilization. Oil had flooded the Middle East with money, which, in turn, flooded the area with corruption and lack of faith. On the path to purification and salvation, fanatical mobs attacked and destroyed every one of the oil rigs in the Gulf, beseeching Allah to rid them of the infection."

"That means . . ."

"That means hundreds of oil wells in the Gulf are still burning over a year later. The Middle East is not the answer. If we don't find a solution soon, we'll go from being screwed to being really and truly screwed. A new Dark Ages is right around the corner."

I shook my head, overwhelmed. I realized that the golden paradise I'd pictured the Canaries to be, the oasis I'd dreamed about all those dark months, was actually a poor, desperate, besieged place where daily life was a struggle. I wondered what would become of me, and my friends. But then an obvious question flashed in my mind.

"I'm very grateful for your welcome, for catching me up, and taking care of all that paperwork, but one question keeps running around in my head. Why me? Why the hell're you telling me this?"

"Because we have a serious problem," she replied with a strange smile. "And we believe you and Mr. Pritchenko can help us solve it."

1 6

For a second, I thought I'd heard her wrong. I was stunned by that last sentence.

"Prit and me? Why the hell do you need our help?"

"It can't be any clearer. Mr. Pritchenko is a helicopter pilot with thousands of flight hours under his belt, many of those hours in combat, not to mention flying a helicopter from the mainland to the Canary Islands. He's not only valuable to the community, but a gift that literally fell out of the sky."

"What about me? Where do I figure in all this? I'm just a lawyer, or I was before civilization collapsed. I don't think my knowledge and experience will help get an oil well. And if you're thinking of suing the Undead, I strongly advise against it. I don't think they're solvent. If you ask me, they won't even appear in court."

"Cut the crap!" Alicia cut me off. "I said we need you for your skills, not your jokes. You survived out there longer than any of our raiding parties. I don't know if you're skilled or just lucky. Mr. Pritchenko is one of the most valuable professionals today. We need you *badly*—both of you."

"I can see how you need Prit. But after everything we've been through, neither of us wants to leave this island for a very, very long time. We're mentally and physically exhausted. All we want is a safe place to live and work, away from those creatures. And," I added, still the comedian, "I still don't see why you need an attorney."

"Oh! You've got it wrong." Alicia seemed genuinely surprised. She shook her head and said softly, "It isn't the government that needs an attorney."

"What do you mean? So, who the hell . . . "

"It's Mr. Pritchenko who needs your help." Alicia slowly strung out her words. "And I hope you're really good at your job, because he's really going to need your help."

For a moment, I was too stunned to speak. I wouldn't have been more surprised if they'd told me to take a bite of the *Galicia*'s radar antenna. I didn't understand a thing.

"Prit? My help? What the fuck?"

"At 9:45 this morning, Mr. Viktor Pritchenko was being led from his cell to the examining room to discharge him from quarantine and provide him with documentation for residency, like yours." Alicia had a stern look on her face. "In one of the corridors, he crossed paths with another member of your group, Sister Cecilia Iglesias, headed for the same place. Suddenly, without a word, Mr. Pritchenko grabbed the guard's billy club and, before guards could subdue him, beat Sister Cecilia on the head, leaving her senseless on the ground."

I staggered as if I'd been punched in the stomach. Prit assault Sister Cecilia? No way! There must be a mistake. My Slavic friend sincerely venerated that smiling, plucky, vivacious nun, who'd comforted him and guided him out of the deep well of depression with long conversations and loads of understanding. Attack her? That was totally ridiculous.

"I regret to inform you that Sister Cecilia is in a coma in the infirmary onboard and may die from her injuries in the next seventy-two hours."

"There must be a mistake," I said, in the calmest tone I could summon. "Prit loves that woman like his mother. That can't possibly be true."

"I'm sure it's hard to accept, but the facts are irrefutable," Alicia replied, with a sad note in her voice. "The three security guards escorting them were eyewitnesses. One of them is the head guard, a man we have complete confidence in. There's no discrepancy in their stories."

Prit, a murderer. Impossible. I needed to see him and find out what the hell happened. Once again I was trapped in the jaws of a situation that was out of my control. The last time I felt like that was on another ship, the *Zaren Kibish*, a thousand years ago. Captain Pons's eyes were boring into me. My mind was racing to come up with a plan.

"You want Prit's and my help? For starters, take me to him now. Not tomorrow, not in ten minutes, not when you get around to it. I need to see my friend, *now*."

"Of course," Alicia said, a bit cowed by my reaction. "Follow me."

We walked down a narrow staircase to a locked room where two grim-faced officers stood guard. Once inside, I stood there petrified. My friend lay in a corner, shirtless, covered with bruises. Prit's right eye was swollen shut, he had a fat lip, and his mustache was caked with blood.

When he saw me, the Ukrainian rose, limping. He looked shattered.

"Prit! What the hell'd they do to you? You okay?" I probed his sides for broken ribs.

"Listen," he said between coughs. "I don't know what they told you, but I didn't do anything! Hear me?" He clutched my sleeve. "Don't believe a word they say!"

"Prit," I said calmly, throwing my arm around his shoulder. "I know you're telling the truth. If I doubted you, even for a second, I wouldn't deserve to be your friend. Don't worry, man. I'll get you out of this mess."

"I hope you're a better lawyer than you are a nurse," Prit replied sarcastically and raised his left hand, which was minus two fingers.

Thinking back to my pitiful efforts in doctoring his wounds back at that Mercedes dealership brought a thin smile to my lips. That damned Ukrainian and I had been through a lot together. There was no way I'd leave him in the lurch.

"Hey, show me some respect, pal! I'm the best lawyer you can afford!" I joked and gave him a friendly punch on the arm.

Prit shot back with an indecent reference to my mother's virtue and cracked a smile that tore open his cut lip again, making him wince.

"Well, you have us over a barrel, Ms. Pons. Now, where the hell's Lucia? And Lucullus?"

Before she could answer, I saw a tall, willowy silhouette in the cabin doorway. She hesitated, afraid to enter. In the light filtering through the porthole, I could make out the freckles on her arms. I'd studied them so many times I could've traced a map of them with my eyes closed. She was trying to control a struggling ball of orange fur. With an indignant meow, Lucullus broke free, took four short hops, landed in my lap, and purred contentedly.

Before I could make some wisecrack, Lucia crossed the room and we clutched each other in a long kiss. When we finally came up for air, I got a better look at her. She had a nasty bruise on her left temple and was visibly thinner and paler, but otherwise she was as beautiful as ever. Anger glinted in her tear-filled green eyes.

"Know what they've done . . . those . . . those . . ." She was so angry, she could barely speak but I got the message.

I grasped her shoulders and whispered soothing words in her ear. As I did, determination welled up in me. For the first time in months, I was full of energy and that strange strength that had kept me alive as the world fell apart around me.

Captain Pons said we should go ashore at once, but I tuned her out. I was relieved to have almost all my "family" around me. Sister Cecilia's absence weighed on me, but I was convinced she'd pull through. Given time, we'd work everything out. We'd face whatever lay ahead and everyone else be damned.

With our battered friend propped up between us, Lucia and I emerged from that cabin without a backward glance. We were finally going ashore to face this new world and whatever was left of the hu man race.

1 7

TENERIFE

We were back on land. Before we left the boat, we were given a huge packet of documents: passports, quarantine certificates, ration cards, transportation passes, and a laminated card that identified Prit and me as "Auxiliary Navy Personnel Class B." They gave Lucia an orange card, which classified her as "Civilian Resident." We didn't know if that was going to be a problem.

I was warned to keep an eye on Lucullus. The few cats that had survived were in "high demand." I didn't know what that meant, but it didn't sound good.

We made the ten-minute trip to port in a small boat that looked to be a hundred years old. Powered by a sputtering two-stroke engine that kept backfiring, it'd been put back into service because that old engine ran on the low-grade diesel that more modern engines couldn't use. The whole trip, I was afraid we were going straight to the bottom of the bay on a boat that must've dated back to Spain's Africa wars.

Tenerife Port was bustling with hundreds of people, going about their jobs, dressed in clean clothes, undernourished but otherwise healthy. They didn't look particularly happy, but at least they were calm. They were probably still pinching themselves over surviving the Apocalypse.

The captain of the boat was a witty guy who had a lot to say. According to him, over eight hundred thousand people lived in Tenerife before the pandemic. That number climbed to several million in the early days of the Apocalypse, when wave after wave of refugees from Europe and America reached the islands. Now the population was down to a million and a half.

What the hell happened to that mass of humanity? Where'd they go? If what that guy said was true, there were a helluva lot of missing people.

A guy in uniform was waiting on the dock to check our documents. I was surprised to see flags flying everywhere, as if the survivors had had an attack of patriotism. Even the bus that took us to our new home sported flags, and not just the Spanish flag, but also the one with that strange blue insignia I'd seen flying from the *Galicia*'s mast. I didn't know what it stood for—and nobody was in any hurry to explain.

1 8

It was a really surprising weekend. I'd vacationed on the Canary Islands several years before and had always wanted to go back. Never in my wildest dreams did I imagine coming back under those *special* conditions.

At the dock, a sweaty, stressed-out guy in a uniform, who was doing five things at once, checked our documents, gave us a quick handshake and rushed off on urgent business. Prit, Lucia, and I just stood there on the dock, all our luggage at our feet, waiting for the bus. We didn't know what else to do.

Something made me uneasy and set my nerves on edge. The look on Lucia and Prit's face told me they felt the same. The Ukrainian licked his lips; his eyes flitted nervously in every direction as he reached for a gun he didn't have. Lucia rocked back and forth almost imperceptibly as she clutched Lucullus. Even the cat was twitching.

Finally it dawned on me—that crowd of people was making us jumpy. People were dashing here and there, going about their business, bumping into us, barely glancing at our frightened trio. I had to close my eyes to keep from passing out. Noises engulfed us: shouts, snatches of conversation, laughter, a child crying, a horse neighing, the hum of hundreds of mouths talking at once in the background. After a year of tomb-like silence, that multitude was a shock to our nerves.

Lucia pointed something else out: There was no smell of rotting flesh. Thousands of smells floated in the air, some pleasant, some not. We were in a port, after all. But they were human smells.

The strangest part was we had nothing to do. We didn't have to run away. Not a single Undead was on our tail. For the first time in months, we were absolutely idle.

However, that picture of normality was misleading. Before the Apocalypse, there'd never been a crowd like that on that dock. There were no cars on the road except for a URO, Spain's version of a Humvee, but there were a lot of draft animals dragging carts made from car chassis. In fact, the "bus" that took us to our new home was actually a cart pulled by two oxen.

They put us up in a former three-star hotel, built in the seventies. For decades it welcomed legions of European tourists, eager for sun and sand. Although clean and neat, the shabby building had seen better days. Even before it was turned into refugee housing, it wasn't the best hotel on the island. The former reception area was now a communal playroom for the screaming children of the families in the complex. We hadn't seen many children since very few had survived. And the number of babies and pregnant women overwhelmed us. Half the women looked like they could deliver any day. A primitive survival instinct must compel survivors to reproduce at all costs. I'd read about a similar phenomenon among Holocaust survivors, but I never imagined I'd witness it first-hand

The residents in that building were classified as Auxiliary Navy Personnel, like Prit and me, and lived there with their families. Most were mechanics, engineers, highly skilled construction workers, electricians, even a vet, with all the skills essential to the community's survival. *Everyone but me*, I thought bitterly. I was there because the island bureaucracy had lumped Pritchenko and me together as "experienced survivors." If that weren't so tragic, I'd laugh.

We were assigned three adjoining rooms on the fifth floor. There was electricity for only six hours a day, from six pm till midnight, which proved to be a real pain in the ass. With no elevator, we had to trudge up all those flights of stairs.

Fortunately, the previous tenants had torn down the walls, connecting the rooms into an apartment. The rooms were dingy but clean, and there was running water, just no hot water. When the electricity was on, we could pick up the signal from the island's TV station on the television screwed to the wall above the bed. All in all, things were okay.

The downside was, in twenty days, Prit and I had to report to a "special work group" at a barracks downtown. Something told me we weren't going to like that "special work" one bit.

1 9

Hard to believe we'd only been on the islands for a few weeks and were already mixed up in a bad situation! I was so angry I wanted to scream. In frustration, I kicked a trash can as we were walking out of the office and sent it rolling down some stairs, making a shitload of noise. All that got me was a glare from a secretary and a sore foot.

We'd had a few short, happy weeks of vacation. We relaxed, gorged ourselves, slept like the dead, and baked on the beach. Then one morning, a messenger came to our home with a summons for Prit and me. At noon we were to report to the former headquarters of MALCAN, the command center and logistic support group on the islands, in Weyler Plaza downtown. Dozing beside Lucia, I could hear Prit arguing with the guy in the next room. He finally gave up and signed the receipt. I got up, my hair standing on end, my eyes bloodshot, and found my friend with a worried look on his face. That couldn't be good.

"What the hell'd that guy want?" I asked, as I filled the coffeepot with the vile stuff they called coffee.

"See for yourself," the Ukrainian muttered, holding out the paper. "They want us to start earning our keep."

After breakfast and a shower, we headed out, our stomachs in knots. We weren't sure what they wanted from us. To say we had our guard up was putting it mildly.

A beat-up URO was parked in front of the old hotel. At the wheel was a young kid, barely eighteen, in an ill-fitting uniform. I'd have bet a million euros that boy had just enlisted. He'd probably been a refugee like us just months before. During the first weeks of the Apocalypse, the military took a huge hit as it tried to defend the Safe Havens. Now they filled the gaps in their ranks with anyone they could find.

After five minutes on the road, it became clear the kid had little experience driving a heavy vehicle the size of a URO. He lurched through the crowded streets, laying on the horn like a Cairo taxi driver at rush hour, nonchalantly whizzing past cars, trucks, and pedestrians. He even drove up on the sidewalk. Every time he shifted, it sounded like he was going to rip the transmission to shreds. Forty minutes later, we miraculously reached Weyler Plaza in one piece.

When Prit and I looked around, we couldn't believe our eyes. Most of the historic, art nouveau buildings that surrounded the plaza had been burned to some degree. Their walls were pockmarked by shrapnel and bullet holes, a sure sign the area had been the scene of a fierce battle. I wordlessly pointed to a dark black spot that stained the ground under our feet like a sinister carpet. Prit reached down, scratched the surface, and took an expert sniff. Shaking his head, he mumbled, "Napalm."

The building was packed with office workers running around, doing God-knows-what. They kept us waiting for a long time in a small room decorated with the flags of dozens of regiments that probably no longer existed except in memory. By the time a sergeant finally hurried us into an office, the sun was high in the sky.

A bald, pudgy little guy who looked to be pushing fifty sat at a desk. His black goatee stood out against his pasty white skin and bobbed up and down as he talked. He wasn't wearing a uniform—surprising since up till then, we were the only people we'd seen in street clothes. He was talking a blue streak on two phones at once as his hands flew over a computer keyboard. Beside him, one assistant held a ton of folders, while another madly rifled through documents piled on a side table. People streamed in and out of that office in a systematic way like a well-organized anthill. The guy motioned for Pritchenko and me to sit in chairs in front of his desk, but kept on barking orders into the phone.

As we waited for that guy to finish all his conversations, I checked out the mess piled around him. Most of the folders bore the seal of the Second Operational Quartermaster Corps, a unit I'd never heard of before. From what the guy was yelling into the phone, I surmised that that building was the unit's administrative headquarters.

Our host brusquely introduced himself as "Luis Viena, administrative head of the Second Quartermaster Corps" then went back to arguing with someone at the other end of the line about acquiring several hundred liters of helicopter fuel. He wanted the fuel immediately and the person on the other end of the line was refusing to provide it. He finally reached an agreement, citing something called "Presidential Priority," then hung up looking pleased with himself.

He sat there, lost in thought for a few long seconds. Then he blinked, pulled out a handkerchief, wiped his sweaty brow, and turned to us with a broad smile on his face.

"Good morning, good morning." His words poured out in a torrent. "I'm very sorry to keep you waiting so long, but organizing an operation of this size is difficult, very difficult, yes sir, especially with so few resources and the staff . . . the *staff*," he snorted contemptuously and waved his hand theatrically. "Oh sure, most are good people, hard-working men and women, dedicated, very dedicated of course, but their training and experience . . . know what I mean? You don't get training and experience overnight, no sir." His hand cut the air like an imaginary ax. "No way."

Prit and I kept our mouths shut. That hyperactive little man stood up, still ranting, as he rummaged around in a file cabinet. Finally he found folders with our names on them and turned toward us, triumphant, waving the folders as if they were fans.

"Organization. Organization and a system," he said proudly. "Those are the keys, yes sir." He rattled on as he sat back down, distractedly extracted some reports from the mountain of papers piled on his desk, then stuffed them into the folders he was holding.

He read our names aloud and, for the next ten minutes, delved into our considerably thick files. Occasionally he let out an "uh-huh" or an "ah-ha" and even a couple of surprised "oh's" and looked up at our faces. Finally, he set the folders back on his desk, took off his glasses, and rubbed his weary eyes. Then he started talking again.

Over the next half hour he told us all about himself, saying he headed up a task force. He wasn't in uniform because, although he'd served in the army, he was no longer a soldier. Before the Apocalypse, he'd been an executive at Inditex, the world's largest fashion conglomerate. For over fifteen years, he'd run the company's giant clothing distribution center in Zaragoza. He'd been enjoying a quiet holiday at his home in the islands with his wife and daughters when the world went to hell. Powerless, he witnessed the world's collapse, the defeat of humanity at the hands of the Undead, and the arrival of shattered survivors. At first they flooded in, but that downpour slowly became a drip that ended with us. Once things settled down, the army recruited him to be its quartermaster and bring order to the broken supply chain. Given his background, he was the right person, the only person with experience in organizing huge amounts of resources. So far, he'd done a remarkable job.

I envied that chatty, high-strung guy. Not only had he survived the Apocalypse, peacefully, in the Canaries, in his own home, surrounded by his family, but he worked comfortably behind a desk, hundreds of miles from the nearest Undead and all that shit. A piece of cake, compared to what we'd been through.

My instincts told me Prit and I—not that guy—were going to have to smell that shit up close.

TSJ hadn't just carried off useless people or criminals. Many of the fallen were people with knowledge and skills essential to society's survival. Engineers, architects, agronomists, nurses, pilots, doctors, soldiers— all missing in large numbers, especially the latter. Medical personnel and the military had suffered huge losses, since they were the first line of defense in the losing battle against TSJ. The government was trying to rebuild the military and medical corps as fast as possible, but that took time.

And that's where we came in. Prit was one of the few surviving helicopter pilots; all the flight hours he'd logged made him invaluable. As for me, the fact that I'd spent over a year in the Wild West, as the military called areas infested with Undead, made me a seasoned veteran, able to survive in a hostile environment and look out for less experienced members of my team.

As Viena spoke, I felt the blood drain from my face. He must be fucking joking. Me? A *seasoned veteran*? I spent most of that year running from one place to another like a scared rabbit or hidden in the basement of Meixoeiro Hospital! I was no Rambo!

I politely pointed that out to Mr. Viena. And, in case he hadn't noticed, Viktor Pritchenko, although certainly an exceptional pilot, had lost half a hand in an explosion. We weren't who they thought we were—just two exhausted survivors who wanted to start a new life. We'd do any job they entrusted to us, but we were no soldiers. Not for all the gold in the world would we go back to that so-called Wild West. I said all this in a long speech, then sat back and studied my interviewer.

Viena sat perfectly still for a moment, staring at us. Then he cleared his throat and spoke. "Gentlemen, I think you've misunderstood. I'm giving you an order that comes from much higher up. If you think you can resume the orderly life you led before the Apocalypse, think again. The world has completely changed and that change affects all of us. *All* of us. Including you, gentlemen." He turned to Prit. "And Mr. Pritchenko's in a very delicate situation. True, he's one of the most experienced pilots on the islands and God knows we need good pilots. But there's that ugly business with the nun."

I grabbed Prit's arm to stop him from leaping across the table, as the Ukrainian muttered a string of curses in Russian.

"That brings us to the next situation." Viena nodded, deep in thought, indifferent to Prit's reaction. "If Mr. Pritchenko voluntarily enlists in the quartermaster corps, we could . . . how should I put this . . . find a solution agreeable to all parties in the matter of the *Galicia*. There wouldn't be a trial and all charges would be dropped."

"As for you." Now he turned to me. "Surely you can see how much we need a person of your experience to face those monsters. Our raiding parties have been to the Wild West three or four times, tops. However, you and your friend," he stopped to glance at my file, "survived for more than a year out there. Few of us here can say that," he said with a smile.

I sat there in silence for a few seconds. The way he put it made sense. They had Prit by the balls; he had to accept. Just the thought of turning my back on my only friend made my stomach clench. Plus, if I didn't accept the assignment, I had no idea how the hell I was going to survive. I'd asked around and they sure didn't need any more lawyers.

I looked over at Prit. *What choice do we have?* his eyes said.

"At least we're in this together, right?" he asked, resting a hand on my shoulder.

"Of course, Prit, don't worry," I replied, hiding my distress, my mind racing at top speed. Back into the fucking shit.

"Great, gentlemen!" Viena clapped his hands. He quickly signed some forms and set them in front of us to sign. "After you leave here, they'll take you to your group's headquarters. If you have arrangements to make at home, do it right away." He peered over his glasses. "You head to the Peninsula tomorrow. I don't have to tell *you* what you'll find there."

2 0

That morning was unusually cold for the Canary Islands. You could still see Venus twinkling in the sky. Our group rubbed our hands and stamped our feet on the concrete floor of the Reina Sofia Airport to fight off the bitter cold.

After our meeting with Luis Viena, we only had time to rush home, grab a few personal items and say good-bye to Lucia. The worst part was telling Lucia that we'd been "drafted" and that Prit and I had to return to the Peninsula as part of a support team. In those few hours, my darling girl went through several stages of grief: anger, indignation, tears, anger. She finally accepted the situation with resignation. But, this morning, when she said good-bye, she was distant and cold. I didn't blame her.

She actually didn't hold me responsible for the situation, but there was a wall between us. I didn't understand until Prit explained to me what even a blind man could see. Lucia had experienced a terrible trauma, losing all her loved ones in a very short time. Prit, Sister Cecilia, and I were all the family she had. Now, the nun was fighting for her life and we were leaving on a very risky journey. Lucia was afraid it'd be a repeat of those terrible times in Vigo. I was so thickheaded, I thought she was mad at me. What a damn fool I was! I wanted to hold her in my arms and tell her not to worry, nothing in the world could stop me from coming home, everything would be okay, but I didn't do that when I had the chance.

The past few hours hadn't been easy for us, either. We joined our team at the military base at Tenerife North Airport for training on the weapons we'd use on our mission.

Fifteen minutes earlier, an officer decked out in full dress uniform drove us to an empty hangar at one end of the airport. He climbed onto the hood of a URO and announced our mission. As the words came out of his mouth, I was sure I was having a horrible flashback. It had to be a cruel joke. But it was real. And fucked up. They really were sending us back to the Peninsula. To Madrid, one of the most dangerous places in Europe.

Madrid wasn't a quiet, abandoned corner of the world. Nearly six million people had lived in the city and its suburbs before the Apocalypse. Only about fifteen thousand of the refugees on the islands were from there, so that meant Madrid would be teeming with millions of Undead, just waiting for us.

"Our objective is Safe Haven Three, one of the city's five refuges." The officer shouted. "Said Safe Haven withstood the Undeads' assaults for only four days. We believe more than three quarters of a million people lost their lives there." He cast his eyes over the group as that chilling figure sunk in.

"But you aren't going there to tour the battlefield! The largest building inside that Safe Haven was La Paz Hospital, which housed offices, stores, cafeterias, and dormitories. Next door to it was the largest pharmaceutical warehouse in Madrid. It supplied drugs to other Safe Havens by air." He paused. "Unfortunately, the tide of Undead thwarted that plan."

I looked at Prit, who was as absorbed as I was in the officer's explanations. If the reports were true, tons of drugs had been seized from the warehouses of Bayer, Pfizer, and other manufacturers nearby during the last chaotic days and must still be there. Those drugs were as important as fuel or weapons. Maybe more important. Our health care system was already shaky due to a lack of medical staff. Without those drugs, it would revert back to the eighteenth century. The situation in Tenerife's hospitals was grim. They needed antibiotics, insulin, serums, opiates, painkillers, sedatives—the list went on and on. Supplies were running low and production wasn't keeping up with demand. On top of that, some medicines were impossible to produce, due to the lack of materials and know-how. We had no choice. We had to go there.

The hospitals on the other islands were either infested with Undead or had already been looted by teams like ours. To make matters worse, casualties on those trips had been very high. So they'd decided to try for the jackpot—Madrid.

Before the communication systems failed, Spain and France had shared a spy satellite, Helios II. Its central control was in France, but there was a substation on the Peninsula.

After several attempts, the few surviving computer programmers finally created a replica of that substation in Tenerife. The Helios II's cameras were now our eyes on southern Europe. The fact that they hadn't had any problems taking control of the satellite convinced me that either France wasn't interested or there was no one left at the helm.

Aerial images of Madrid showed that the city was intact for the most part, except for some neighborhoods that had burned to the ground. The warehouse seemed to still be standing, but who knew what we'd find when we got there?

In the half dark before the sun was completely up, we took off in an Airbus A-320 headed for the Peninsula. Nearly every seat had been removed, transforming that bird into a gigantic cargo ship. Our destination was Cuatro Vientos Airport, the former military airfield, about ten miles from the capital. Months before, someone had noticed via satellite that the fence around the airfield was intact; additionally, there seemed to be no movement on the site. After weeks of observation, they concluded that the facilities were empty and probably safe. That word *probably* bothered me the most.

The only way to access the complex was through the main building. The last radio communication, received as the Safe Haven was falling, reported that the airfield was locked up tight. If that report was reliable, the complex was safe and empty.

Our first objective was to secure the airport. To accomplish that, we were accompanied by a platoon that comprised a few surviving Spanish legionnaires, battle-hardened commandos who'd be armed to the teeth. Once the area was secured, they would station themselves around the perimeter and seal off the area. Then it would be our turn. That's when things would get really rough.

2 1

TENERIFE

"Fuck!" Lucia grabbed the pan of milk off the stove so it wouldn't boil over, spilling half the contents on the burner in her rush. The acrid smell of scorched milk instantly filled the room.

Tears welled up in her eyes. She felt like such a fool! She'd only looked away for a moment. She knew perfectly well how strictly milk was rationed—one liter per person every two weeks. But she got distracted and spilled almost half a liter. How could she have been so stupid? Where the hell was she going to get more?

She slumped into a chair and glanced around, discouraged. Since they'd come to the Canaries, everything had gone hopelessly wrong. First, they were quarantined on that damned ship for a month, stuck in a tiny cell, not knowing what was going to happen next. She'd wake up at night, breathing hard, covered in sweat, feeling the walls of the cell closing in on her. The only break in that routine was visits from doctors swaddled in their spectral hazmat suits. Out of the blue, they'd been released. Then, she was horrified to learn that a sadistic guard had beaten Sister Cecilia almost to death like those sadistic guards in Nazi concentration camps.

They'd filed a report against the guy the minute they set foot on land, but three weeks had passed and nothing had happened. The island's bureaucracy was stretched so thin trying to settle the avalanche of refugees and minimally feed them, they didn't have the staff or the time to investigate an alleged crime. And all they had to go on was what she'd seen before she passed out.

Since that day nearly a month ago, the nun had hovered between life and death in one of the island's crowded hospitals, just one of the thousands of sick and wounded cared for by a handful of overworked doctors and nurses and a few exhausted volunteers with very few resources.

And that damned apartment! Before the Apocalypse, Lucia lived with her parents in a big three-story house. The apartment she lived in now was tiny and had practically no furniture. It reminded her of the Krakow ghetto she'd seen in *Schindler's List*, where dozens of people were crammed into very little space. There weren't any walls or guards in Tenerife, but it felt oppressive just the same.

They were lucky; they lived in a "good" sector. Since Prit was one of the few pilots on the island, he'd been classified as essential personnel, entitling the three of them to some advantages, such as better rations and a "luxury" apartment with fewer cockroaches. Lucia knew there were thousands of people living in overcrowded conditions that were much worse. Even the smallest village was crammed with refugees. Famine was a threat to everyone, regardless of housing or classification. Unless you had contacts in the black market—and something interesting to sell.

With her boyfriend and Prit around, Lucia felt safe and didn't dwell on the terrible circumstances that weighed on her like a two-ton slab. She'd been carefree and blocked out everything she disliked. She'd focused instead on her brief, impromptu honeymoon with "Mr. Lawyer," the nickname she'd given him because he rambled on about the injustices of the system and problems the government needed to address.

Lucia was deeply in love, as only a romantic seventeen-year-old girl can be. Some nights she'd lie in bed, trying not to wake him up, and watch him toss and turn, plagued by the monster-fueled nightmares. Lucia knew that she was the best medicine for him. Since they'd arrived, he'd slept better and even smiled a couple of times. Then suddenly, he and Prit had had to leave with almost no time to say good-bye.

They'd all known it was just a matter of time until authorities recruited the "guys from the helicopter" to head back to the Peninsula in search of God-knows-what essential supplies, but that didn't make it easier to say good-bye.

And although she was on an island full of police and soldiers, with no Undead within hundreds of miles, Lucia was more terrified than ever. For the first time since this nightmare began, she was alone and had to rely on herself.

A knock on the door roused her from her thoughts. Dragging her feet, she went to the door and came face-to-face with Miss Rosario, the building manager. She was a small, dumpy, fifty-something woman with terrible varicose veins. She wore her steel gray hair in a tight bun on top of her head. Her dress was made of coarse brown fabric that made her look much slimmer than she actually was. Miss Rosario studied Lucia with her little owl eyes and tried to get a glimpse inside the room.

"Are you all right, dear? I thought I heard voices."

"Don't worry, Rosario," said Lucia, pulling the door half-closed behind her. "Nothing's wrong. I just spilled a little milk, that's all."

Miss Rosario had been given the title of "block leader" by the government and proudly wore her plastic badge. One of the first things Lucia discovered was that there were snitches everywhere. Last week, one of her neighbors, an agricultural engineer who worked on one of the farms at the northern end of the island, stopped her on the stairs. He told her that Miss Rosario was an official informer who was granted oversight of the buildings on that block by the authorities. Just like in East Germany, every building and every neighborhood had a "block leader."

"That's not the worst part," the neighbor added, after looking cautiously over his shoulder. "Besides block leaders, there're dozens, maybe hundreds of undercover informants. Even your boyfriend or roommate could be working for Information Services. It's like the fucking Stasi in the GDR back in the old days."

His bitter comments still echoed in Lucia's head. She hadn't paid much attention before. Everyone was almost obsessively paranoid. She thought his furtive comments were just the ravings of an old man who saw conspiracies everywhere. But now she knew her neighbor was right. Too bad she couldn't tell him. Two days before, he'd been "transferred" to a different housing complex. That wasn't out of the ordinary, but that transfer took place at four o'clock in the morning. And in an army truck instead of one pulled by a team of horses. He must've confided in the wrong neighbor.

"Don't forget, young lady, no visitors are allowed on this block after four," Miss Rosario's jangling voice droned on. "If you have a guest, you'll have to fill out a report."

"See for yourself. There's no one here," grumbled Lucia and reluctantly opened the door wide to let the snoopy woman look inside. Just then, Lucullus materialized out of the dark hallway with speed that belied his size and slipped inside the apartment, brushing against Lucia's legs, back from one of his mysterious walks.

Miss Rosario sniffed with a look of disgust that struck Lucia as really funny. The biddy's face reminded her of a bulldog sniffing a particularly smelly turd on the sidewalk.

Lucia made a heroic effort to keep from laughing. She already had enough problems with that old hag and she didn't want to add to the list. She was a newcomer and the only one in that housing complex who didn't have a job in an "essential" sector. That made the manager especially suspicious of her, coupled with the fact that she was one of the few people in Tenerife who still had a pet that hadn't been cooked up in a stew.

While her boyfriend and Prit had been in the flat, old lady Rosario had stayed away, but since they'd been called up, she'd mounted a ruthless siege. Because her apartment was especially coveted, Lucia suspected that Rosario was watching for the smallest slipup to justify evicting her. Or the old woman just had a wild hatred for a younger, prettier woman. In any case, she had to tread carefully.

"I swear there's no problem," repeated Lucia with a forced smile. "I have to leave right now. I have to go to the hospital. My job, you know."

"Yes, yes, of course, the hospital." The old bat shook her head, and with a look of *you're not fooling me* added, "It's a good thing your husband got you that job at the hospital. That way you can take care of your mother and get out of the mandatory Agriculture Brigade. It'd be a real shame, dear, to ruin your delicate hands with a hoe."

"She's not my mother, she's a nun," Lucia said pointedly, as she grabbed her bag and slammed the door behind her. Rosario had planted herself like a tree in the hallway. To get past her, Lucia had to nudge the old battle-ax aside. The caretaker smelled of strong perfume and stale sweat. "And he's not my husband; he's my boyfriend. About my work . . . "

"Oh, stop your flimsy excuses." Rosario shot her a poisonous look and changed her tone. "You may have fooled Information Services, but you can't pull the wool over my eyes! You and your friends show up one day out of the blue, claiming you're from the Peninsula! You get to live in a good sector, while people better than you have to break their backs in the fields! Ha! What a load of shit! I know you're filthy Froilist spies! Hear me? Froilists, that's what you are!"

As Lucia made her way down each flight of stairs, she could hear the manager shouting, *"Froilist scum!"* But the girl didn't pay any attention. She'd heard it all before. She knew she hadn't given the old bag any reason to write her up, but she knew she was under surveillance. And Rosario might not be the only spy. Lucia was convinced someone was following her. But she was no Froilist. As far as she knew, anyway.

2 2

MADRID

That smell . . . the smell of the burned flesh of dozens of bodies thrown on a pyre.

I thought it would be like grilled meat, but it was a denser, heavier smell, a little spicy. It was unsettling, as if your nose somehow knew it wasn't a normal scent. Strange, after five minutes or so, I didn't notice it anymore. But when I got on the plane and then came back out a few minutes later, the smell assaulted me again, suffocating me.

Sitting on the steps of the Airbus, I watched the legionnaires throw body after body into a pit at the edge of the runway. The first bodies were doused with gasoline to start the fire. After that, the bodies' fat fed the fire, which flared up every time a new body landed on the flames.

I couldn't believe we'd only been there for three hours. It felt like a century. The flight and the muffled drone of the plane's engines had lulled me into a strange calm. Everyone seemed strangely elated. I finally realized why—we were thousands of feet above the ground, safe from the Undead. The entire crew had relaxed, knowing it was impossible for those damned things to reach us.

It was like the break in a horror movie when the actors sit around chatting on the porch in the daylight after surviving the horrors of the haunted house overnight. But that's just a prelude to a night of even more horror. Was that what we were in for?

Our group was made up of a platoon of twenty legionnaires, two officers, three civilians, plus the pilot and copilot. The mission's bombastic leader had called us the "infiltration team." Judging by the forced joviality, you'd think we were on a routine flight over the equator, not flying into the heart of that hell.

The commanding officer was an amazing character. His name was Kurt Tank, but he told us to call him Hauptmann Tank or just Tank. Before the collapse he was in the German army. The Apocalypse caught him, like many of his countrymen, at his vacation home in the Canary Islands. When he realized he couldn't return to his country because there was none to go back to, Tank enlisted in the army of survivors, along with many other foreign soldiers. Risky and dangerous, sure, but at least they were armed and could defend themselves.

You might assume that a German guy with such a militaristic name would have a commanding presence, but he was far from the archetypal Super Arian. Tank was skinny and pale, with green eyes that bored into you. His deliberate, low-key manner gave the impression that he was soft and meek. Nothing was further from the truth. When I shared a cigarette with the legionnaires on our team, I learned he'd led his men into unimaginable situations. On an "infiltration mission" he led two months earlier in Cadiz, he and two other guys were the only survivors. A real tough guy.

Landing at Cuatro Vientos Airport was a real experience. Built in the early twenties as an airbase, its runway was too short for large civilian planes like the Airbus A-320. But we weren't bound by any regulations and didn't have to follow a flight plan.

We could fly over the city at low altitude without getting a ton of complaints and approach very low at the slowest speed possible to improve our chances.

We circled about three thousand feet above the suburbs of an absolutely dead, desolate Madrid as we made our approach. Out the window I could see the huge bedroom communities that ringed the centuries-old capital. Normally those areas would be pretty dead during the day when most of the residents were at their jobs in the city, but the total lack of activity generated a feeling that was hard to explain. All our jokes and laughter stopped. A silence, dense and thick as oil, replaced it and a sticky fear settled in everyone's heart.

I was amazed at how everyone faced that situation. The soldiers seemed to cope better, the way they've done for centuries, at least on the surface. Most of them painstakingly checked their gear. The four legionnaires in Team One napped in a corner, enjoying those last moments of calm. They'd deplane first to secure the perimeter and were taking the biggest risk. We all knew that if things got out of control and they couldn't secure the runway and nearby building, the mission would have to be aborted and we'd have to take off in a hurry, leaving them stranded.

As for the others, those with military experience—like my buddy, Prit—kept busy to distract themselves from the anxiety I'm sure they were feeling. The phlegmatic Ukrainian popped his gum loudly. Using his razor-sharp knife, he carved a wooden figurine with more good intentions than skill. That was the same knife he'd used to kill an Undead in Vigo and save my life.

Next to him were two people I hadn't recognized until I heard the woman's nervous chatter and her brittle laugh: Marcelo and Pauli, from the team that had plucked us out of death's jaws at Lanzarote Airport. Someone must've decided that, since we'd flown together then, we'd work well together on the infiltration team. I wondered if it was our fault they'd been picked for that God-awful mission.

The other civilian was David Broto, a quiet guy from Barcelona, in his twenties, stocky, with black hair. His faraway gaze didn't hide his pain. I assumed he'd lost loved ones in those dark days, like everyone else, and hadn't gotten over it.

Most of the survivors were like that. They seemed normal, healthy, and well adjusted until you looked into their dull eyes. They ate, breathed, talked, laughed, even joked, but they were just going through the motions. Their spirit was dead; they were completely destroyed, lost and broken, looking for a reason to live. They never got over losing their way of life, their family and personal history, and felt guilty for surviving. Nothing had any meaning now.

Post-traumatic stress some said, but that was bullshit. It was a much deeper pain that no one could define. I'd heard that despite such widespread emotional strain there hadn't been a single case of suicide on the islands. Not one. Despite the horror, we survivors were endowed with a will to survive. Or instinct. Or maybe it was faith.

The plane banked hard and the landing gear extended with a loud screech. The engines' whine rose two octaves and the brakes groaned trying to stop the fifty-ton A-320 as it rushed down that short runway. I worried, like everyone else, that the noise was arousing the interest of all the Undead packed into that city, waking hundreds of thousands of them out of their slumber as the plane roared overhead so low it nearly clipped the roofs of buildings.

The phone on the bulkhead gave a loud ring. It connected directly with the cockpit a few feet away. Hauptmann Tank grabbed the receiver, nodded a few times, and hung up with a curt "thank you."

"The pilot reports that we'll be on the ground in less than a minute!" He shouted above the roar of the engines. "Our landing may be bumpy, so buckle up!"

I was scared shitless so I pulled my belt as tight as I could. Prit was muttering something in Russian, probably some comment about the pilot's mother or Tank's, or maybe he was pissed off he had to sit there, like the rest of us sheep, instead of being at the controls of the Airbus. You never knew with Prit.

"When the plane stops, Team One, take your positions immediately!" Tank shouted in his thick German accent, as he clutched a luggage rack and struggled to stay on his feet. "Sweep the area, check the perimeter. Shoot anything that moves! But if any of those helicopters parked on the runway gets the slightest scratch, I swear to God I'll rip the guts out of the guy who fired the shot! Got it?"

A grunt of assent rose from twenty throats, while twenty pairs of sweaty hands cocked twenty HKs and strapped on helmets.

A sharp jolt shook us, then the landing gear gave a terrifying shriek. A dull roar rose from the engines as the pilot threw them into reverse at full speed to bring the huge Airbus to a stop in that small space.

"Too fast," Pritchenko muttered, watching as the runway rushed past us.

Thick black smoke billowed from the wheels. The pilot had locked the wheels in a desperate attempt to slow down the plane. The cabin shook violently, as if the plane were breaking into pieces. The friction was shredding the tires. The smell of burning rubber was overpowering.

If we had a blowout at that speed, the plane would likely tip and roll out of control down the runway, becoming a fireball. My balls shrank in terror. I was convinced we were going to die.

The Airbus gradually slowed down, but it still emitted sounds that weren't very reassuring. Something came loose from the cargo bay and crashed noisily to the floor, but that was it. Finally, with a plaintive screech, the plane came to a complete stop, but its engines still rumbled, exhausted from the strain.

On cue, the legionnaires got to their feet in sync. Two of them manned the door while a third attached a rope ladder that unfurled down to the runway. Before I could blink three times, they'd slithered down onto the cracked pavement.

A few seconds later, we heard the first shot, then a couple of long bursts of machine gunfire and an explosion broke the silence on the runway.

Let the dance begin.

2 3

TENERIFE

Island heat slapped Lucia in the face as she left the apartment building. Out front, a dozen people waited patiently for the bus. Not a single vehicle drove by, except for an occasional bicycle and a beat-up wagon on retreads pulled by a worn-out nag.

Although the hospital was just a few miles away, getting there took a really long time. On account of the strict fuel rationing, there were almost no motor vehicles on the road, aside from the few engaged in essential services. There were very few draft animals and even fewer bicycles. A junk heap with wheels and pedals no one would've looked twice at before the Apocalypse was now worth a fortune. Under martial law, bicycle theft was punishable by hard labor. Gasoline theft was worse, punishable by firing squad. Draconian measures, true, but the fragile law and order on the island had to be maintained at all costs or it could collapse.

Lucia joined the line of hopeful people to wait for some kind of transportation that would take her close to downtown. Soon, Fortune smiled on her. A former Coca-Cola delivery truck came limping along, wrapped in a huge cloud of blue smoke produced by the low-grade diesel fuel refined on the island. Because it lacked chemical additives, engines that ran on it broke down from time to time.

Better than nothing, Lucia thought, as she scrambled aboard. The truck took off with a jolt. She and the other passengers clung to anything they could to keep from being thrown off. Lucia was reminded of the picturesque Soviet trucks and buses she'd seen on the streets of Cuba when she and her parents vacationed there a couple of years before. Those vehicles looked funny at the time, but she never imagined she'd have to ride on a similar conveyance one day. She smiled at the irony and wondered if the epidemic had reached Cuba. Of course it had! That damned TSJ had reached the farthest corners of the globe. It was the deadliest plague in the history of mankind. Only a handful of isolated places like the Canary Islands had been spared.

She knew all too well that the rumors were true. She and her friends had been the last survivors to reach the Canary Islands from Europe. Behind them was only death, desolation, and millions of Undead wandering around for eternity.

She was glad to have made it there. Life on the island wasn't paradise, with all the rationing and overcrowding, but at least she could close her eyes at night without worrying that a horde of Undead would break the door down and end her life.

But the situation was far from ideal. Thousands of people suffered from hunger. Despite the government's best efforts, food supplies were dangerously low. Every day, a fleet of fishing boats went out to sea, hoping to return with their holds full, but catches were meager. And while large areas of the island had been cleared for farming, their output was still very low. Specialists and farmers worked hard to get them going, but the shortage of chemical fertilizers and pesticides prevented a good harvest. The general feeling was that the volcanic soil was too weak to feed the multitude. Fresh meat was available only to a fortunate few. Most people were very thin, their cheekbones jutting out, their eyes shining with hunger. Very few people fared well, but no one said they wanted to leave the relative safety of the island. Not even in jest.

And then there was the matter of the Froilists.

Lucia remembered how confused she and her friends were when they heard people speaking matter-of-factly about "the others," the Froilists. At first they'd thought that was how people on the Canaries referred to the Undead. They soon realized their mistake.

When survivors first crowded together on the Canaries, they had to face a painful reality: The system they'd known in the old world had gone up in smoke. For a little while, people acted as if nothing had changed.

Most of the government had disappeared in the mayhem before the collapse. Only a handful of ministers and a regional president had reached safety. A rumor went around that the Prime Minister's motorcade was lost somewhere between his residence in Moncloa Palace, and Torrejon de Ardoz army base, but nobody knew for sure. The head of the opposition party and his family had made it to the islands, thanks to an old friend who owned an airline but, in a cruel twist of Fate, he died a few weeks later in a car wreck. Most of the Royal Family reached the Canaries, except for the king's son and heir, the Prince of Asturias; the king's daughter, Cristina; and her husband. Their fate was a mystery, but no one thought they'd survived.

At first King Juan Carlos had tried to form a government, although skeptics pointed out that, since the Peninsula was lost, there wasn't much left to govern. Things went well for a few months, until one morning the king was found lying on the bathroom floor, dead from a stroke. His Majesty had the dubious honor of having the last state funeral that part of the world would ever see. Then the situation became almost more chaotic than when the Undead had first attacked.

Without a legitimate government, soldiers grew restless, not knowing what authority to obey, overwhelmed by the heavy responsibility of protecting and feeding more than a million people, with little administrative help or a health care system.

Then, a group of generals took the bull by the horns. Since the king's daughter, Infanta Elena, was next in line, she was crowned Queen of Spain at the town hall in Tenerife in a hasty ceremony few survivors knew about.

It soon became clear that the only goal of that coronation was to legitimize the military junta's de facto power to govern the two plague-free islands—Gran Canaria Island and Tenerife. Queen Elena was just a puppet in their hands. Just three weeks after she was crowned, Queen Elena I was assassinated during a visit to a communal farm by a member of the Communist Party, or what was left of it.

Chaos erupted. For fourteen days the islands were embroiled in riots between the defenders of the Third Republic and the supporters of Froilán, Elena's son and therefore the new king. Each side knew all too well that it was too weak to prevail and that a long civil war was out of the question.

Finally, the two sides called a truce. With little Froilán as their figurehead, Royalists (derogatorily called Froilists by the Republicans) would control Gran Canaria, under the protection of the military junta. Tenerife pompously declared itself the "Third Spanish Republic" and elected a prime minister and a "National Emergency Democratic Government." The truth was, democracy was just a nice word that both groups hid behind as they took power and tried to survive. The way an old lady, down on her luck, holds onto a dress she wore in better days and her grandmother's silver spoons, both governments tried to clothe themselves in the last scraps of legitimacy, while still throwing punches under the table. Although they weren't officially at war, neither side recognized the other's legitimacy. Raiding parties frequently stole supplies, leaving more casualties than the Undead had.

When Lucia and her friends reached the islands, confrontations between Republicans and the Froilists were at an all-time high. Both governments seethed with paranoia over enemy infiltration. Each side knew it had thousands of supporters on the other island . . . and thousands of infiltrators among their own ranks. It was only a matter of time before a fifth column would jump into the fray.

2 4

MADRID

Hearing the shots, I pressed against a window, trying to see what was going on. After they'd deplaned, the legionnaires had divided into groups of three. Four groups spread out on the runway around the Airbus, while the fifth group sprinted toward the terminal at the far end of the airbase. Those guys had clearly drawn the short straw. They were headed for the hangars, out of our line of sight. If they encountered any problems, they'd be too far away for help to reach them in time. But I felt sure they knew that.

I was taken by surprise by a new burst of gunfire coming from the terminal building. Through the doors that opened onto the runway staggered three Undead—a middle-aged man whose wide mustache was covered with clotted blood, and two women, one of whom had had her arm torn off at the shoulder.

There they were—the tireless fucking Undead.

I shuddered at the sight of them. The passage of time had had little effect on those things. I'd hoped they'd rotted after all this time, but their bodies seemed to be holding up well. I was sure they'd decayed in some way, but it was a slow, subtle change I couldn't put my finger on. They just didn't seem as "fresh" as they did at first. It would take years or centuries for them to "die," a lot more time than we survivors had.

The clothes those three were wearing were in very good condition, so they must've spent most of the time inside the terminal, not subjected to the elements. The one with the bloody mustache had on a green jumpsuit like the airport cleaning staff wore. The other two looked like civilians or flight attendants, but I couldn't say which since their clothes were covered in blood.

Those Undead didn't faze the legionnaires closest to the door. They very coolly let them get about six feet away before they acted.

Their system struck me as odd. In each team, there was a long-range shooter, a short-range shooter, and one soldier who stood in the middle watching to make sure no Undead got too close without being noticed. The middle guy also loaded the other soldiers' weapons. The two shooters switched positions frequently and if need be, carried out the same role.

Just then, the team slung their HKs across their backs, quickly put on plastic safety goggles, and drew their pistols. For almost a minute, they allowed the monsters to approach, until they were almost an arm's length away. On the order of the group leader, they all pulled their triggers.

Almost simultaneously, the heads of the three Undead exploded in a fountain of blood, bone chips, and viscera. Their bodies collapsed onto the concrete, convulsing. I couldn't suppress a loud "Fuck" as I involuntarily took a step back and fell backward over a seat. It was so unexpected and macabre I felt breakfast rising up my throat.

"Explosive bullets," Prit murmured, wearing a wolfish grin, as he helped me up. "Even a misplaced shot becomes a hit. Those guys know what they're doing."

The three legionnaires hopped over the bodies and kept running toward the building. Another group had already entered the control tower, while a third group hurriedly put new batteries in one of the airport's electric vehicles. After a moment, the little bus came to life and started to roll slowly on tires that had gone flat after months outdoors. It wouldn't run for very long, but long enough to check the perimeter.

More shots rang out inside the terminal. Prit jumped to his feet, with the look of a hungry hunter. The Ukrainian wanted to get off the plane and, as he put it, "shoot some ducks on the pond." I wasn't so eager to get out there.

"What the hell're we waiting for?" the Ukrainian growled. "Let's go!"

"Don't be in such a hurry, Mr. Pritchenko." Pauli stretched out her arm to restrain my restless friend, who was slipping down the aisle like an eel, headed for the door. "Listen to me, please! The legionnaires have drilled this operation for weeks. We have to stay in the plane until they've secured the perimeter. Then can we leave. Plus, your mission is to fly a helicopter. That's it. Got it?"

"They may need our help!" Prit snorted, casting an urgent glance at the door. "They're mopping up out there while we're sitting on our asses in here, damn it!"

"They know we're here," I intervened, trying to reassure my friend. "If they need us, they'll radio us. Besides, if we go out there now, they might confuse us with the Undead. We have to wait, Prit. Try to understand that."

The Ukrainian turned his back, sulking and cursing under his breath. He wanted to take on those monsters, but he was being held back. How different we were! I'll admit it—those Undead terrified me. Not only wasn't he afraid, he hated them and wanted to unleash his wrath on them.

There was a crash of broken glass as a huge window in the terminal exploded. Through the shower of glass, I saw flashes from guns turn the room a sulfur yellow. Then several bodies with mangled heads fell out the window and landed on the tarmac with a thud. For a second, there was silence inside the plane. Suddenly, someone's radio violently crackled, startling us.

"Alpha Three in position. Terminal secured. Doors barricaded from the inside. Twelve varmints down. No casualties of our own. Awaiting instructions. Over."

"Alpha Three, hold your position," Tank replied as he waved us down the rope ladder onto the runway. "Teams Two and Three, entering the building. Hold your fire!"

Tank turned to us, cocking his gun. His sea-green gaze rested on me for a second, then he surveyed the rest of the group. A chill ran down my back. I could guess what was coming next.

"We're up, gentlemen. Let's go!"

2 5

The rope ladder swayed violently; its rough surface burned my hands as we descended on it to the runway. Preceding me was tall, silent Marcelo. Unlike most Argentines, he was a man of few words, but he seemed confident in everything he did. Next down the ladder was Pritchenko. In his excitement, he was humming an indecipherable tune under his breath. Broto, the computer tech, and Pauli were waiting for us on the runway.

My thoughts were a bit scattered, so when my feet touched the ground, I gave a little hop. "Once more into the breach dear friends," I said, quoting Shakespeare's *Henry the Fifth*. I looked up at the plane, thinking how safe we'd be in there. The copilot watched us out the side window and gave us a mock salute, then slammed the Plexiglas window shut. Those sons of bitches. They'd be safe in there while we dragged our asses through Undead-infested Madrid. But that was how it had to be. There were only a handful of people left in the world who knew how to fly a plane that size, so they were worth their weight in gold. No point in brooding. We all had to play the cards we were dealt.

I joined the other members of my group. With sweaty hands, I grabbed the gun I'd been issued—a nine-millimeter Glock, like the one I took off the soldier back home a million years ago. I also had a dozen magazines stashed in my backpack and a sheath full of spears stitched to the leg of my wetsuit.

The legionnaires looked at me funny and made wisecracks about my wetsuit, but I wore it anyway. It was the main reason I'd survived. If something works, why the hell change? Plus, I was superstitious enough to believe that nothing bad would happen to Prit or me as long as I had it on. Bottom line, it made me feel better and that alone was worth it.

One of the legionnaires looked worried as he conferred with Tank. Something had gone wrong. I overheard him say that the group that had headed for the airport's Aviation Museum wasn't answering radio calls. Shit . . .

The hairs rose on the back of my neck and I broke out in a cold sweat. If we didn't secure every access to the runway, thousands of Undead would overrun it in minutes. There'd be so many, the plane wouldn't be able to take off. The engines would suck in dozens of bodies and explode, trapping us forever.

The heavy-duty wire fence surrounding the runway was over twenty feet high. The first dozen Undead—men, women and children—had gathered there and were shaking the fence, sending up a cacophony of sounds as they beat against the steel mesh like a bunch of drunk monkeys. If that fence gave way, we'd really be screwed.

In less than ten minutes, a huge crowd of Undead had already gathered. Within an hour there'd be tens of thousands. I pictured a long procession of corpses parading down what remained of Highway M-30 that encircled Madrid, headed straight for Cuatro Vientos Airport. Not a surprise with all the racket we'd made.

"You two! Come here!" Kurt Tank waved us over as he spread a map on the ground. "We don't have much time. There's no sign of Alpha Four and that means they must've suffered a serious setback."

"Serious setback." That's one way to put it. More like they were fucked up.

Tank peered through his binoculars. "The door to the hangar is closed. We're safe out here. They must be trapped on the other side, but we don't have time to check. We have to stick to the plan, before a million of those things get here."

"The fence seems to be holding," the computer guy argued hesitantly. He looked as scared as the rest of us.

"That fence wasn't designed to withstand several thousand bodies pushing against it, sir," replied the sergeant standing next to Tank. He was tall and dark, with a deeply wrinkled, weathered face. "In no time, a lot more of those bastards will join them. Then that fucking fence will give and you won't like what happens next, sir."

"No time to waste!" Tank barked pointing to a lone helicopter parked near the control tower. "Get that helicopter up and running NOW! I don't care what you have to do, but get that chopper in the air! You have fifteen minutes, not one minute more, or we'll be in big trouble." He turned back to the legionnaire who stood expressionless beside him. "Sergeant, organize your men in patrols around the perimeter, but don't get within five feet of the fence! And burn those damn bodies. They're starting to smell!"

Not knowing why, I started running toward the helicopter, with Pritchenko at my side. Someone had handed each of us a large, very heavy package wrapped in oilcloth. I started to pant, cursing every time that damned bundle slipped from my hands. Pauli and Marcelo ran in front of us carrying equally heavy wooden boxes. Broto followed at a trot, clutching his backpack, looking more worried with every step.

When we reached the helicopter, I fell against its side, puffing like a freight train. The other team ran to the small planes parked on the edge of the runway. The electric bus was heading toward them, carrying several red cylindrical pods. I guessed they were empty containers they'd load with drugs when we got to our destination.

If we got there.

Every time I turned toward the fence, I got chills. The Undead were streaming. Before the Apocalypse, this was a densely populated area two miles from a huge mall. It must've been a fucking "hot spot." That sight wiped the smile from Prit's face.

"Here, kid." Marcelo held out a closed fist. "Take this, just in case. You might need it. Use it wisely."

The computer guy stared at the Argentine and closed his fist around what Marcelo was handing him. Then he slowly opened his hand and looked up, confused. It was a shiny copper nine-millimeter bullet.

"What's this for?" he asked, surprised.

"It's yours, dickhead. In case you haven't noticed, there're more of those rotten bastards out there than we have ammunition. Even if we make every one of our shots, we won't have enough bullets. So, if you get in a tight spot, you can . . . POW!" Marcelo pointed an imaginary gun at his head.

Broto paled and, with trembling hands, stashed the bullet in his pocket. He was the only one on that mission who was unarmed. He must've been kicking himself for turning down the Glock they'd offered him in the Canaries.

"Oh, come on, Marcelo, don't be an asshole. Leave the kid alone!" Pauli snapped, as she gave the Argentine a friendly punch in the arm.

"Do the math, kid," said the Argentine, ignoring Pauli, as he pointed to our guns and then to the savage crowds behind the fence. "Do the math." Then he turned to the helicopter and started unwrapping the package Prit and I had brought.

"Don't pay any attention to him," Pauli said to David. "He's just fucking with you. He doesn't like being here, he doesn't like the Undead and doesn't like babysitting rookies like you, so he's in a bad mood. If all goes as planned, you won't be any closer to the Undead than we are now. Don't worry, okay?"

I looked at the petite officer and saw worry in her eyes. We both knew things weren't going to be that simple. But her words seemed to calm the computer guy.

Meanwhile Pritchenko had slipped into the cockpit. His hands were flying over the mass of controls, checking fuel levels and fluids of that huge SuperPuma. Most of the control panel lit up, indicating that at least the electrical system and battery were intact.

Something about the chopper caught my attention. Although it was a military plane, it was painted entirely white, from nose to tail, except for a red and blue stripe down the side. You could barely make out SPANISH AIR FORCE beneath the months' worth of dust and ash that covered the huge bird.

I mustered up some courage and pulled the lever on the door. It opened with a groan and folded down as a ladder. Adrenaline roared through my veins as I cocked my gun and climbed the three steps.

Instead of the usual bench seats, it had comfortable leather arm-chairs, covered with a layer of fine dust. I cautiously stepped in. The interior was dark and gloomy since its windows were encrusted with dust, so my eyes took a few seconds to adjust. Nearly blind as I made my way down the aisle, I kicked a long, cylindrical object lying on the floor, sending it rolling into a corner with a muffled thud. When I bent over to pick it up, I saw that it was a mahogany cane; its silver handle was engraved with a seal. I carried it to the door to get a better look.

I couldn't help gasping. The handle was engraved with a fleur-de-lis, the symbol of the Bourbones, Spain's royal family. I froze for a few seconds to let my mind process that information. There weren't many Bourbones in the world; even fewer were so old they needed to walk with a cane. I knew who this cane's owner was—King Juan Carlos! I'll be damned . . .

Broto entered the cabin, dragging his heavy backpack, and found me with the cane in my hands. "They must've evacuated the royal family from the Zarzuela Palace in this helicopter," he commented like a guy talking about yesterday's game. "A plane was waiting for them here. You know the rest."

Just then Pauli appeared in the doorway, dragging one of the wooden boxes. "What the hell're you guys doing back there? Give me a hand. These fucking boxes aren't going to load themselves!"

Chastened, Broto and I grabbed the first box. A hieroglyph of acronyms, stenciled in black, were scattered across the top; I could only decipher "7.62 x 51mm." Machine gun ammunition. I looked up. Marcelo had unwrapped the package Prit and I had dragged there. A huge, evil-looking MG3 machine gun, glistening with oil, lay inside. I whistled softly. We sure weren't hurting for firepower. Who knew if that would be enough.

The SuperPuma's engines let out a hoarse cough, along with a cloud of smoke and dust. The propeller blades started to rotate slowly as the engine came alive with a hiss.

"All aboard!" Prit bellowed from the cockpit. "Let's go!"

The huge chopper's blades picked up speed as Prit revved the engine. It was a tight fit in the cabin with eighteen team members and all our gear. Kurt Tank sat next to Prit in the forward cabin.

With a jolt, the bird rose into the air. Suddenly, an alarm began to wail in the cabin and a huge red indicator light lit up the dashboard.

"What the fuck's happening, Prit?" I asked over the intercom, alarmed.

"Quiet back there!" The Ukrainian sounded calm as he fought the cross currents that shook the helicopter. "The engine temperature sensors must be clogged with dust or they've been damaged by moisture! According to the dashboard, the main engine is about to burn up, but that's impossible. We just took off!"

"You sure?" I asked again. That was to be expected. Any plane would be in bad shape after months of neglect and exposure to weather.

"I can't be a hundred percent sure!" Pritchenko snapped. "It is what it is! We can't land again to do a tune up! Look down there!"

I looked out the window. A throng of thousands of angry Undead had gathered at the fence along the runway. Every inch of the perimeter was covered with those things, two or three abreast. They clutched the fence and furiously shook it. Their groans were so loud you could hear them above the whir of the helicopter's blades. Some had stuck their arms through the gaps between the concrete supports and the steel mesh.

You had to see that scene to believe it. There were all kinds: young, old, children, fat, skinny. They all were a waxy yellow and had that tattoo of exploded veins scattered across their skin. Their clothes were in bad shape, and some were completely naked, covered with dirt from head to toe. As we rose, those Undead monsters stretched their arms toward the helicopter, their lifeless, watery eyes drilling into us. Even from that height, I could see inside their grisly, dark mouths.

They knew we were there. And not just because we were making all that noise. They'd detected our vital signs somehow. Something drew them to us.

We were all petrified at that ghoulish sight. Someone muttered, "Dear God in Heaven." Another voice quietly said the Lord's Prayer, over and over. My mouth was too dry to say a word. I would've killed for a whiskey.

The Undead just kept coming—down side streets, singly or in small groups. They swarmed the M-40 highway and skirted dozens of huge pileups, wobbling toward us.

"Will the fence hold?" Broto asked over the intercom glumly, as he took it all in.

"Let's hope so." Tank shrugged. "The two pilots and the soldiers on the ground have orders to take refuge in the Airbus, out of sight of the

Undead, and make as little noise as possible. We hope that'll keep more from approaching the perimeter. Plus, the noise our helicopter makes will draw them to us."

"That's reassuring," murmured Broto, as he paled.

"Why not shoot?" I asked Marcelo, who'd leaned the MG3 out the left rear window. The Argentine coolly held the machine gun and carefully scrutinized the crowd.

"What for? That'd be a waste of ammunition. From this distance most of my shots would miss their marks." He gazed at that crowd, a shadow of fear in his eyes. "It'd be like shooting into the sea."

We sat in silence, watching the parade of Undead below the helicopter.

"Six minutes!" Pauli's voice broke our silence. "Get ready, everyone. This'll be a very short flight."

2 6

TENERIFE

"Oh, shit!" shouted the truck driver, as he swerved hard onto the shoulder.

Passengers were thrown to the bed of the truck in a jumble of arms and legs, cursing in several languages. Bruised and battered, Lucia got to her feet and looked around. The white cloud of steam pouring from the truck's engine and the glum look on the driver's face told her the truck wasn't going any farther.

"Are you crazy?" an old man asked, indignantly, as he helped a little boy to his feet. "Do you think we're just a load of gravel?"

"Don't blame me!" The driver shrugged, pointing to the smoking engine. "This heap's been patched with parts from three different trucks! It's a miracle it still runs! Be glad we're not stranded on the highway!"

"Whadda we do now?" someone else asked.

"Get out and walk," the truck driver said matter-of-factly and gave his cap a tug. "I'm staying here with the truck. Some bastard might try to steal my gas."

A chorus of groans rose at that. It was still early in the morning but the sun was already beating down. Everyone knew the walk wouldn't be pleasant.

Lucia leapt like a deer out of the truck and got her bearings. Her shift at the ICU started at two and it was already twelve thirty. The hospital was about four miles away, so she had just enough time to get there on foot. Thankful she'd gotten an early start that day, she began walking down the shoulder, glancing behind her like the other passengers, hoping another vehicle would come along.

No sweat. It's a beautiful day and I don't mind walking.

A lot of people were walking up and down the same road. Until a couple of weeks ago, there would've been a fruit and vegetable stand by the side of the road, but the Government of the Republic had decreed that collective farming would increase yield. Time would tell if that strategy would pay off. Lucia couldn't be bothered with that at the moment. She had more pressing matters to focus on, like how the hell to get more drugs for Sister Cecilia on the black market.

Lucia visited Sister Cecilia every minute she could. She was devastated at the nun's wan, bandaged face that blended into the white sheets where she lay motionless.

The week before, Lucia had sold a pair of diamond earrings that had belonged to her mother. It was a miracle she'd been able to hold on to them for so long. Selling them broke her heart. They were the last memento of her former life, a reminder of the girl who got on that bus a thousand years ago and embarked on this difficult life. She thought bitterly, *These new times forced people to grow up so fast. Back then, a seventeen-year-old girl was still a kid. Not anymore.*

In exchange for the earrings, that sweaty guy who worked at the Port Authority had given her a half dozen ration coupons; for Sister Cecilia, she'd gotten one of the rarest, most expensive items on the island—four boxes of morphine. The doctors had already used up two of those boxes. Lucia wondered what would happen when the nun's meager allotment of analgesics ran out.

That wasn't the only problem. The doctor said Sister Cecilia badly needed a drug called mannitol to reduce the swelling in her brain, but the medical board had ruled that her friend was a lost cause and precious vials of mannitol would be wasted on her. But Lucia didn't lose hope.

She'd been walking for twenty minutes when the driver of an overcrowded bus with a ridiculous-looking fuel tank bolted to the roof took pity on Lucia's group and picked them up. At a little past one, the girl finally arrived at the hospital.

Health services had totally collapsed. There were five hundred physicians on the island at most, and that number included med students from the University of La Laguna whom authorities had rushed to graduate.

In the lobby was an endless flow of patients, medical staff, and people claiming they had the most ridiculous ailments. Being admitted to the hospital guaranteed three meals daily and a break from the oppressive Mandatory Labor Service for a few days. Every day, exhausted doctors weeded out the fakers from among the genuinely sick.

She entered through the employee entrance, nodding at the armed guards manning the metal detector. With a quick, practiced gesture, she pinned her badge to her lapel. The guards knew her and gave her a quick glance, then turned their attention back to the relentless stream of people trying to finagle their way in. Security was no laughing matter at the island's only functioning hospital. There'd been several attempts to rob the pharmacy. On the black market, medications were the most valuable currency.

"Hi, Lucia!" The nurses' aide who greeted her was a real pistol, barely five feet tall. She was making eyes at one of the guards as she pinned her ID to the neckline of a blouse that was better suited for a bar than a hospital.

"Hi, Maite! How's it going?" With a knowing smile, Lucia walked up to the girl she considered her good friend. They'd only known each other a couple of weeks but survivors made friends amazingly easily. Those who'd emerged from that Undead hell desperately needed to interact with other people to feel alive.

"Great!" Maite replied with a mischievous grin. "Fernando's taking me out to dinner tonight. We may even have some wine! He's got some special ration coupons."

"Fernando . . . who the hell's Fernando?" Lucia asked, but one glance at the guard and the starry-eyed look on Maite's face explained everything. She shook her head. Her friend had a new boyfriend every week. They all promised the eternal love Maite was so desperate for. Of course there'd be a new guy the next week, but that didn't matter.

Life goes on, Lucia thought as she pulled on her uniform in the locker room and listened to her friend chatter away. *Despite all the shit we've been through, we still fall in love and have dreams. Even living the way we are, we survivors are fairly happy. Incredible, but true. Our will to live is so strong.*

" . . . Cecilia?"

"What'd you say, Maite?" Lucia abruptly turned from her thoughts.

"I asked you if there'd been any change in your friend's status."

Lucia thought for a moment, with a bitter look on her face. "No change. I'm going to go see her before my shift." She wanted to say, *No fucking change. She'll probably be a vegetable forever, but I can't accept that. If I did, I'd start to lose her and I'm sick of losing the people I love,* but she checked herself and forced a smile, as she took Maite's hand in hers and made a pouty face. "Will you come with me? Please?"

"Sure," said Maite. "First let's swing by the nurses' station and get some of that crap they call coffee, okay?" Maite gave Lucia a loving hug and walked out of the room, not knowing that in less than half an hour, she'd be dead.

2 7

MADRID

Madrid was dead.

There was no one left in a city where almost six million people once lived, breathed and dreamed. Nobody, except *Them*.

The metropolis extended for miles; not a sound broke the silence. The SuperPuma flew really low over streets and plazas as it crossed the city at top speed. Prit said we'd be less visible that way since the engine noise would ricochet, making it harder for those monsters to locate its source.

Passing so close to those rooftops made me extremely nervous, especially in such an unreliable helicopter. Everywhere the scene was the same: wide, empty streets; here and there a vehicle lying across the road. Trash, broken glass and worm-eaten skeletons were everywhere.

Retiro Park, located in the heart of Madrid, had once been a showcase. Now it had become a jungle. Weeds had devoured its walking paths. Its little lake gleamed in the sun, almost buried under tons of algae that gave it a greenish cast. On the lake's banks, the Crystal Palace was just a skeleton of steel beams and broken glass.

La Castellana, the main thoroughfare through the heart of the city, looked ghostly. Massive clouds of dirt rolled down that ten-lane road, rattling the few streetlights still standing. It was completely free of cars, since it had been closed to traffic right before the final collapse. A lone Volvo SUV with bars on its windows looked out of place on that deserted avenue. Why had its driver stopped in the middle of nowhere?

Here and there we spotted mounds of mummies and decaying skeletons where defense forces had taken a stand against the Undead. In every case, those mounds were surrounded by empty, shiny copper shell casings. Unfortunately, all those dead Undead were just a drop in the vast ocean of Undead that infested the streets.

It was a chilling sight. Sidewalks and roads were crawling with thousands of those creatures who were stopped in their tracks as if in a trance. It was like looking at an aerial photo of a street, frozen in a moment of normal city life. But the crowd's torn, blood-stained clothes destroyed that illusion—those who still had clothes, that is.

Only when the noise of the propeller blades and the shadow of our helicopter passed over them did the Undead awaken out of their trances.

"Look over there!" Broto shouted in disbelief, pointing to a spot on the ground.

We were passing by Santiago Bernabeu Soccer Stadium. Heavy vehicles and huge, steel, industrial containers blocked all the entrances. The number of worm-eaten bodies littering the sidewalks around the stadium was even greater here. Scaffolding ran halfway up the south facade, connecting two open holes in the side of the stadium, but none of us understood why.

Clearly large crowds had mounted a resistance there, but the stadium was deserted now. Tumbled-down shacks lined the bleachers, and torn plastic bags were caught on rusted iron poles and floated in the air like ghosts. The grass playing field was a vast quagmire; dozens of small irregular lumps covered more than half of it. In a corner, where goal posts should've been, someone had spelled out *HELP* with seats ripped from the bleachers.

"What the hell're those mounds?" I asked pointing to the lumps in the grass.

"Graves," Marcelo muttered grimly. "It's a graveyard."

We were all speechless, in shock. I imagined the anguish of the people holed up there. As the months went by, their supplies ran out and no one answered their silent cries for help. They must have felt despair every time one of them died from hunger, disease, the Undead, or God knows what. For a moment I felt that suffocating panic. As time passed, they realized they were doomed. No one was coming to their aid.

"Look," Pauli said. "The graves on the end are almost level with the ground."

"Maybe at the end they didn't have the strength to dig an actual grave," someone muttered.

"Think there's still someone there?" I asked.

"I doubt it," said Marcelo. "Anyway, we can't stop to find out." He stared into my eyes. "You know as well as I do—this isn't a rescue mission."

I didn't say another word. Marcelo was right, but I refused to accept it so coldly. I knew if I hadn't left my house in Pontevedra, I'd have gone insane, wallowing in my misery, a prisoner in my own home. I imagined how I'd have felt seeing a helicopter overhead and not be rescued. I put that thought out of my head.

"Ready back there?" Tank's voice boomed over the intercom. "We're here."

I craned my neck to see where we were and instantly regretted it. The massive buildings of the La Paz Hospital rose sharply on the horizon, like monoliths. Amid the shattered remains of what once had been Safe Haven Three, a roaring mass of Undead turned toward the noise that had awakened them out of their lethargy.

We waited. I couldn't imagine how we would get through that crowd.

"How the hell can we land there?" Broto's voice quavered. "They'll make mincemeat out of us before we even get out of the helicopter!"

"Take it easy, *che*," said Marcelo, curiously calm. "Don't worry. We've got it covered." He nonchalantly lit a cigarette as he kept an eye on the crowd below.

I wanted to be as calm as he was, but in my heart I was convinced the computer guy was right. As Prit flew lap after lap over the hospital parking lot, the situation grew worse. A crowd of five or six thousand Undead milled around below us. More monsters converged upon the parking lot by the minute.

The main door looked like the exit of a stadium at the end of a match. Dozens of those beings were crammed together, staggering and stumbling, trying to get out.

I watched in horror as some of them fell out the shattered windows and plunged to the ground. When the swarming mass on the upper floors saw our helicopter hovering overhead, their desire to reach us was stronger than their sense of survival. Thirsting for our blood, they threw themselves out the windows in an attempt to grab us. They somersaulted in the air, like bags of dirty laundry and crashed to the ground with a thud, some twenty feet below.

"I don't fucking believe that!" Pauli muttered, nudging Marcelo. "That bastard's still moving after falling from the tenth floor!"

The Argentine craned his neck to see where she was pointing. The poor devil was a young guy, naked from the waist up. His spine must've broken in the fall, because he was stretched out on the ground, dark liquid oozing from his body, probably his internal organs that'd been crushed upon impact. He jerked around, struggling to stand up. Too bad he hadn't broken his skull and ended that nightmare.

"Don't worry, Paulita," Marcelo said matter-of-factly. "His days are numbered."

"Why do you say that?" I asked. "What the hell're you going to do?

My question was interrupted by Tank's scratchy voice crackling over the intercom.

"That's good! Most of them should be out of the building. Go ahead, Group Two!"

The helicopter traced a long ellipse, away from the plaza. Before I had time to wonder what the hell was going on, a raspy sound cut short all conversation in the cockpit. The helicopter leaned slightly as the entire crew moved to the windows, trying to spot the source of sound.

After a few seconds, I spotted two small dots in the sky heading right for us at top speed. As the dots grew larger, we could make out all the details of those planes that purred along, chewing up the distance between them and the plaza.

Totally amazed, I uttered a loud *Fuuuuck*. "What the hell are they?" I stammered. I felt like I was in a really weird dream.

"Buchones!" David Broto cheered, pressing his nose against the window. "*Damn!* Look at 'em go! Incredible." The computer guy bounced in his seat, pointing at the propeller planes as they made a graceful turn around the hospital tower.

"Will someone please tell me what the hell a Buchon is? Where did they come from?" I asked over the uproar in the helicopter. Everyone was talking and shouting at once. It was a madhouse.

"Those are Hispano Aviación HA-1112 M1L Buchones!" Broto shouted, not taking his eyes off those small fighter planes.

From the look on my face, he realized I didn't understand. "After World War Two, Franco somehow secured the plans for some Nazi fighter planes and had them manufactured for the Spanish Air Force. But since the German factories were destroyed in the war, they outfitted them with Rolls-Royce Merlin engines. They patrolled Spain's African colonies till the late fifties. Now there're just a few in museums. Two Buchones! Amazing!" he blurted out, his eyes glued to the planes.

Fucking Tank, I thought, marveling at the German's audacity. In just a couple of hours, the other team had managed to start those relics that had been gathering dust in the Air Museum. The crowd of Undead was going wild because of the engine noise as those old birds hovered menacingly above them.

"Watch closely, *che*." Marcelo made room for me beside him at the open window. "The show's about to start."

The Buchones made a final turn about a mile from us and headed straight for the plaza with a deafening roar. Only then did I notice that hanging underneath each plane's wings were the red containers I'd seen the other team laboriously ferry on the airport bus. I suddenly realized what was going to happen.

"NAPALM!" I cried. I couldn't contain myself. This was gonna be good!

The planes flew very low—around three hundred feet—over the parking lot. On cue, the red containers broke away, did a slow roll, and fell onto the crowd below.

The fuses were activated as soon as the containers hit the ground. Two huge balls of fire and black smoke exploded almost simultaneously. The flames rose to a staggering height and a tremendous explosion echoed across the city.

The helicopter lurched suddenly, as if it'd been punched by a giant fist of air. Prit let out a long stream of Russian words. The fireballs changed into a single, gigantic, orange ball, streaked with dark smoke.

Globs of the gelatinous Napalm splattered everywhere. I had to turn away from the window. Although we were several hundred feet from the fire, the unbridled heat rising from that hell was suffocating. The tall buildings surrounding the parking lot transformed the place into a giant stewpot, concentrating the effect of the napalm. The swirling air generated by the heat fueled the flames.

Judging by Kurt Tank's comments on the radio, he was thrilled with the outcome of the operation. He had every reason to be. There wouldn't be much left down there.

Those few moments seemed to go on forever, but finally the fireball died down once all the fuel was consumed. The columns of black smoke combined into a single tall column visible from miles away.

"Look at that!" howled one of the legionnaires. "Not a single one is left standing!"

Excited shouts erupted in the helicopter. The huge crowd that had been knotted together in the parking lot just a moment before was now reduced to just a few hundred smoking torches that stumbled around and finally collapsed. The vile blue or green flames the smoldering bodies on the ground gave off blended with the black smoke that blanketed the entire parking lot. The pungent smell of burning flesh stung my nose and made my eyes water. Dante's *Inferno* couldn't have been worse.

"Why do they burn like that?" Broto asked Pauli, staring at the charred tapestry. "That's fucking amazing! They burned to the bone in minutes. Jesus Fucking Christ!"

"Simple," said the Catalan, as she tightened the straps of her bulletproof vest. "Most of those things have been dead—or undead—for over a year."

"What does that have to do with it?" Broto was clueless.

"It means," Pauli patiently explained, "they're undergoing the process of putrefaction, albeit slowly. The process of decomposition generates—"

"Gases," I blurted out, suddenly grasping what had just happened.

"Methane gas, mostly. The longer they've been in that state, the higher the concentration of gases saturating their body fat. The ones who burned like matches succumbed in the early days. The rest," she nodded toward the few figures still staggering around, "have only been Undead for a few months."

I looked down once more at the furiously burning bodies below. Jubilation flooded the cabin in waves, as the helicopter slowly descended. But out of the corner of my eye, I noticed the tense, worried faces of the crew. A few veterans made jokes to take their minds off their fear.

I was hard-pressed to describe what I felt. Fear, mostly. Anguish, thinking about the thousands of lives we'd just cut down. Those things weren't just rag dolls; they'd been people who'd had a life and dreams and who didn't deserve to end up like that. And I felt heartsick, thinking that if it weren't for dumb luck I'd have ended up one of the horde of Undead.

Mostly I was scared.

Panicked.

In just a few moments, those soldiers, who were so young and should've had their whole lives ahead of them, would bravely head into that building. Viktor Pritchenko and I knew too well the horrors awaiting them.

2 8

TENERIFE

Basilio Irisarri was in a foul mood. The look on his face and in his narrow, vacant eyes was homicidal. Lately he'd snarled over and over, "Get my drift, pal?" Basilio didn't know he had that tic, but it had gotten worse recently. As an idea took shape in his mind, that phrase became a mantra he said to anyone who'd listen.

Things had gotten complicated since that ugly business with the nun. Basilio was already in the hot seat with the higher-ups. He always had trouble with bosses, but this time he was really in the hot seat.

For starters, he was no longer stationed on the *Galicia*. During the internal investigation required by navy protocol, he'd been "temporarily relieved" of his duties. He didn't mind that part. The *Galicia* was nearly empty these days. The flow of refugees had completely dried up. That damned nun and her pals were the last to be quarantined on that ship.

Basilio had resented standing guard in an empty boat anchored in the middle of the bay. He'd never admit it, but he got the creeps patrolling that gigantic ship in the dark, with only a flashlight, hearing the creaking and groaning of a thousand bulkheads.

On the plus side, he was the first to get wind of any new "business opportunities" in the port. Everyone knew that all the best deals in the black market were cooked up on the docks under the watchful eye of inspectors and officers. Pull out a few packs of smokes or gold earrings at the right time and a guard would suddenly need to take a piss or the harbor patrol boat would develop engine failure that mysteriously fixed itself a couple of hours later. In that world, Basilio was like a fish in water, a true genius with an innate talent for discovering some juicy deal.

For the first time in his life, things were going well, *very* well, for Basilio. His contacts were coming through after weeks of "negotiating." He was raking in the booty, gold especially.

The lack of legal tender on the islands was a real pain in the ass, even for the black market, but it was inevitable. With a continent in shambles, there were billions of euros lying around, free for the taking—if anyone dared face the Undead to get them. Many refugees arrived clutching millions of dollars, euros, and pounds they'd found strewn across their home countries. They flooded the local market with useless currency that no government backed. Gold, silver, and precious stones—those were the real currency and Basilio knew how to get them.

But a few weeks before, things had gotten fucked up again. First there was that damned raid that cost him a huge shipment of bootleg rum. Then he got the news that that damn nun was still alive!

Basilio's methods were crude, but he was nobody's fool. If the nun was alive, it was just a matter of time before she woke up and told the real story about what happened. Then he wouldn't have jack shit—no bright future, no black market deals, just a one-way ticket to the cranes in the port and a quick hanging.

So, when he learned through one of his customers (a doctor hooked on the dwindling supply of cocaine) that that old bitch was clinging to life, he realized he needed to come up with a plan.

Basilio was no coward. He had no problem bumping someone off in a dark alley, but sneaking into a hospital full of guards, in broad daylight, to knock off an old woman lying in a crowded hospital room would be tricky. Basilio would have to tread lightly. If the old bitch died in a dramatic way, he'd be the first person they'd suspect.

For several days Basilio considered letting the situation play out. According to his contact, the old hag was in a coma and there was a good chance she'd never wake up. He could get lucky and the nun would kick the bucket.

But the day before, a team had left for the Peninsula in search of medicine. They might bring back some drug that would revive the old bat. On the other hand, with all the Undead around, there was a good chance they wouldn't make it back. But Basilio couldn't take that chance.

He finally made up his mind: He'd take care of the nun himself. That thought made him feel a whole lot better.

So the next morning, he disguised himself as an orderly, pushing a wheelchair. In it was Eric Desauss, a wiry, red-haired, freckle-faced Belgian, with a convincing cough. Under a blanket, he gripped a nine-millimeter Beretta he'd insisted on bringing "just in case."

Getting the uniform and the pass was simple, although he'd had to pay Dr. Addict a fortune in white powder. Getting Eric to collaborate was easy, too. An old acquaintance from Basilio's little world, he'd been diagnosed as schizophrenic. Just the thought of killing the nun gave him a morbid thrill and a painful erection he had to hide under the blanket.

Basilio was having a hard time getting his bearings in that fucking madhouse. Dr. Addict had told him how to get to the nun's hospital room but had refused to go with him, saying, "I don't want to know what the fuck you're up to. I don't even want to know you."

Basilio and Eric roamed around the hospital for nearly twenty minutes. Basilio's bad mood was quickly approaching the red zone, like mercury in a thermometer left on a hot stove. They couldn't keep wandering around aimlessly. Sooner or later, someone would notice that the same orderly with the same patient had passed that same spot three times—and then they'd be in deep shit.

"Eric, I think we have a problem. Get my drift, pal?"

"You're telling me. We've been in this hallway twice. That guard looked us over real good. Maybe we should come back another day."

"No fucking way," Basilio whispered. "I've got enough morphine in my pocket to bring down an elephant. They frisk everyone leaving the hospital, including staff. What do you think they'd say if they found the piece you're hiding under that blanket?"

"We could stash everything here and come back another day," Eric whined. His enthusiasm was waning.

"There's not going to be another day. Get my drift, pal? It's gotta be today. We can't take a chance she'll wake up. Hey! Look! We found it!"

Basilio pointed to a sign that said RECOVERY ROOM 12 with an arrow pointing to the right.

Basilio pushed the wheelchair faster. Before the Apocalypse, that room had been a parking garage for ambulances. Now, the hospital was so crowded, they'd turned it into a hospice with just a coat of white paint and four picture windows on the south wall. The stench of sickness and death was so strong, the two gunmen gagged as they walked through the door. The hospital staff called that room "the Morgue." Many patients were brought there, but few left it alive. Most often, there was no way to heal those patients; they were the sad ghosts whose lives were cut short. In the old days, they'd have recuperated from their ailments in a couple of days. Now the desperate ill were locked away there so no one had to see them and everyone could go on with their lives, pretending everything was fine. It was way worse than hell.

Fifty beds filled the large room, lined up in two neat rows, with a wide aisle down the center. Most of the beds were occupied, except for a couple whose mattresses were rolled up to let their springs air out. A bloodstain on one of the mattresses made Basilio stop short for a moment. His eyes flitted from bed to bed, searching for the nun's face among that dying crowd. Finally, he spotted her.

Two nurses in the far corner of the room were leaning over a patient in crisis. One of the nurses hurried out the far door for help. The other nurse had her back turned, so she didn't see Basilio and Eric stop in the middle of the aisle. The Belgian got out of the wheelchair and pressed himself against the wall, Beretta in hand, keeping an eye on both doors.

Basilio wasted no time. He stuck his hand into his pocket, pulled out a syringe filled with morphine and sidled up to the bed where the defenseless Sister Cecilia lay. The sailor-turned-hit-man studied her for a second. In just a few weeks, the old woman had shrunk. With that giant bandage on her head, she looked like an enormous insect in a cocoon. *Sorry, old gal,* he thought as he gripped the saline drip and injected the drug in the syringe he was holding. *Nothing personal. You shouldn't have gotten in the way . . .*

BANG! The shot was amplified a million times in that huge room, startling Basilio out of his thoughts. He whipped around to face Eric, who'd gone down on one knee and fired the Beretta three times in rapid sequence. At the back of the room, a doctor stopped in his tracks, as if he'd hit a concrete wall, then collapsed as a fountain of blood spurted out his neck. A nurse lay sprawled on the floor at his feet. The nurse who'd had her back turned was now draped over her patient in a strange, deadly embrace awash in blood and brains.

"Eric! What the hell're you doing?" Basilio roared.

"That nurse saw us," replied the Belgian, in a strangely slow voice. A demented smile drew up the corners of his mouth. "They were going to set off the alarm, Bas! What else could I do?" He shrugged as if to say *Don't blame me.*

Basilio's anger was oozing out every pore, but he didn't lose control. Two thoughts fired through his cold, dark mind. First, he shouldn't have brought that maniac Belgian along. Second, they had to get out of there—fast. People were yelling and screaming all over the hospital, and he could hear an alarm blaring in the distance.

"You've fucked things up real good, pal!" Basilio growled, as he finished emptying the contents of the syringe into the nun's IV. He spent a few seconds of the little time they had to escape making sure every drop entered the old woman's body. He wouldn't have time to calmly smoke a cigarette and watch the old woman die the way he'd planned. He wanted to be sure the morphine was in her body and there was nothing they could do to save her, especially in all that confusion.

"Done." He put the syringe in his pocket, cast a last glance at Sister Cecilia's pale face and barreled out the door. "Let's go before . . ."

Basilio's words froze in the air. The old sailor's eyes opened wide as saucers and he zeroed in on the two figures silhouetted in the doorway. One was a short nurse wearing a lot of makeup and a plunging neckline, but the other nurse . . . Basilio would've recognized that figure and those green eyes anywhere. They'd haunted his dreams for weeks.

"It's her," he muttered in disbelief. Then overcome by his rage, he yelled, "It's the other bitch! Kill her!"

With a twisted smile that would've struck fear in the devil himself, the Belgian raised his pistol and licked his lips.

Two shots rang out.

2 9

MADRID

The SuperPuma landed with a jolt on the parking lot, its blades sending up swirls of smoke. As soon as it touched down, there was the sound of tearing metal. Instantly alarms went off and red lights lit up the dashboard.

"Jesus Christ, Prit! What's that?" I shouted, my voice shrill with fear.

"Don't know . . . " The Ukrainian mumbled as he focused on controlling the plane. With just its two front wheels on the ground, it was spinning out of control, like a top. Everything that wasn't tied down or screwed into the wall went flying, amid shouts from the passengers, who clutched their seats, white-knuckled.

After one very long minute, the spinning slowed down and the SuperPuma finally came to a complete stop. For a moment there was complete silence in the cabin.

"Everyone okay?" someone finally asked. A chorus of grunts answered as we stood up cautiously, afraid Prit might treat us to another crazed ride. We were bruised, but in one piece.

"Can somebody tell me what the hell happened?" Tank asked.

"Ask the pilot, sir," a sergeant replied acidly. "I'm still trying to find my stomach."

But Tank couldn't ask the pilot. Prit had unbuckled his harness, bolted outside and headed for the back of the helicopter, leaping over charred bodies. After a few seconds, the Ukrainian hopped back in the cockpit.

"The tail rotor came loose," he said calmly, as he unscrewed the top of his flask. "We can't take off."

"Whadda ya mean we can't take off?" one soldier asked in a hushed voice. "How long till we *can* take off?"

"Never." Prit answered, matter-of-factly, the way you'd talk about the game on Sunday, and scratched his head thoughtfully. "The napalm explosion or debris knocked the tail rotor rennet loose. Or maybe it just fell off. This Puma has been sitting out in the open for months, so it's hard to say. I do know this bird is *kaput*. Dead."

"Can't you fix it?" Tank asked.

"Maybe . . . if I had a new propeller, a complete set of differentials, a case of beer, a couple of expert mechanics to help me, and twenty hours to do it. So, no, I can't."

"Whadda we do?" asked a voice that couldn't hide the fear. "How do we get back?"

"Find other transportation," Pritchenko said with a shrug. "What choice do we have?"

A chill ran through the helicopter. You didn't have to be a genius to realize that our chances of survival were severely reduced.

"Prit," I said in a frightened voice. "That means we have to go with them . . . in there."

"I know," he said casually, as if we were talking about a walk on the beach.

"How the hell can you be so calm!" I exploded.

"*Fatalism*," he said with a sad smile.

"What the hell're you talking about?"

He took a long swig from his flask. "Well, the helicopter is damaged and can't take off. But, staying here won't fix it. It's fate, *kapish*? It is what it is. Getting upset won't do any good. *Niet*?"

I glared at him. "Sometimes you really piss me off! The way you think is too damn Russian for me!"

"Ukrainian," Prit corrected me with an unflappable smile. "*Ukrainian* thinking. The Russians are farther north."

"Whatever you say, Prit," I answered, my spirits deflated. That guy was impossible. Times like these brought out Prit's Slavic peasant soul. He accepted hard times with resignation, like his ancestors had done for centuries. He just gritted his teeth and kept moving because there was no way to turn back.

Some of the team members had already slid open the door and were about to jump out. I hesitated. Suddenly I felt very cold, even though sweat was pouring down my back. I tried to swallow, but my throat was dry as a desert. I patted my pockets in search of a cigarette, but my hand was trembling so hard I couldn't unbutton the pocket flap. Anxiety squeezed my heart like an invisible hand. In that state I'd screw up before I took two steps outside. A thought flashed before me—I was going to die there. My vision got blurry, my head started spinning . . . Dear God!

"Hey! Take it easy." Pritchenko's familiar, reassuring voice brought me back to reality. The Ukrainian rested a hand on my shoulder and stared at me, a couple of inches from my face. With measured calm, he pulled a pack of cigarettes out of my pocket, lit one, and stuck it between my lips.

"Prit, I can't go out there." My voice cracked. "They'll kill me. They'll catch me in the blink of an eye. Fuck! What the hell're we doing here?"

"You'll be okay." The Slav helped me to my feet with one hand and slung his rifle over his shoulder with the other. "You did great before and you'll do great this time, too. Don't worry. We've been in tighter spots, you and me, and we got out okay, right?"

I nodded hesitantly. Everyone else had climbed out of the helicopter. Tank was shouting our names as the rest of the team divided into their groups.

"Remember the little store in Vigo, with the Pakistanis?" A smile spread across Prit's face. "We were in deep shit, alone, unarmed, no vehicles, surrounded by those monsters, crammed into that fucking crawl space. If we could get out of that, this is—how do you say it—a piece of cake!"

I nodded, with a shaky smile. Pritchenko was right. I thought being classified as "veterans" was strange, but few people had spent as much time among the Undead as we had and had lived to tell the tale.

I let out a long, deflated sigh. If we were the best hope the human race had for its salvation, things were more fucked up than I'd thought.

I took a deep drag on my cigarette and watched the Argentine attach the MG3 to its tripod with the tired look of an expert who's done that a million times. Okay, so we were back in the middle of that shit, but at least this time we had a plan, and we were surrounded by people who were really good at what they did. Plus, Prit and I had each other and that was no small thing. Maybe those guys with the napalm would take another pass to clear the area. Maybe we'd get out of this with our hide still intact.

"Ready?" The Ukrainian cocked his HK.

"Ready, comrade," I replied, cautiously pulling out my Glock. "Stick close, okay?"

"Okay. Lucia'll kill me if anything happens to you and I have no desire to lug your cat around." He gave me a sly grin. "Let's go."

When we jumped down onto what I thought was the surface of the parking lot, one of my legs sunk into what felt like a hole, and a putrid stench flew up my nose. Pauli watched me, half-worried, half-amused.

"Careful. You just stepped in that poor devil's lungs," she said with a smirk.

What I'd taken as the parking lot's scorched surface was a carpet of charred, smoldering bodies. When I jumped out of the helicopter, my right leg sunk into the chest of a burned corpse, shredded its ribs, and came to rest on what was left of its spine. Grossed out, I stepped back and pulled my boot free, nearly losing my balance.

Tank's steel grip on my arm stopped me from falling onto the charred remains.

"Stick with your team," he said dryly, his shark eyes glaring at me. "Protect the computer guy. Without him, this entire mission is pointless."

I shrugged him off, wondering what was so special about that fucker Broto and walked over to Prit, carefully stepping over all the charred bodies.

"We go with them," Prit said pointing to Pauli and Marcelo. "Apparently we have to babysit that freaked-out computer hot shot."

"Any idea why?"

"Not a clue," Prit said with a sigh. "But surely in a few minutes—look out!"

The Ukrainian jumped back like he'd seen a snake and he shoved me out of his line of fire. I turned just in time to see two horribly charred Undead less than five feet away from us. They were burned so badly you couldn't tell their ages or sex, but they moved pretty well, considering their condition.

Prit raised his HK and opened fire at the one on the right. In a split second the rattle of his rifle merged with bursts from other weapons. All the Undead still standing in that parking lot were headed right for us.

The napalm had killed most of those monsters, but three or four dozen still ringed the helicopter and were closing in. The roar of HKs mixed with the bark of the Glocks, and in the background you could hear short, rhythmic bursts from the Argentine's MG3.

Our two Undead were awfully close and Prit and I faced them alone. The rest of the team was hurriedly shooting in other directions, focusing on their immediate area. The deafening noise drew more and more Undead. They just kept coming.

Pritchenko's first shot ripped a hole in the Undead's chest. It staggered back, shaken by the impact for a moment, but kept coming toward us. The Ukrainian corrected his aim and fired again, this time at its head, transforming it into viscous pulp that splattered in every direction. That Undead collapsed in a heap, but Prit and I didn't have time to watch. He calmly aimed at the other Undead, took a deep breath, and pulled the trigger. His gun emitted a horrifying metallic *clank*. We froze, as the Undead approached, unstoppable.

"It's jammed!" Prit shouted. "Fuck! It's jammed! Shoot at that one, fast!"

As if in a dream, I raised the Glock. I watched my thumb free the safety the way the instructor had taught me in Tenerife. I focused all my attention on the creature advancing toward us. I shut out the rest of the world. All that existed was that charred monster, the sight on that heavy Glock, and me.

I heard myself breathing. I felt my finger slowly press the trigger—and fired.

But the hammer made just a muffled *clank*.

3 0

TENERIFE

The gunshots got Lucia's attention first. As she pushed through the heavy fire doors, she was struck by the eerie silence in that room. Next, her gaze flew to the burly orderly bent over Sister Cecilia, his head pressed against the nun's head as if he were telling her a secret. Then, out of the corner of her eye, she noticed a red-haired guy sliding along the wall to her right with his hand behind his back.

That guy's got a hard on like a horse in heat, she thought, puzzled and amused. Just then, the redheaded guy (who looked a lot like the lead singer in the Spin Doctors) drew his hand from behind his back and aimed a black gun at her and Maite.

Lucia didn't believe the expression *time stopped*—not until five seconds after she opened that damned door. The instant that guy pulled the trigger, Lucia felt time stand still and become something very gooey and thick, like melted caramel.

The first shot sent slivers of the wall flying by her right ear and shook her out of her daze. She automatically stepped out of his line of fire. But Maite froze in the doorway, that cup of bad coffee clutched to her chest, her eyes glued to the shooter as he raced along the wall, raising his gun again.

The second shot hit Maite right below her heart with enough force to lift the small girl into the air, spraying blood and coffee in every direction. She pirouetted like a dancer in the Russian ballet, slumped against the door, then slid to the floor where she lay motionless, a bewildered look in her eyes.

"Not that nurse, you idiot! The other one! Get the other one! The tall one!" Lucia heard the orderly say.

That voice triggered a memory and Lucia knew instantly that the nun was a goner. If she didn't run for it, her number would be up, too. Groaning in fear, Lucia retreated down the hallway.

The hospital was in utter chaos. Alarms were going off everywhere. Groups of armed men (some in uniform, some not) ran past dozens of panicked patients and confused, overwhelmed doctors.

"Froilists! Fucking Froilists!" howled a guy in a military uniform Lucia didn't recognize, as he led a group of soldiers into the building.

From another part of the building came a series of hiccups Lucia instantly recognized as bursts from HKs. Then came a muffled explosion and the rattle of another weapon she couldn't identify (Pritchenko could've told her they were AK-47s). In the pandemonium of panicked civilians and soldiers afraid of a Froilists' incursion, two groups of guards were shooting at each other. It was a fucking madhouse.

A gurney flew out of nowhere and hit Lucia in the hip, knocking her to the ground. A red-hot pain shot up her leg. The crowd and the shooting swirled around her as she struggled to her feet. She glanced down the hallway and spotted the redheaded guy with the gun standing next to Basilio. When he saw her pushing through the knot of people, he jabbed the gunman in the ribs and pointed at her.

Lucia wasted no time. Gripping the gurney, she stood up, knocking aside equipment that had fallen in the corridor. Knowing her way around the hospital gave her an advantage, but she had less strength to push her way through all the people running in every direction. Not daring to look back, she sensed that her pursuers were gaining ground.

Lucia spotted the intersection of two hallways. She knew if she turned right, she'd come to the exit. Even in all the chaos, there must be a guard at the door. She was just a couple hundred feet from the hallway.

As she approached the intersection, machine-gun fire nearly tore Lucia's head off the minute she stepped into the hall. She instinctively dropped to the ground. Shots rang out behind her, coming from the same direction as the first shots. Before she knew it, she and fifty other people were caught in the crossfire between two groups shouting commands and rallying cries.

Get out of here or you're screwed, she told herself as she gritted her teeth and crawled toward a side door. A nurse she didn't know was slumped on his side, his head blown wide open. The air smelled of gunpowder, blood, and shit. The groans of the wounded mingled with the hysterical screams of those hit by an explosion.

A disheveled officer in the Civil Guard came out of God-knows-where, shouting himself hoarse trying to bring order to the chaos.

"Hold your fire! We're shooting at each other, dammit!" His words convinced a few of the confused shooters to stop firing.

Lucia felt relieved. Finally someone was taking control of the situation. She started crawling in his direction, but stopped midway when she saw that smiling redheaded creep who killed Maite come up behind the officer.

With a flourish, like a barber removing his customer's cape after a haircut, Eric Desauss raised his gun and shot less than an inch from the neck of the unsuspecting officer. The soldier dropped to the ground, a red fountain gushing from his neck. Security guards took aim at the gunman, but before they could fire, a machine gun at the other end of the hall took out three or four of them.

Chaos erupted again. The guards completely forgot the lone gunman and concentrated on the group that had fired on them. Basilio took advantage of the situation to grab one of the HKs on the floor.

"Over there! She went out that door!" Basilio yelled.

Humming a little tune, Eric the Belgian stepped over the soldier's bloody corpse and headed for the door, looking down the barrel of his gun, with Basilio following close behind. His fly felt like it was about to explode as intense pleasure spread through his body. As he sprinted through the crossfire, he pictured himself jacking off over that slut's corpse and a huge smile lit up his face.

3 1

MADRID

For a very long second, I stood there, frozen like a store dummy, staring at the Glock in my hand. What had happened didn't sink in. The fucking gun hadn't fired, but I didn't have time to ponder the situation. With a murderous roar, one of the half-charred Undead launched himself at Prit as he loaded his HK, grabbed him by the shoulder and hurled himself on top of the small Ukrainian.

Instinctively, Pritchenko raised his rifle and drove its muzzle into the Undead's chest like a stake, which sent both of them careening backward. The Undead stopped in his tracks. The blow probably broke his ribs. Caught off balance, Prit stumbled and fell backward onto the ground, totally helpless.

That was all the Undead needed. He dropped to his knees and slumped over my friend who was struggling to get free from that deadly embrace. Everything was moving in slow motion. I peered at the monster's rotten teeth through his lips that'd been reduced to a thin grimace by the fire. He snapped his jaws like a bear trap, just inches from the Slav's face that was pale with terror.

"Get him off me! *Dabai, dabai!*" Prit shouted.

Getting a running start, I kicked the Undead's ribs as hard as I could. That kick would've knocked the life out of a normal person, but those creatures were made of sterner stuff. Wobbling from my kick, the Undead guy dropped Prit, who crawled away.

Then the monster focused all its attention on me. I took a couple of steps back as the Undead struggled to his feet. Prit stood silently behind him, holding his huge hunting knife, poised to hack off the thing's neck.

Before the Slav could make a single cut, the Undead's temple erupted in a miniature volcano. Bits of the guy's brain splattered everywhere and his body collapsed in a heap. Prit and I looked at each other, stunned but relieved.

"What kind of fucking game are you two playing?" Pauli's shrill, sarcastic voice was the most wonderful sound on the earth. She was down on one knee, blue smoke wafting out the barrel of her HK. She'd come along just in time.

"Looks like you boys prefer hand-to-hand combat," she said mockingly. "You know better than anyone that wrestling with monsters is a really bad idea. You could catch something really bad." She slowly got to her feet and brushed off her knees.

"Prit's fucking gun jammed," I protested, pointing to his HK. "My pistol didn't fire either." I waved the Glock under her nose. "So don't give me any shit, dammit!"

"For starters, that's a rifle, not a gun," Marcelo corrected me, rubbing his shoulder that was sore from shooting the MG3. "You guys jammed *two* weapons? That's a first."

I held out my Glock, with a scowl. The Porteño took out the magazine and examined it carefully. He raised his eyes with a look of disbelief.

"Did you chamber the first bullet, asshole?"

"Uhhhh . . ." The blood rushed to my face. Fuck. Despite the training in Tenerife, I'd never gotten over my fear of accidentally shooting myself as I drew the gun. I'd decided to take the first bullet out of the magazine, so there was no bullet in the chamber.

I knew perfectly well I had to cock the gun before I shot it, but in the confusion, I'd forgotten. The Glock hadn't fired on account of my own negligence. I was mortified. I wished that that Undead lying at my feet *had* killed me.

"Who'd they send us? Rookies wet behind the ears!" one of the younger legionnaires shouted, spitting on the ground in disgust.

"Careful what you call me, you sniveling brat." Prit turned on the legionnaire, a homicidal gleam in his blue eyes. "When you were still running around on the playground, I'd already slit a bunch of Mujahideen's throats in Chechnya." The Ukrainian's voice was icy and controlled. He'd rip the guy's guts out right then and there if the loud-mouthed kid gave him the slightest excuse. Prit pointed at me. "This guy's been through more than you can imagine. He's survived tight spots that would've scared you shitless. So shut the fuck up!"

The legionnaire glanced around for support, but the rest of his team was out of earshot. He swallowed, raised his hands and backed off. "Take it easy, pal! Just watch your ass, because I'm not going to lift a finger to help you. Got it?" He turned and walked back to the warehouse door with his tail between his legs.

"What happened to your HK, Prit?" Pauli asked, unfazed. "Did it jam?"

Not saying a word, the Ukrainian took the magazine out and pulled the hammer. A shiny bullet flew out and hit the ground with a clink. Prit scooped it up and handed it to Pauli.

"Oh, shit! It's a series forty-eight!" The Catalan frowned and handed it to Marcelo.

He examined the shell and winced. "The motherfucker's calibrated wrong!"

"What is it, Marcelo?" Clearly something was wrong, but I couldn't figure out what.

"We've used up a shitload of ammunition fighting the Undead," Pauli said, as she checked her own gun's magazine. "Each incursion consumes hundreds of rounds. Six months ago our supply of bullets reached a critical low. We had to start making our own. The problem was there were no machines on the Canary Islands to produce the shells with the necessary precision, so we had to build the machines from scratch."

"But that's good, right?"

"Not really," Pauli said with a weary shake of her head. "Not all that ammunition met quality standards. Occasionally some defective ammunition can slip in. We lost a couple of teams before we figured out what was going on. We assumed the ammunition for this mission had been tested several times. Guess we assumed wrong."

"A mistake?" David Broto asked, wide-eyed. All in all, the computer guy had survived his first contact with the Undead pretty well.

"Or sabotage," one of the sergeants glumly interjected, as he checked one of his magazines. "This one's defective too! Son of a bitch!"

"Froilists?" Broto asked.

"Could be." Marcelo stretched like a cat and started walking toward his MG3. "All I know is, Tank's not going to like this."

Sabotage? My head was spinning. What was that all about? Before I had time to ask, Tank landed like a mortar round in the middle of our group, barking orders.

"What the hell're you doing standing around? Get the lead out, dammit! We don't have all day!" He pulled one of the legionnaires by his backpack toward the building.

Wrestling with my backpack, I followed the rest of the group toward the warehouse's rusty fire escape a few feet away. Thinking about that defective ammunition sent chills up my spine. It could be the death sentence for a lot of our group.

3 2

TENERIFE

Lucia ran down a hallway in an unfamiliar wing of the cavernous hospital. Unlike the rest of the building, it was deserted and was lit up by flickering fluorescent lights. There wasn't a single bed or wheelchair . . . and not a damn thing to hide behind. She rubbed her throbbing hip where the gurney ran into her. She'd have one helluva bruise, but she wasn't concerned about that.

She could hear the muffled sound of gunfire through a heavy double door she'd just slipped through and her pursuers' excited voices. Dripping with sweat, she ran faster, hoping that the corridor led someplace safe or, better yet, outside.

Lucia turned a corner, then stopped suddenly at an abandoned checkpoint with a metal detector. There wasn't a soul in sight. A newspaper lay on a table. Beside it was a cup of steaming coffee. A radio resting on a pile of folders softly played some music. The guards must have run down the main hallway when the alarms went off and were probably shooting on the other side of the door.

She searched the table for a weapon, tossing a pile of papers on the floor in her rush. All she found was a gun-lovers magazine and a pen-knife.

She jiggled the drawers but they were locked. *Damn! Think fast or you're fucked. Really fucked.*

Her gaze fell on a colorful poster of smiling soldiers passing rations down from an army truck. The caption read "The Third Spanish Republic is looking out for you." Below the poster was a file cabinet, its top drawer standing wide open. The guards had left in such a hurry they'd forgotten to lock the drawer.

Lucia rifled through it but all she found was a handful of magnetic cards and papers on a clipboard where someone had scrawled some names and hours. Lucia assumed it was a record of who'd been given the cards. Her heart sank. Just as she was about to toss the clipboard aside, she spotted something written across the top in bold: 71410NK.

She ripped off the sheet of paper, stuffed it in her pocket, and took off running. She could hear footsteps getting closer.

After a few feet, she hesitated at the top of a staircase, panting, swallowed hard. She'd been so sure that that hallway led outside, and yet here she was, at the top of some stairs headed down to the basement.

No, fuck no! What're the odds I'd have to hide in a fucking hospital basement twice in a row? It's almost funny.

About the same as winning the lottery or being struck by lightning. But one thing was certain, if she didn't go down there, those maniacs would corner her. The look in that red-haired guy's eyes had made her feel really scared—and dirty. She wasn't going to stick around and argue with him.

She sighed and started down that long flight of stairs. It was well lit and meticulously clean with the faint smell of disinfectant. If it weren't for the lack of windows—and people—those stairs would've seemed completely harmless.

Lucia ran all the way to the bottom. The ugly, light green tiles on the floor and walls were different from the upper hallways, but otherwise it looked the same. Red arrows and a symbol she couldn't identify set it apart from the rest of the hospital.

Lucia stopped for a few seconds to catch her breath. She felt as if her heart would explode and the bruise on her hip was throbbing. The sound of footsteps flying down the stairs spurred her on. She followed the red arrows without hesitating, as a voice in her head screamed, *What the hell will you do if it's a dead end!*

The hallway led to a square room. A heavy steel door with the same unfamiliar symbol took up an entire wall. She was sure she'd seen that symbol before, but she was so scared, she couldn't think where.

Beside the door was a panel with numbers, buttons, and a slot. It was an alphanumeric keyboard, like on a cell phone; each key corresponded to letters and numbers. She grabbed the magnetic card from her pocket and inserted it into the slot. A screen lit up with a welcome message, along with a digitized photo of a confused-looking, gray-haired doctor wearing glasses.

GOOD AFTERNOON, DR. JURADO. PLEASE ENTER YOUR PASS-CODE.

Lucia froze. Then she remembered the code scribbled on the piece of paper. With trembling fingers, she pulled the paper from her pocket and punched the code into the keyboard. The screen went blank for a millisecond and then a new message appeared.

WRONG PASSCODE. YOU HAVE TWO (2) TRIES LEFT. PLEASE ENTER YOUR PASSCODE.

Lucia brushed a sweaty lock of hair out of her eyes. "You idiot, you can't even type a damn code right!"

She typed it in again, as calmly as she could, making sure it was correct. She pressed ENTER and the screen went blank.

WRONG PASSCODE. YOU HAVE ONE (1) TRY LEFT. PLEASE ENTER THE PASSCODE.

She felt her stomach clench into an icy fist. If this wasn't the passcode, she was done for. She wouldn't get another chance. Plus, those footsteps sounded really close now. She beat her fist against the door. That was stupid. The second to the last character of the code was not the letter O but a zero. She typed it in a third time, this time her fingers flew over the keyboard, as Basilio appeared around the corner, breathing like a bellows. The screen flashed a third time and a new message appeared.

WELCOME TO THE ZOO, DR. JURADO. HAVE A NICE DAY.

The door opened with a hiss. Lucia had just enough time to slip in before a blast from an HK kicked up splinters of plaster from the wall she'd been leaning on. Another bullet hit the control panel. It exploded with fireworks and gave off a faint singed smell. Lucia tried to close the door, but the system had been fried when the panel blew up. With death at her heels, Lucia headed into that room. As she did, she recalled the meaning of the biohazard symbol emblazoned on the door.

Then an alarm went off.

3 3

MADRID

The spiral staircase creaked and shook beneath our feet. Flakes of rust showered down as we climbed flight after flight. That staircase was in such bad shape, it mustn't have been used before the Apocalypse. A thick layer of ash and dust rose up in white clouds making us sneeze and giving the stairs an unworldly, sinister look. Someone behind me whistled through his teeth nervously.

When we finally reached the third floor, an emergency door, criss-crossed by a thick chain, cut us off. I collapsed onto one of the last steps, like most of the group, gasping for breath. The bone-dry air, the heat generated by the napalm, and the dust swirling around us made us desperately thirsty.

With clumsy hands, I unscrewed my canteen and took a couple of long gulps. I passed the canteen to Broto, who'd flopped down next to me, his two-hundred-plus pounds shaking the staircase. The computer geek took a very long drink. I couldn't take my eyes off his Adam's apple, bobbing up and down as he gulped down half the canteen. Finally he took a deep breath and handed it back to me, with a loud belch.

"How're we gonna get that damn door open?" he asked, after a long silence.

"No idea, but I'll bet Tank has thought of something," I said, rummaging around in my backpack for a cigarette. Then I remembered I'd left my last pack on the SuperPuma.

"Everybody get back!" One of the legionnaires was unrolling a cable away from a plastic substance that one of his team had stuck around the frame of the door. The cable was connected to a metal box the size of a cigarette pack with a button on top.

"Shit! That's going to make a lot of noise. Let's go, pal," Prit muttered as he pulled Broto to his feet. Our computer whiz had gotten his backpack stuck between two rungs in the staircase. He looked like a huge snail as he struggled to get free. Prit and I jerked him free and got the hell off the landing.

We stood behind the legionnaire with the detonator. When he was sure no one was on the upper floor, he flipped up the lock on the button. I opened my mouth to keep my eardrums from bursting in the explosion, the way I'd been taught back on the island.

Just then machine-gun fire and excited shouts rang out from the bottom of the stairs. The Undead had started up the stairs and the guys in the rear were taking them out. Their position gave them an advantage, but with so little ammo, they couldn't hold them long.

The same thought must have occurred to the soldier with the detonator. With a flick of his wrist, he pressed the button. A muffled explosion and a cloud of chemical smoke wafted down over us. A large piece of concrete shot over the railing and landed on the crowd of Undead below, but that was as much as we could see.

"Get climbing!" Tank roared. "You guys in front, move your fucking asses!"

Prit and I looked at each other. We'd been the last to get off the staircase so now we were at the front of the line, along with the explosives expert and the sweaty computer guy. The rest had known what was coming and had "allowed" us to take the lead. They got a good laugh as we wrestled Broto to his feet.

"We're fucked, aren't we, pal?" I asked as I pulled on the top of my wetsuit.

The Ukrainian gave me a wry smile, as he checked the clip in his HK for the umpteenth time. "Who knows . . . but stay close, got it?" And with that, he scrambled up the last flight of stairs, ready to enter the building.

Remembering all the dead Tank had left in his wake on previous missions, I climbed the last flight of stairs on Prit's heels. The door on the landing looked like a giant hand had ripped it off the wall. It lay twisted against the railing where we'd been sitting. A fine rain of concrete and pulverized brick trickled out the holes where the hinges had been.

Prit knelt in the doorway, his HK pointed inside. Panting, I stood next to him, waiting for his next move. The Ukrainian handled situations like this much better than I did.

"It's darker than a cricket's ass in there," he said softly.

"Wait," I said, turning back. "Broto! Broto! Get your fucking ass up here, dammit!

As he trotted to our position, the computer guy dropped his rifle. Flustered, he stooped to pick it up, but in the process he swatted the legionnaire behind him with his backpack. A stream of curses trailed the poor geek.

"Hey, pal," I laid a reassuring hand on his shoulder. "Stay calm, okay?" Broto nodded, rolling his eyes, clearly wishing he were anywhere else in the world.

"Got a flashlight in your backpack?" I asked.

"Uhhhh . . . yeah . . . " Broto dug around in his backpack and finally pulled out a Polar Torch, like the one I'd had that day a lifetime ago when I had to leave my home in Pontevedra behind, or stick around there and starve.

I shook the flashlight and turned it on, aiming it into the building. The smoke and dust from the explosion hadn't cleared completely. Millions of little specks danced wildly in the beam I shined in every direction.

Suddenly a loud explosion shook the air. The whole staircase trembled violently, followed by a heart-stopping rip, as if a giant sheet of paper had been torn in two.

"What was that?" I asked, alarmed.

"They must've blown up the stairs below us," Prit replied, glancing over the railing. The rusty step he was on slumped under his feet with a groan, sending up a cloud of rust. He backed away carefully, casting a wary glance at the landing.

"The whole fucking staircase could come down at any time, even without explosives," he said, dragging our backpacks to the door. "Let's get out of here while we still can."

Prit was right. The staircase had been on its last legs before we got there. Now it was at a breaking point. The explosion to cut off the Undead had been the last straw. That old structure could collapse any second from the intense heat of the napalm and the vibrations we made as we climbed up. It was creaking and shuddering; cement dust streamed down all around.

"Get a move on!" someone yelled behind us, spurring the legionnaires on. I recognized Tank and Marcelo's voices hustling their men up the stairs.

The situation was growing worse by the minute. The foot-long bolts holding the staircase to the building became deadly projectiles as they flew out with a clang. A section at the very top came loose. With a loud bang it bounced down several floors then came to rest on the ground, hundreds of feet below. I heard a cry of pain when someone was hit by a piece of steel, but I couldn't see who it was. A cloud of cement dust enveloped us and I couldn't see more than a few feet in front of me.

I grabbed Broto by the sleeve and vaulted into the building. Prit followed, leaping like a gazelle. Right on his heels, a knot of two dozen terrified legionnaires rushed up the tottering structure. Suddenly, everyone wanted to be first inside.

It was pitch black inside, but wonderfully cool compared to outside. Even with the flashlight, I could barely see through the dust. Broto recoiled with a muffled shout; someone must've run into him. I turned, my arms outstretched, blindly feeling my way. I took a sharp jab to the groin and doubled over in pain, trying to breathe. A shadow knocked me down and a heavy boot tripped over my leg. All around, guys were shouting, cursing, and gasping for breath. We couldn't see a thing with all the dust in the air. Just then, the ladder fell completely away with a monstrous roar that shook the building. A second later, we heard hundreds of tons of rusted steel crash onto the parking lot; the Undead answered with an enraged roar. The structure had crushed hundreds of those bastards. A drop in the bucket, but at least it was something.

Coughing, I tried to sit up. All around me the shouting multiplied. I heard Tank yelling orders and another voice shouting for a john, but everything else was gibberish.

Tank gradually regained control of the situation. Here and there flashlights gradually lit up the room with a dull glow. I looked around. The first image that came to mind was of the firefighters at the World Trade Center on 9-11. Covered in a thick layer of dust and ash, we all looked ghostly. When the staircase fell, the plaster ceiling in the room came down around our heads. The floor of that airless room was covered with a layer of ash nearly a foot thick. When we rushed in, we'd stirred it up. Through a crack in the door, I could make out the faint afternoon light falling on Madrid.

Tank called out our names. Each name was answered with a raspy "yes" or "present," along with coughs and sneezes. But seven names didn't answer. They must've been the guys who were bringing up the rear who now lay dead (one would hope) on the parking lot, felled by the twisted wreckage of the stairs.

Prit crawled to my side, his thick mustache completely white. "You okay?"

"Nothing's broken," I said, as I patted down my body.

"You're bleeding." Always a man of few words, the Ukrainian simply pointed to my forehead.

"Oh, man, that sucks!" I muttered. I touched my face and my hand came back bright red. Blood was streaming down my face, but I hadn't noticed. In all the confusion, a piece of plaster must've gashed my scalp.

"I'm fine too, thank you. Don't worry about me," Broto said bitterly, sneezing hard.

"Lucia'll kill me," Prit said, ignoring the computer guy as he bandaged my head. "I promised her you'd come back in one piece. You've been trying to break your neck from the minute you climbed out of the helicopter. Your head looks like a cocoon," he said, punching my shoulder.

Then he turned to Broto. "You sure you're okay? Let me take a look." He grabbed the computer guy by the arm and pulled him close. After giving him a thorough going-over, he handed him his canteen.

"Flush your nostrils first, then take a drink. Just one. Got it?" he said menacingly. "We're not gonna find any water here, so we have to ration what we have."

Broto wasn't listening. He was in shock over the scene before us. In fact, it was a miracle he didn't drop the canteen.

I whispered, "Prit, what the hell is all this?"

3 4

TENERIFE

Gasping for breath, Lucia dashed into a three-foot-square cubicle. The floor and walls were covered with a smooth, springy material instead of tiles. At the back of the room was a door with a small window. Lucia shook it hard but it was locked tight. Bolted to one wall was a small metal bench. On another wall was a flashing red button.

Lucia didn't think twice and pressed the button on the wall. A red light went on overhead and a small horn went off behind the door. Frightened, she stepped back but another door, concealed in the wall, locked behind her. She was trapped. Lucia's ears plugged up when a blast of air sealed the room. Before she had time to wonder what was going on, she heard a fist pounding on the door behind her.

She turned quickly. On the other side of the small glass window, Basilio Irisarri peered in, red-faced, trying to catch his breath. The sailor shouted something Lucia couldn't hear.

We're completely cut off, she thought, fascinated. *Not a sound coming in or out.*

The sailor made it crystal clear he wanted her to open the door.

"Oh, sure, that's just what I'm gonna do," Lucia mouthed and flipped him the bird.

Basilio's icy, shark-like gaze turned diabolical. He pointed at Lucia, stepped back, double-checked his HK, and aimed it at the door.

"Shit!" Lucia screamed and dropped to the floor.

The door was so thick all she could hear was the muffled patter of the bullets as they struck the airtight door. She looked up in amazement. That door was not only waterproof, it was bulletproof. The only damage she could see was a deep scratch on the window. Slowly and cautiously, she stood up. Just then, a fine mist that smelled like disinfectant started to fall from sprinklers in the ceiling. At the same time, another dense chemical cloud wafted out of conduits in the wall, making Lucia's eyes water and her throat burn.

That bastard is gassing me, she thought, but Basilio's puzzled expression proved he'd had nothing to do with it.

She realized she was in a decontamination airlock. *You idiot! What were you thinking? You activated the system when you pressed the red button.*

The next thing she thought was that she wasn't wearing a hazmat suit.

On top of that, she didn't know if the gas would kill her.

On the other side of the glass, Basilio looked like he was on the verge of a heart attack. The sailor hurled the empty HK at the door and turned to the red-haired guy.

The Belgian pressed his face to the window. At first all he could see was a lot of steam. He finally spotted Lucia, who stared back at him, helpless, huddled on a metal bench, her eyes red and raw from the chemicals.

Eric's smile would've seemed loving and tender if it hadn't been for the cold, dead look in his eyes. The Belgian rarely smiled, which was fortunate since people didn't live long after seeing that creepy smile. But that afternoon he was having a damn good time. In the last ten minutes he'd racked up so many fantasies, he'd be jacking off for days as he relived them. Catching that chick would be a perfect end to a perfect day.

Excited, he licked the glass. A small sliver of glass pierced his tongue and left a trail of blood, but he didn't notice; his eyes never left Lucia. She was mesmerized like a rabbit with a snake. Then she threw up from all the chemicals.

A siren wailed in the room and the sprinklers stopped spraying. Lucia's eyes were red, puffy slits as she leaned against the bench to stand up. Her ears popped, telling her that the room was depressurized. One of the doors had opened, though thankfully it wasn't the door she'd come through. The pressure between the room she was in and the adjacent room equalized. She staggered through the door and into the next room.

For the first time in that long day, she wondered how long she had to live.

3 5

MADRID

"What the hell is that?" Pauli muttered behind me, echoing my question to Prit.

The flickering beam of our flashlights lit up a room about forty square feet. Scattered across the floor lay the remains of the plaster ceiling. A thick layer of ash covered every inch of the room. I reached in and pulled some out. Burnt paper. Some of the paper was only half-burned, but it was still illegible.

"Looks like they burned half the National Library," I muttered. My gaze wandered along the blackened walls to the metal drums stationed around the room. They must've done all that burning in those drums.

"Someone was in a big hurry to destroy all these documents," Broto said, kicking a pile of ashes piled up in a corner. "Either they got very cold or they didn't want to leave papers lying around for the next guy to find."

"I doubt the Undead care what's on these papers. Hell, those bastards can't read," I pointed out.

"Whoever burned those documents must've thought the Undead wouldn't be the only ones stopping by," Pauli replied as she got to her feet. "Obviously, he was right. We made it, didn't we?"

"Yeah, we made it," Prit nodded, then quietly added, "but we still have to get out in one piece."

"Or find a way in there." I pointed to the huge steel door at the back of the room.

It was about eight feet by eight feet, reinforced by steel bars. It looked like someone had ripped the door off a fucking bank vault and planted it in the middle of that concrete wall. Several bags of cement and wooden beams lay tossed in the corner. Someone had hurriedly built a concrete wall before installing the door.

"They turned this building into a fortress. I'd bet my last euro that every access to the building was either walled up or has a door like this one."

Across from the door, standing guard, surrounded by sandbags, were two machine gun nests with MG3 mounts identical to Marcelo's. They were lined up perfectly with the door we'd entered through. It would've been next to impossible to get in that door.

Tank was kneeling on the floor, holding a flashlight, with the building's floor plan spread out in front of him. He looked tense, but seemed to have the situation under control.

"We're here," he told two sergeants who listened attentively. "According to the Safe Haven's records, the pharmacy's supply room is two floors below. Access ladders are here, here, and here." His finger danced across the map. "Two of them are closed off by half a ton of concrete, but the other has only one door."

"Which one, sir?" asked one of the sergeants.

"No idea. Nobody who worked in this sector of the building survived."

"What was here?" another sergeant asked, pointing over his shoulder at the huge steel door.

"On this floor, what was left of Madrid's government joined units from the army's Second Regiment of Communications," said Tank, reviewing notations on the map. "Supposedly, they were evacuated three days before this Safe Haven fell, but their convoy never reached Barajas Airport. I'm sure they're all dead."

"While they were here, they really protected their asses," replied one of the sergeants, a seasoned veteran who seemed to have a lot of confidence in Tank. "How're we gonna get through that damned door, sir?"

"That's what this guy's for." Tank pointed to the computer whiz. "Mr. Broto! That door isn't going to open by itself. Get started ASAP."

David Broto gulped and got to his feet, breathing heavily. He ran a trembling hand over his eyes, leaving a trail of ash that made him look like a raccoon. He pulled a laptop, a long cable, and a toolbox out of his backpack. With a small drill, he expertly removed a cover fitted into the base of the door and attached the cable that was plugged into his laptop.

A series of characters ran across the screen when Broto activated the hard drive. To my surprise, an image of the mechanism inside the door suddenly appeared in a corner of the screen.

"A fiber optic camera," I muttered, stunned, as I watched our computer whiz handle it with remarkable skill.

"Who is this guy?" I asked Marcelo. He shrugged, as stunned as I was.

Tank's voice, dripping with irony, boomed out behind us. "Mr. Broto's an expert in opening doors and breaking into *impenetrable* systems. We were pretty sure we'd come up against something like this." He pointed to the armored door with a casual wave. "So, we 'invited' him along. Good thing you were living in Tenerife, Mr. Broto."

David turned bright red and ducked behind the computer screen. He looked like a huge bird about to lay a giant egg.

"What exactly did you do in Tenerife, Broto?" Prit asked, innocently. He had an amazing knack for asking uncomfortable questions as if he were just making conversation. To the casual observer, he was just curious or tactless, but I knew the Ukrainian took note of every detail. He was a sly old dog.

"Mr. Broto has been living in Tenerife for two and a half years . . . in Tenerife Prison II, to be exact," Tank said in a slow, deliberate voice. "Mr. Broto's last job didn't turn out the way he'd planned and . . . I'll let him tell you the rest."

David Broto hung his head and mumbled something incomprehensible, his eyes glued to the computer screen. Prit and I weren't the only "volunteers" on that mission.

After fifteen tense minutes, during which Broto only got up to attach a second cable, our "computer guy" finally gave a satisfied grunt and struggled to his feet. With his right hand he disconnected the cables; with his left he typed a rapid succession of codes into the keypad on the armored door. Then he stepped back.

"It's open." His voice sounded calm, but with an artist's pride in a job well done.

"That was fast!" Tank stood up. "Great! Díez, Huerga, open that door. The rest of you, cover us. We're going in."

The two soldiers ran up, grabbed the door's huge wheels and turned them simultaneously. Gently, with just a slight purr, the heavy door turned on its oiled hinges and opened onto the last stronghold of Madrid Safe Haven Three.

3 6

TENERIFE

"Goddamn it! I can't see that bitch!" Basilio peered through the window, trying to make out his prey. "Where the hell'd she go?" he snapped, his mind racing. He was furious that his careful plan was falling apart.

They hadn't heard any shots fired on the upper floors for a few minutes. Someone must've finally brought order to the chaos and calmed nervous trigger fingers. You didn't have to be a genius to realize that it was just a matter of time before guards came down to take a look, and then they'd be trapped. The light above the door turned green, accompanied by a long beep. Basilio grabbed one of the hazmat suits hanging beside the door and threw one to Eric.

"Here, put this on and help me fasten mine. Let's go after her."

"Do we really need these?" Eric eyed them suspiciously. "What the hell's in there?"

"Flu vaccines and shit like that," ventured Basilio, as he stuck his legs into his suit. "This is where they make drugs and hazardous chemicals. Acids and shit like that."

"That little hottie went in without one and she didn't keel over," challenged Eric, still not convinced.

"Suit yourself," Basilio shrugged. "But if your dick falls off, don't say I didn't warn you."

That finally convinced the Belgian. He sighed and picked up the suit. Not saying another word, the gunmen struggled into the bulky suits. The narrow visors of their headgear reduced the field of vision and muffled sounds. The suits had a breast pocket for battery-operated walkie-talkies, but there weren't any in sight. Basilio gave an impatient wave. They couldn't waste any more time looking for them.

Once inside the airlock, he hit the red button on the wall. In seconds, the disinfectant enveloped them in a dense fog. Eric nervously fiddled with his Beretta; Basilio kicked himself for not bringing more weapons.

When the door opened, the two gunmen walked in back to back. The room was deserted. A long table covered with beakers and microscopes stretched from one end of the room to the other. In one corner, a flickering monitor gave off a soft light. At the far end, a centrifuge was running with a low hum. There was no sign of the girl.

With a nod, Basilio told Eric to check out one corner of the laboratory, while he made his way to the other. His gut told him the girl was still there.

Warning voices in his head that had saved his life more than once were shouting themselves hoarse that something wasn't right in that lab.

3 7

MADRID

In groups of three or four, we filtered through the armored door into the building's dark interior. The beams from our flashlights danced nervously in every direction.

"We're an elite unit, so why the hell don't we have night vision goggles?" Pauli grumbled, as she peered into the darkness. "We're blinder than moles in a tunnel."

"Pipe down and keep your eyes open," Marcelo snapped. "Drill any asshole you see full of lead."

Everyone was alert, watching for the slightest movement of Undead lurking in the shadows. Someone tripped over a metal trash can and sent it rolling to the other end of the room. It careened off a filing cabinet with a clang that echoed all the way to the top floor of that God-forsaken building. Tank let out a furious hiss and lunged at the poor jerk with the speed of a cobra. *Glad I'm not in that guy's shoes*, I thought. My gut told me Tank had just chosen the next "volunteer" to be point man.

The strong, musty smell of rotting garbage was making me light-headed. To take my mind off it, I examined the rooms we walked past. Most had been turned into offices. A thick layer of dust covered the empty desks, dark computers, and piles of paper.

One of the offices was particularly disturbing. Its desk, chair, and filing cabinet were piled high with paper birds, too many to count, maybe three or four thousand, all colors and sizes. At first I was amused at the thought of some government official, sitting idly at his desk, folding paper birds all day. Then a chill went down my spine. That was the work of an obsessed maniac, not a bored bureaucrat passing the time. I could almost picture the guy, hunched over his desk in the dark, folding sheet after sheet into birds, his mind sinking deeper and deeper into a dark hole.

With a shiver I backed out of that room and looked around for the beam of Prit's flashlight, but I couldn't see a thing. My stomach clenched when I realized I'd wandered away from the group. I was all alone.

I traced my steps back into the hallway, as I tried to get a grip on the panic rising from the pit of my stomach. I'd come from the right, but that hallway branched off in two directions. My sense of direction had never been very good. I confess, I'd let Prit and the legionnaires choose a route through the building while I admired the view.

Cursing under my breath, I stood in the intersection of the two hallways. I thought I heard a faint noise coming from the hallway to my right; it sounded like whispered commands. I checked my Glock, then headed for those voices.

Along the way, I'd stepped over piles of empty army rations. There'd been a lot of them back at the armored door, but the number tapered off the farther I headed into the building.

Turning a corner I stumbled upon the first body—a rail-thin guy, dressed in military trousers and a black T-shirt bearing his unit's insignia: a fist clutching a sheaf of lightning bolts with the words FIERI POTEST written below it. Bracing myself, I bent down to check out the body. The guy'd been dead for months, judging from how decomposed his body was. In his right hand, he clutched a crumpled paper cup. I couldn't make out what was in his left. I took a deep breath, trying not to throw up, and wrenched the object out of his desiccated hand. It was a picture of two kids, about five or six years old, smiling into the camera, their hair blowing in the wind on a sunny day at the beach.

I looked up from the photograph and studied that decayed corpse again. There were no bullet wounds or visible injuries, although I could've missed them in my hasty examination. I was sure of one thing: That man's last thoughts weren't about a dark hallway. In his mind he'd been running along a beach on a bright summer day.

Clutching the photo, I could almost smell the ocean and hear the seagulls. On an impulse, I stuck it in my pocket and carefully stepped over him, trying not to disturb his dreams.

Twenty feet away, I found two more bodies sitting at a table. One guy had on a T-shirt with the same insignia and was also clutching a paper cup. The other guy was wearing a colonel's dress uniform. On his chest gleamed three medals, like ancient jewels looted from a pharaoh's tomb. In his right hand, he held a service pistol, the muzzle stained with the blood that had splattered when he blew his brains out.

Voices in the distance drew me out of my stupor. I backed away from that macabre scene and followed lights reflecting off the ducts in the building's massive ventilation system. With a sigh of relief, I realized I'd only taken one wrong turn. I was walking parallel to the group, but on the opposite side of the duct. All I had to do was follow that wall and turn right where it dead-ended and I'd run into my group.

Obsessed with that thought, I started to walk faster. Wandering around alone in the dark wasn't my idea of fun. Feeling abandoned in a building full of corpses was a thousand times worse, like walking through a haunted house.

My imagination started to play tricks on me. A couple of times I almost shot at my own shadow reflected on the walls. Then I heard whispers or shuffling footsteps following me. In my fevered mind, I saw the colonel stand up and come after me, his medals clinking softly as he stretched out his fleshless hands to grab my neck and drag me back to that room and force me to stay there forever.

Panic washed over me. I wasn't walking anymore—I was running. Up till then, I'd controlled my fear, as a matter of pride. I didn't want to look like a fool in front of the whole group. (*What an asshole. He got lost the minute we entered the building. He's so clueless he can't take ten steps without screwing up. He was shaking in fear when we found him.*) But by then, I didn't care if I looked like a coward. I was calling Pritchenko, Tank, Broto, and every other name I could remember. I didn't want to be alone in that darkness that smelled of despair, fear, and death.

If I'd been paying attention, I could've avoided the body, but I was in a daze and I ran right over him. My left boot sank into something soft with a faint *chooooofff*. There are no words to describe the nauseating smell that burned my nose. I got the wind knocked out of me when I fell on my side. My flashlight flew out of my hands, slid five feet, then came to rest upside down next to some clothes piled on the floor.

For a few seconds I lay there, trying to catch my breath. Finally, I got up on all fours and dragged myself over to the flashlight, which cast a faint, ghostly glow. I grabbed it and shook it, muttering a prayer to all the gods that it wasn't broken.

To my relief, the beam glowed bright and steady. I shined it on the body I'd stepped on. It was the corpse of a woman in civilian clothes, bloated by gasses. My left boot had punctured her abdomen allowing all the fluids to drain. The body looked like a grotesque, inflatable doll. Disgusted, I looked away. When I passed the beam of light around the rest of the room, the horrified scream I'd held in flew out of my throat.

3 8

TENERIFE

Lucia couldn't see a thing. The chemicals had irritated her unprotected eyes so badly she could barely open them. *What if my corneas are burned? As if I didn't have enough to worry about.*

The first thing she noticed was a faint smell of ozone and the hum of the air conditioner. She felt her way along a wall until she came to a sink where she splashed her eyes with lots of water. When the burning subsided, Lucia convinced herself she wasn't going to go blind, but she'd have a bad case of conjunctivitis for a few days.

With water streaming down her face, she looked up. The airlock was closed again and the red light above the door was back on. Through the disinfectant steam, Lucia could make out two figures. Those bastards just wouldn't give up.

The disinfection process only lasted a couple of minutes. Lucia had spent half that time flushing out her eyes. That left very little time to decide her next move. In desperation, she reached for the phone on the wall. It didn't have any buttons but she got a line out the second she picked up the receiver. Wherever the terminal was, no one was at the other end, so she hung up in frustration. Her eyes fell on a tray of surgical supplies. She grabbed a small scalpel the size of a butter knife. It wasn't much of a weapon, but it was better than nothing.

A door at the back of the room caught her eye. When she opened it, she felt a gentle stream of air. A lab technician could have told her that it was an osmotic pressure lock and that the difference in the pressure in the rooms caused the air to circulate inward to prevent leakage. But Lucia didn't know a thing about airlocks or osmotic pressure. She mistakenly thought there was a window that opened to the outside and that she could get out that way.

Feeling confident, she strode through the door. Ultraviolet lamps lit up a corridor that led to a line of rooms with large windows. In the first room, someone who wasn't wearing a hazmat suit was bent over a table, moving clumsily around something hidden by his body.

"Hey! You! I need help!" Lucia pounded on the glass to get the technician's attention. "Hey! Can you hear me?"

When the man turned, the smile on Lucia's face froze. The guy's face was covered by the burst veins and had the vacant look Lucia knew all too well. He was an Undead.

With a groan, the Undead guy pounced on the glass with such force, he shook the entire structure. Terrified, Lucia stepped back, braced for the glass to give way, but whoever designed that cubicle had done a good job. The window withstood the barrage of punches.

A siren wailed nearby. The entry lock had just opened and her two stalkers were in the next room. Lucia fled down the corridor past more rooms. She was mesmerized by what she saw: Each cubicle held Undead in different states of decay. In one room, an Undead's head and torso were strapped to a gurney. In another, a half dozen heads floated in formaldehyde in jars arranged on a shelf. To her horror, the heads opened their eyes and glared at her, snapping their jaws as she passed by.

The back door opened into another laboratory similar to the first. Her heart pounding wildly, Lucia realized that that last door had a lock on the inside. She pushed with all her strength, closed the door behind her, and bolted it.

She quickly backed away from the door and tripped over a chair that a technician had left in the middle of the room. She tried to keep her balance and for a second she thought she was going to stay on her feet, but she was falling too fast. She threw out her left hand in desperation to grab hold of a control panel, but her fingers slid over the buttons, pressing them randomly as she fell. The razor-sharp scalpel in her right hand cut a wide arc on her leg. The thin slit in her white nurse's uniform was immediately stained red. That cut was thin and shallow but it was bleeding profusely.

"Awwww fuck!" she cried out in pain and cursed her clumsiness.

There was a thud on the other side of the door. Dragging her leg and cursing, Lucia braced herself on the control panel and got to her feet. Her eyes fell on the buttons she'd accidentally pressed. Horrified, she read the label on the panel: CELL OPENING SYSTEM. The muffled groan she heard outside the door told her exactly which cells she'd stupidly opened.

3 9

MADRID

My cry of horror faded as my lungs ran out of air. I was so overcome, I forgot to breathe for a few seconds. The room was a huge mausoleum, a scene from a movie that ends tragically.

Dozens of bodies were scattered everywhere in twos and threes. Most were swollen like the body I'd tripped over, but a few were dried out like thousand-year-old mummies. There were an equal number of men and women, mostly civilians, but a few wore military uniforms. Everybody clasped the same kind of crumpled paper cup.

"There you are!" I heard Prit's familiar voice behind me as he rocketed into the room. "How the hell'd you get in here?" he asked, when he was sure I was in one piece. "If I hadn't heard you screaming like a madman, I'd never . . . " Prit's last words hung in the air.

The two legionnaires behind him stopped short when they got a look at the scene. "What the hell . . ." one of them mumbled.

A terrible thought occurred to me. I stepped carefully around a body and walked over to a table in the middle of the room. An enormous pan sat on a camp stove. Dozens of empty soft drink bottles were scattered around it, along with two smaller bottles. I picked one up and shined my flashlight on it. A skull and crossbones printed on an orange label smiled at me. Below it were a chemical formula and the hospital's logo. Across the label, someone had scrawled "hydrocyanic acid."

"Mass suicide," I muttered, letting the bottle fall into the pan.

Any liquid left in that pan had evaporated long ago. No doubt it was once filled to the brim with soft drinks laced with that powerful poison.

"Who are they? Why'd they do that?" Prit asked.

"They are the last survivors of the Autonomous Government of Greater Madrid," Tank said, "the ones whose evacuation convoy never made it to Barajas Airport." My gaze wandered over those dirty, thin bodies dressed in suits and ties.

One of the legionnaires whistled through his teeth. "That must've been a fucking bitch to discover all convoys had left."

"They must've felt so safe in this bunker that it didn't occur to them to look outside until days later." I looked down at the body of a middle-aged woman sitting in an expensive leather chair, her head resting on her chin, her arms limp at her side. She was elegantly dressed. Her very pricey pearl necklace was partially covered by her dirty, matted blonde hair. I shuddered when I realized who she was. Before the Apocalypse, I'd seen her at a number of press conferences.

"They were stranded with no provisions or weapons," Prit said as he picked up my train of thought. "They had two choices: throw their lot in with the Undead or slowly starve. The bravest ones probably tried to leave." The Ukrainian clicked his tongue at the thought. "Those who stayed behind chose a faster, less painful way to escape."

"They had radios," objected another legionnaire, pointing to a huge military radio lying between two bodies. "Why didn't they radio for help?"

"No power, kid." Prit shined his flashlight on the dark lights in the ceiling. "They must've realized how bad things were when the generators ran out of fuel and died."

We were silent for a moment, imagining the anguish those people felt in their final moments. Tank and seven other members of the team walked in and broke the gloomy spell.

"We found the stairs!" said Tank. For a moment he was speechless as he looked around. Even with all his Germanic stoicism, he paled. Then he blinked and shook his head wearily. "Come on, gentlemen, we still have to go down two floors. Our job is only half done."

Tank turned and walked out, not saying another word. We followed him, dragging our feet. That oppressive place was getting everyone down.

The staircase was located at the end of the ventilation duct. The door to the stairs was crisscrossed with thick chains. My eyes met Prit's. It was the same system they'd used to seal off the doors at Meixoeiro Hospital in Vigo. I pictured some military pencil-pusher drafting protocol for what to do if you were entrenched in a building during an invasion of Undead. I'd love to tell that genius how well his brilliant plan had worked.

Marcelo walked up with heavy-duty clippers and cut the chain with ease. He stepped aside and a group of soldiers crossed through the door. A second later, I heard a single shot, followed by, "Clear." Then we all headed through the door. At the foot of those stairs lay the body of an Undead, bleeding from a shot to the head. I swallowed and eased past him.

If there was one Undead on that side of the door, there'd be more. A lot more.

40

TENERIFE

For want of a nail . . . the kingdom was lost.

On account of a stupid accident caused by a panicked, terrified girl trying to save her life, Chaos escaped from Pandora's box again. But at that moment, no one knew. Not even the heroes of this story. And they never would.

Eric and Basilio quickly checked out every inch of the lab. Basilio stepped to the door and motioned for Eric to stand in front of it. With a nod, the redhead took his position, ten feet in front of the door, gripping his Beretta with both hands. Basilio slowly reached for the doorknob and flattened himself against the wall. If that damned girl was crouched on the other side, waiting to jump them, she'd be sadly disappointed.

He looked up at the Belgian, counted off three seconds on his fingers, yanked the door open, then jumped to the side.

A lot happened in a few short seconds. First someone completely naked barreled through the open door. *Something, not someone,* Eric thought, terrified by the Undead headed for him. The warm, sexual arousal the Belgian felt changed to cold, clammy fear. His eyes seemed to pop out of his head, he raised his Beretta and shot the Undead twice at close range.

The first bullet pierced the creature's neck, releasing a jet of thick, black blood. The second bullet hit him in the face, leaving a gaping hole where his nose had been. The thing collapsed in a heap, but Eric couldn't relax as three more creatures rushed in.

Cursing in French, the redhead retreated a few feet from the creatures, firing his weapon as he went. Blood spewed like a fountain out of the gaping head of the next Undead, an African man, over six feet tall, and splashed all across Eric's visor. Eric ran his gloved hand over the visor, which blurred his view completely and made matters worse.

A claw-like hand gripped his arm. Blindly, the Belgian elbowed someone—or something—hard and he fired blindly into another bulky shape coming at him. At that moment, he felt something grab his knee and then a burning pain shot up his calf.

The Belgian turned and fired twice at the Undead that had circled the table and ambushed him. Sweat poured down his face. It felt like a million degrees inside that damn hazmat suit. Through his blood-streaked visor, he could only see a narrow wedge right in front of him. That's how the bastard had gotten the jump on him.

A piercing howl made his blood run cold. Backed into a corner and unarmed, Basilio faced two Undead at once. His eyes bloodshot, the sailor threw a right uppercut at the Undead that would've brought down an ox. The Undead didn't dodge Basilio's fist, and that sledgehammer punch didn't even slow him down. The creature's jaws snapped together like a rusty trap and broken teeth flew through the air. The other Undead seized that moment to sink its teeth into Basilio's outstretched forearm, its fangs easily piercing the plastic hazmat suit and the thin cotton uniform underneath.

Basilio spun around like a tornado and let fly devastating kicks that would've made Chuck Norris proud. The creature dropped onto his back like a turtle, then struggled to stand up, chewing on that hunk of Basilio's arm.

"Eric!" Basilio cried out in a ragged voice. "Fucking help me!"

The Belgian's face drained of all emotion as he shot the Undead on the ground. The creature died instantly, with Basilio's flesh sticking out of his mouth, like a playful, little pink tongue. A sadistic smile spread across Eric's face, even in that grisly situation.

The last two Undead had piled on top of Basilio. One of them had ripped off his headgear. The Belgian fired twice at one of them, who collapsed like a rag doll, but the other one was faster and clamped down on Basilio's neck. With a muffled roar, Basilio made a last ditch effort and launched his assailant's body over the table, sending test tubes, beakers, and microscopes crashing to the floor.

Eric fired his last two bullets into the Undead's twisted body. He whipped around like a cobra, but he was the last man standing. Six Undead lay on the ground, their heads blown off.

Basilio Irisarri had slid to the floor and sat propped up against the wall. Eric watched in fascination as blood pulsed out of the wound in Basilio's neck in time to the beat of his heart.

"Eric . . ." Basilio's voice sounded strangely waterlogged. A clot of blood slid out the corner of his mouth, then down his neck and joined the river flowing between his clenched fingers. "Eric, help me the fuck up. Eric, I can't . . ."

The Belgian pointed to his headgear and gestured that he couldn't hear him. Then he shook his head and waved good-bye.

"No . . . you bastard . . . " Basilio gurgled. "Get me out of here . . . "

"Can't hear you, Basilio. I don't know if you can hear me, but this isn't fun anymore. I'm hot and tired and I want a cold beer. I'd be willing to bet those beasts devoured your little slut. And in case you haven't noticed, you're dying."

The burly sailor stared up at him, speechless. With each heartbeat, a little bit of life slipped away, out the terrible wound on his neck.

Eric pursed his lips and shook his head. "Gotta go, buddy." He chattered away happily as he bent down and placed the empty Beretta in Basilio's free hand. "I don't want you to think I'm deserting you or that I don't care about you. I really do. So here's a little souvenir. The authorities'll think *you're* responsible for this mess, not me."

He looked around, with the pained look of someone whose yard was torn up in a night of crazy partying.

"Say hello to Satan for me, old pal," he said. He looked at Basilio one last time, then headed back to the airlock. As he pressed the button to open the door, he heard the click of the Beretta's hammer. He turned and saw Basilio pointing it at him with his last ounce of strength. The old boatswain looked at the empty pistol in defeat, realizing he'd been scammed.

"We're rabid beasts, Basilio," Eric muttered, knowing the dying sailor couldn't hear him. "We turn on each other every chance we get. We can't help ourselves! Take these shitty islands. What's the first thing the survivors did? Kill each other! We're on the brink of goddamn civil war, if you believe the media! Those monsters took away the little humanity we had left. At least die with some fucking dignity!"

The door opened behind him. He gave a mock salute and stepped into the little room. Although clouded by death, Basilio's eyes followed him, his vision growing more and more blurred. His brain was dying, but coursing through his veins were thousands of tiny beings that were multiplying like crazy in his warm body. In a few hours, a new Basilio would arise. But Eric Desauss wouldn't be around to see that.

The Belgian pressed the button and immediately the jet of disinfectant enveloped him. The liquid burned as it washed over the gash in his calf. He was shocked to see a large, bloody hole in the pant leg of the suit. His fingers clumsy in the hazmat gloves, he lifted up the torn fabric and inspected a string of evenly spaced puncture wounds.

The sweat on his skin froze. He muttered to himself, "One of those fucking beakers must've cut me. Yeah, that's gotta be it. When that last SOB flew across the table, a million glass tubes broke. One of them must've sliced my leg. Yeah, that's it." His voice didn't sound as confident as he'd like, but it made him relax a bit.

Breathing easier, Eric waited patiently for the disinfectant shower to end. When the red light went off, the Belgian pushed the outer door open and headed back into the hallway. Still wearing the suit, he slipped through the security door that Basilio had blown to pieces and walked calmly out of the demolished lab.

A few feet before he reached the guard post, he met up with a ragtag crew of civilians and military guards racing down the hall.

"In the lab! A guy with a gun! And a girl! They shot up the place! I got away but there're still people inside!"

"Shit, not the Zoo! Hope they didn't reach the Zoo!" The highest ranking soldier turned pale. "Are you all right, Doctor?"

"A bullet grazed the back of my leg," Eric lied convincingly, pointing to his bloody leg. "It's just a scratch. I'll get one of the other doctors to take a look at it."

"Of course, Doctor. They'll patch you up on the next floor. The Froilists made a real mess, but everything's calmer now." The officer turned to his men. "Let's go, but be careful. If the doors to the Zoo are open, shoot first and ask questions later. Got it?"

The group trotted off to the lab. With a smirk, Eric took off his hazmat suit, leaned it against the guard post, brushed his sweat-soaked hair off his face, then hobbled through the metal detector. The throbbing pain in his leg grew worse with every step.

Two minutes later, Eric went through the hospital doors. The place was in complete chaos. Dozens of soldiers rushed in and out, and long lines of patients in pajamas were crowded together on the sidewalk. Whistling through his teeth, he walked downtown, limping slightly.

Maybe I should disinfect it when I get home. What the hell, it's just a fucking cut.

You know perfectly well it's not a cut, asshole, howled the reasonable, logical part of his mind. *It's a fucking bite. And you know you should shoot yourself in the head right now, motherfucker.*

No, I'm sure it's just a cut. I clearly remember—some flying glass cut me.

You're lying to yourself! yelled the little voice, but weaker this time.

Eric had heard voices since he was fourteen and had learned to tune them out. *It can wait.*

Eric realized he desperately needed a drink. What a fucking great idea! It was the Mother of All Brilliant Ideas. A couple of drinks would numb the pain in his leg. Maybe they'd even warm up his balls, which fear had turned to ice. And stop the voice in his head that wouldn't fucking let him think straight, that was screaming about the millions of little shepherd's crooks multiplying in his leg. Hell, it was worth a try.

For want of a nail, the kingdom was lost.

For want of a single, fucking nail.

4 1

MADRID

The lower floors of that hospital were in shambles in contrast to the deathly serene bunker and command center the first floor had been transformed into. As Prit and I walked silently, side by side, I figured his mind—like mine—was crowded with memories of the day we ventured into Meixoeiro Hospital, exhausted and half-dead. It felt like we were returning to the scene of a crime.

Our dwindling group made its way quickly, only stopping for Tank to glance at his map. Occasionally we came across some Undead, but the soldiers on point mowed them down with lethal efficiency. From the center of the group, Prit and I didn't have to fire our weapons once.

We made our way down one hallway after another until we came to the medical supply room. I figured it would have a heavy, armored door since those medications were valuable and scarce, but there was just a double wooden door with a simple lock that looked like it would fall open if you just looked at it. The soldier in the lead kicked that door wide open to reveal a vast room with rows and rows of shelves, and thousands of neatly arranged boxes of medicines.

"This is huge! There must be tons of medicines. We can't take it all!" I protested.

"We don't want to take it all," Pauli replied as she rushed past me. "Just what's on the commander's list."

Marcelo added, "Just the reagents." His gaze flew down a shelf, then he tossed me a plastic bottle that I caught in midair. "They're the most important."

"Why?" I asked, cramming those boxes and bottles into my backpack.

"We need them to make our own medicines. If we take back a lot of reagents, we won't have to come back here."

"I'm all for that!" Prit's mustache flapped up and down as he nodded and stuffed box after box into his backpack.

It took just fifteen minutes to fill our backpacks with medicines and the reagents. The list had a bit of everything on it: antibiotics, opiates, stimulants. I didn't have a clue what most of those things were. To save space, we took the medicines out of their boxes and tossed them on the floor. The mountain of empties grew. Sitting on one of those mountains like a Buddha, Broto took bottles out of a bin, examined them, then pitched them over his shoulder. When he found what he was looking for, he shouted for joy.

"Great! I was afraid I wasn't going to find these." He leapt to his feet and came over to us, unscrewing the lid of a bottle. He popped a couple of nondescript, white pills into his mouth, looking very pleased with himself, then handed me the bottle.

"Want some? You'll be glad you did."

"What are they?" I asked suspiciously.

"Methamphetamines, my friend," Broto said with a wink. "It's the best buzz. You're not sleepy or hungry or thirsty, and you're more alert than an Indian scout."

I didn't want any drugs in my body, so I shook my head, but Prit eagerly took a couple of the pills. He swallowed one and held the other out to me.

"Don't be stupid. Take it," he said sternly. "If it helps right now, it's a good thing, even if it's speed. We don't know what we'll face in the next few hours."

I understood the Ukrainian's logic and swallowed the pill. I didn't feel anything, but I assumed it would take a while to feel the effects.

I stood up, strapped on my backpack, and groaned—it weighed a lot more than I thought. Prit handed me the flashlight and the Glock I'd carelessly left on the floor.

"This thing weighs a ton. I'll be sweating like a pig in five minutes."

"Don't be a baby," Prit said cheerfully and slung his equally heavy backpack over his shoulder. "Every week, my Aunt Ludmila lifted fifty sacks of potatoes that size at the kolkhoz, that collective farm the Soviets forced on us Slavs. Of course, my Aunt Ludmila weighed three hundred pounds, had a glass eye, and was ugly as sin." Then he launched into a wild story about his aunt, a burning barn, and a dairy cow trapped in a mud pit.

Listening to Prit ramble on about his family, I wondered if the speed was kicking in. If he kept on chattering like that, I was going to strangle him.

"Then my cousin Sergei, who was still naked, jumped out the window with a hoe in his hand and—" Prit was still talking when two shots rang out on the other side of the shelves. In a split second, the Ukrainian's cheerful chatter ceased. He cocked his HK and crept over to where the shots had come from. I struggled to keep up with him, half-buried under my backpack. Marcelo threw off his pack so he could man his MG3.

We reached the door as more shots rang out and I heard warning shouts. Three legionnaires were trying to hold back a group of Undead amassed at the door to the supply room. We'd run out of time—our presence was no longer a secret. The building rumbled as hundreds of creatures howled, beating the walls or clumsily climbing the stairs, heading right for us. In a moment the place would be swarming with them.

"We gotta get out of here!" one of the sergeants screamed.

"Head for the ground floor!" Tank yelled over the rattle of guns. "In the satellite photos, I saw some tanks in the parking lot behind the building. We gotta get outta here fast! Let's go, let's go, let's go!"

His words spurred us on. We closed ranks and headed for the stairwell. Every few feet, a group of Undead appeared out of nowhere, but the soldiers were well trained and they hit their marks every time. Yet it was slow going, just a few feet at a time. If they'd caught us in a larger space, we wouldn't have had a chance, but being inside the building worked in our favor. The narrow stairs were our greatest ally. Those creatures could only attack us from the front or back, no more than two or three at a time.

Nestled in the center of the group, I focused on not getting out of step or tripping on the trail of bodies as we were leaving.

The deafening clack of the guns bounced off the narrow hallway. When a soldier in front needed ammunition, he'd turn and tap the shoulder of the man behind him. Broto and I grabbed those empty magazines and passed them to the soldiers behind us. Like magic, they filled those empties with ammo they carried in a backpack and kept walking. Gunshots tinged the darkness with a spectral orange glow. Flashlight beams swung wildly from side to side. The smell of gunpowder, blood, and sweat filled the air.

The soldier in front of me turned for a magazine. Just then an Undead came around a corner, wrapped his arms around the soldier's neck and dragged him out of the group. I heard the guy's desperate cry, but before anyone could do anything, the creature dug his teeth into the unfortunate soldier's arm. Without slowing down, Tank raised his pistol and fired at the Undead that fell at his feet. Then he turned his gun on the wounded soldier.

"NO!" was all the poor devil had time to yell before Tank blew his brains out.

I froze. I knew the guy was doomed; it was the only humane thing Tank could do, but I wasn't prepared for his brutal reaction. I felt the blood drain from my face.

Tank leaned toward me and said something, but deafened by gunfire I couldn't make out a word he said. All I heard was a high, steady whine in my ears. Even the gunshots sounded muffled, as if my ears were packed with cotton. Someone pushed me from behind and before I knew it, I'd taken the fallen soldier's place at the front.

Three Undead swayed a few feet from us. On my right, Marcelo carried the MG3 on his back. The shooter would have to be a real Hercules to fire that gun without resting it on something. He coolly fired his pistol at everything that crossed his path. On my other side, the veteran sergeant with a scar on his neck leaned toward me and shouted something. I didn't need to hear him to know what he meant.

Gritting my teeth, I raised my HK and started shooting.

4 2

MADRID

llllllllllllllllllllllllllllllllllllllllllllllllllllllllllllllllllllllllllllllllllllllllllllllllllllllllllllllllllll

I don't know at what point things started to turn around. It's hard to calculate time when you're on dark stairs shooting at everything that moves. To be honest, I don't think I contributed a lot to the team. Most of the time Marcelo and the veteran sergeant had already cleared out the Undead before I even aimed. However, once we made it to those stairs, we made better time and came across fewer creatures. Maybe the cacophony of gunfire bouncing around all the recesses on the stairs and in hallways made it hard for the Undead to locate us.

Whatever it was, it was a blessing. In just a few minutes, we'd used up almost all the ammunition that wasn't defective. Once the magazines were empty, the soldiers threw down their rifles and grabbed their handguns with desperation in their eyes.

"Magazines! A fucking magazine, dammit!" Marcelo yelled.

"Here!" Broto said, sweating profusely. In a trembling voice, he added, "It's the last one!"

To make sure the Argentine had understood him, he held out his empty hands. I turned to him in disbelief. We still had to go down a flight of stairs, cross the ground floor, go out the exit and head to the lot where supposedly the tanks were parked. Without any more ammo, we wouldn't make it to the exit.

My eyes met Tank's. He was in the right column near the back. The other sergeant and Prit covered our retreat, holding off any Undead that showed up. The German shot me a grim look and shook his head. *There's nothing we can do,* his eyes said.

Just then, as if the gods took pity on us (or prolonged our suffering a bit more), we came to a landing with a window. It was tall and grimy and let in only a small square of dim light, but it was a window nevertheless. I pointed it out to Tank.

"We're on the first floor. We can get out through that window! It can't be very high!"

The German herded our group like a sheepdog to that window and stood in the most exposed position to protect the last men as they reached the landing. When we were all leaning against the wall, I breathed a sigh of relief. All we had to do was protect our flank, but our situation was still terribly compromised. There were only eleven survivors and we had less than half of our ammunition left.

"Get on my shoulders!" Pritchenko yelled in my ear so loud, I thought my eardrum would explode. Several hands grabbed my backpack and lifted me onto Prit's shoulders. With a shove, Prit lifted my head level with the window.

The window was about two feet square. It looked like it hadn't been opened since the building first opened its doors. Its hinges were ringed with rust; a layer of dirt let in only a thin film of gauzy light. I clung, white-knuckled, to the metal frame and looked out the window. I could barely make out a small parking lot. Over time, sand, ash, and cracks had obliterated most of the lines painted around the parking spots. At the back of the lot, two heavily armored, olive green vehicles sat quietly. Their cannons had been carefully wrapped to protect them. There wasn't a soul around. Any Undead wandering around must've been drawn inside by our gunfire.

I jiggled the lock, but it wouldn't budge. I didn't have time to ponder the situation. With the butt of my Glock, I bashed the window. It broke with a loud crash and a shower of glass fell outside. Hurriedly, I brushed the glass off the frame and stuck my head out.

The air smelled fresh and clean compared to the stuffy air in the building. To my right was a metal pipe bolted to the wall. It might've been an electrical duct but it was too thin to be a drain. It seemed to be well anchored and strong enough to support our weight. Although we weren't very far off the ground, I decided it'd be better to climb down that pipe than to jump.

"We can get out through here!" I shouted, looking back inside.

In quick succession, the others lifted the eleven backpacks full of drugs up to me and I threw them out the window. Twisting and turning, I slipped through that gap with the grace of an arthritic acrobat, and descended hand over hand, clinging to the pipe for all I was worth.

The first thing I did was look around nervously. There were only four bullets left in my Glock. If any Undead had come around the corner, I'd have had to run for it. I got lucky; there weren't any around. For the moment.

I watched Prit slip down the pipe, his trusty knife bouncing against his kidneys. Then came Marcelo and the veteran sergeant in the neckerchief. In a tense moment, David Broto got stuck in the window. Marcelo had to climb back up to get him unstuck.

Meanwhile, the situation inside degraded with each passing moment. I heard only two guns firing. They could hardly contain the crowd of Undead. One of the soldiers went out the window, with a panicked look on his face, and decided to jump to the ground. When he landed, his right ankle gave a terrible crack. For a second we all forgot about the situation and watched the poor bastard writhe in pain.

I could hear the rhythmic hiccup of only one gun inside the building. Tank headed out the window and turned back, extending his hand to the next guy, a very dark-skinned, pimple-faced soldier. Tank had him by the wrist, but the soldier let out a piercing scream, as something pulled him back into the building.

"Aaaaah, fuck, it hurts, it hurts so bad!" The kid screamed, desperately trying to hold on to the commander's arm.

Unceremoniously, Tank mumbled a brief "sorry" and released the guy's wrist. In less than a second, his body was swallowed up and disappeared as fast as a rabbit into a magician's hat. His screams of agony echoed for a moment and then there was silence.

We were speechless when Tank reached the ground and brushed the dust from his jacket, which was smeared with someone—or something's—blood. In addition to the young soldier, we were missing another legionnaire and a sergeant, who'd also been left inside. We all did a head count but no one dared say a word. Of the original eighteen who'd started out less than an hour before, only eight remained: Marcelo, Pauli, Tank, Broto, the veteran sergeant, the soldier with the broken ankle, Pritchenko, and me.

"What're you waiting for?" Tank growled. "Get in those tanks before we have company!" So much for German sensitivity.

Without a word, we grabbed our backpacks (we had to leave three of them behind at the wall) and followed Tank.

Those were some weird-looking vehicles. They had four huge wheels instead of tracks, and a turret with a humongous cannon. They'd been designed by an engineer with no sense of aesthetics, but they looked really powerful.

"What the hell is that?" I asked, trying to catch my breath.

"A Centaur," the veteran sergeant said as he untied the handkerchief around his neck and wiped his forehead. "A light armored reconnaissance SUV. It's really ugly but it runs great! I had one under my command in Bosnia years ago."

"If it can get us out of here, it'll be the sweetest ride in the world," I muttered, not sharing the soldier's enthusiasm for that pile of steel. "Think it'll start?"

"Sure!" said the sergeant with a smile as he climbed aboard and opened the hatch. "Those babies are tough. If it's got some fuel, it'll run."

While the soldier bent over the vehicle's controls, I walked over to Prit. The Ukrainian was sweaty, but he didn't look tired. Gasping to catch my breath, I made yet another promise to quit smoking.

"Why do you think they left them behind?" I asked between breaths.

"Good question. Either this heap won't start or they didn't think it was worth taking."

"Why's that?"

"Look at them. That huge cannon won't do *us* any good and only four people can squeeze in them. They wouldn't be very valuable in an evacuation, compared to a bus or a truck. If they had only a few drivers, it's logical they left them behind."

Just then, the Centaur engine let out an asthmatic cough, followed by a series of mechanical gasps. Amid a dense cloud of black smoke, the tank sprang to life with a roar, as the sergeant revved the engine.

The sergeant poked his head out the hatch and said, "All set. Let's get outta here!"

Eager to go, I picked up my backpack and started to climb in. I was halfway up in the tank when Broto made a noise like he was choking, his eyes wide as saucers.

"Not so fast, sergeant," Pauli said menacingly. "Get out and raise your hands where I can see them. Let's go."

Stunned, I looked up. Pauli pointed her HK at the stunned sergeant. Marcelo stood beside her, aiming the MG3 at us from the turret of the Centaur. The soldier with the broken ankle limped over and disarmed us, tossing our weapons inside the tank.

Marcelo's voice was as cold as a dagger. "Gentlemen, you're staying here."

4 3

TENERIFE

"Who are you? How'd you get in here?" Heavy protective gear muffled the voice. "Hey, you aren't wearing a hazmat suit! You can't come in here!"

Lucia turned. Behind her, a woman in her fifties peered through the visor of a hazmat suit. She was standing next to a microscope, holding a tray of beakers in one hand and a clipboard in the other.

"You're injured!" The woman cried out in alarm, pointing to Lucia's nurse's uniform. "This is an isolation zone! You could get contaminated!"

Before Lucia could utter a word, shots rang out on the other side of the door, followed by grunts and banging noises, then more shots. Then Basilio Irisarri's booming voice shouted, "Eric, help me the fuck up!" And then silence.

The older woman approached the door and pressed her face to the small window. What she saw made her jump back.

"They're out! The Undead are out! Six cubicles are open!" She turned to Lucia, her eyes flashing with anger. "Did you let them loose? Answer me!"

"Hey, calm down," the girl replied, coolly. "Those two guys out there are—"

"I can't see anyone out there," the woman muttered, as she rushed over to a computer and keyed in a code. A siren immediately started blaring.

A doctor in the next office, also dressed in a hazmat suit, stuck his head in, clutching a gun, disoriented by the alarm. "Eva! What the hell's going on?" When he caught sight of Lucia, his eyes grew wide. "Who's she?"

"I don't know," Eva said and turned to Lucia. "That's a good question. Who are you, young lady?"

"My name's Lucia and I work in this hospital. People are shooting at each other on the upper floors. It's a madhouse. There're dead and wounded everywhere! Two men followed me down here and are trying to kill me. They killed Sister Cecilia! You have to help me!" Lucia realized her story didn't make any sense, but she couldn't calm down after being so close to dying.

"Calm down. Security will be here soon and they'll handle everything, okay?" Eva put a hand on Lucia's shoulder. "While we're waiting, why don't you take a seat and try to calm down?"

A wave of relief flooded Lucia's body. She was safe. Everything would be okay.

She dropped into a chair, exhausted. As she stretched, she felt the sting on her leg where she'd cut herself with the scalpel. She looked up to ask those nice people for a little hydrogen peroxide, but the woman had her back to her.

She focused her attention on the other doctor as he stood under some bright lights; his visor reflected the female doctor like a mirror. Just as Lucia was about to open her mouth, Eva made a gesture that struck terror in Lucia. The doctor pointed to the man's gun, then drew her hand across her neck.

The woman said, "I think we'd better wait inside that—hey! What're you doing?"

Lucia sprang to her feet and threw her arm around the woman's neck, holding the scalpel at eye level. Then it dawned on her that she didn't have a clue what to do next.

"I want outta here. Now!"

"Calm down! Let Dr. Méndez go! Please!" The other doctor's voice trembled as he raised his gun.

Lucia was pretty sure that this guy, probably a lab assistant, didn't have the nerve to shoot. "You have to be a special breed to shoot someone as you're looking him in the eyes," Prit once said. Lucia was pretty sure the assistant didn't have what it took. So she took a deep breath and squeezed the doctor's neck tighter.

"I want outta here. Now! Or I swear to God, I'll slit her throat from ear to ear."

"Listen, you can't leave!" Dr. Méndez gasped. "The Undead in the lab have hurt your leg; you may be infected. Just let me go."

"Nobody hurt my leg," said Lucia, tersely.

"You're bleeding," the other doctor pointed out, as if that wasn't obvious.

"I cut *myself*! I was holding a knife and I stumbled and fell. I accidentally cut myself. Got it?" She had little hope they'd believe her.

"Sure, sure you did. You cut yourself with half a dozen infected Undead surrounding you. I heard that story at the Valencia Safe Haven a million times." Eva gasped. "Hey . . . you're . . . choking . . . me . . ."

"Is there another way out?" Lucia asked slightly loosening her grip on the doctor's neck. She didn't want to hurt anyone, but she had to escape. If they thought she was infected, she knew all too well what the "treatment" was.

"There's another airlock that leads to the dispatch area." The lab assistant's voice wavered as he pointed to the door behind him.

"Dammit, Andrés! Shut the fuck up!" Eva snapped, her eyes shooting daggers.

At that moment, Lucia loosened her grip. That was the chance Dr. Méndez had been waiting for. The doctor drove her head backwards, bashing her headgear against Lucia's forehead. For a moment, colored spots danced before the girl's eyes. She elbowed Lucia in the chest, knocking the wind out of her, then broke free and jumped to one side.

"Shoot, Andrés, shoot! She's infected!"

"I can't shoot, Eva! I can't! You do it!"

"Give me that, asshole," Dr. Méndez growled and yanked the gun out of his hand.

That struggle gave Lucia time to slip into to the next room, whose open door beckoned to her. She flung herself through the airlock and slammed the door behind her. At the last moment, a hand appeared through the door, clutching her arm.

"I've got her, doctor, I've got her!" The assistant's voice sounded triumphant until Lucia plunged the knife deep into his forearm, forcing him to withdraw. "Aaayyyy, I'm hurt, doctor! I think she bit me!"

Lucia slammed the door and pressed the button on the wall. Seconds later, the chemicals burned her eyes again. After two long minutes, the light turned green and she entered a cluttered office with papers and books piled everywhere. Lucia stumbled through the mess and came to a window that opened onto a dimly lit ventilation shaft. Attached to one wall was a fire escape ladder that led to the upper floors. Without hesitating, the girl started to climb up to street level.

Outside there was chaos. Hordes of people pushed their way through the crowd and shoved each other down the stairs, stumbling, shouting hysterically. A group of nurses were trying to treat the wounded in the hallways, but the flood of people overwhelmed them. Gunshots still came from inside the hospital. Some of the security forces must not have realized they were chasing their own shadows.

"Hey, you, come here!" A stocky, dark-skinned male nurse grabbed her arm. Terrified, Lucia tried to break free, but the man was too strong. "Calm down, honey, I just want to help you! Here, let me see those cuts."

Before Lucia realized what was happening, the nurse swept her into a garden area where a doctor had set up a makeshift hospital.

"The cut on your leg isn't very deep, but your forehead took a good hit. What the hell did you get in your eyes? Someone must be spraying tear gas," he said as he flushed her eyes out with distilled water. Lucia instantly felt relief.

"I'm fine, thanks, I'm fine," was all Lucia could mutter.

"You don't *look* fine. Better take it easy for a while, at least until things get sorted out." The nurse gave her a scrutinizing look. Just then, two orderlies set down a stretcher; on it lay a soldier with a gaping gunshot wound in the chest. When the nurse turned his attention to the wounded man, Lucia slipped out the side of the garden.

A few feet from the hospital, she stopped, hoping her head would stop spinning.

She leaned against an empty shop window and stared at her reflection. She looked like she'd been through a hurricane. Her hair was matted from the chemical showers, her white pants were stained red from the cut, her eyes were red and swollen, and she had a huge bump in the middle of her forehead.

No wonder people're staring at me. It's strange that they aren't running away in terror. I look like a junkie strung out on crack.

A group of civil guards came running down the sidewalk. Lucia's first impulse was to tell them what had happened. Sister Cecilia and Maite had been killed before her very eyes. The police needed to catch the killers. They might still be in the area. She shuddered and glanced around fearfully.

She started to cross the street, but a dark thought stopped in her tracks. If you tell those guards that crazy story about gunmen, a nun, and some Undead, they'll probably lock you up while they investigate that mess. Especially looking the way you do. Those doctors in the lab (the Zoo, they'd called it) were probably giving the hospital guards a detailed description of a nurse with red eyes who was "wounded" by the Undead.

Those doctors wanted to kill me. I didn't do anything wrong, but they wouldn't listen. They'd wanted to kill me. But why? She was on the verge of tears.

Because they're afraid of you, idiot. They're terrified of another outbreak of that virus and they think you might open that door to hell.

But I haven't done anything wrong! I didn't even get near the Undead.

Think anyone cares about that? The voice in her head laughed bitterly. *Now, be a good girl and run along. Save your own neck.*

Keeping her head down, Lucia walked past the guards. The honk of a horn startled her. A heavy military truck roared up and screeched to a stop in front of the hospital. Heavily armed legionnaires jumped out and ran inside.

With a shudder, Lucia took off running in the opposite direction. She realized she had nowhere to go. She was a fugitive.

4 4

MADRID

"What the hell is this?" growled the sergeant, too stunned to move. "Some kind of sick joke!"

"This is no joke, asshole," Marcelo replied slowly, almost chewing his words. "It's simple. We're leaving, you're staying."

"Are you out of your fucking mind?" Broto shouted. "The Undead'll be here any minute! We gotta get the hell out of here!"

"Oh, we're going, just not to Tenerife. We're headed to Gran Canaria." Pauli kept her eyes glued on us. "Those drugs are the property of the *legitimate* government of Spain. Is that clear?"

Tank had been too shocked to talk, but he couldn't stay silent anymore. Fuming, he walked up to the soldiers perched on the vehicle, ignoring the weapons pointed at him.

"Fucking Froilists! You royalist scum! You miserable traitors! Where's your honor and dignity?" he spat out.

"You're the traitors!" Pauli shouted. "You people think you can blow off the laws! You betrayed the legitimate democratic government and installed that phony Republic!"

"You call that damn Froilist government *democratic*!" Tank was livid. "What's legitimate about it! You're just a gang of soldiers hiding behind a child. You're using him to promote your own interests and calling it a democratic monarchy!"

"That child is the King of Spain! *He's* the legitimate government! Only a traitor or a communist would set up a republic behind the people's back!" Pauli's voice broke.

"Nobody went behind the peoples' back, you fool! The republic is democratic!"

"Democratic? Like hell it is! When were elections held? Or a referendum?"

"What about you? Has your damned monarchy held an election? *Nein!* You don't give a shit about legitimizing what you claim!"

Marcelo suddenly fired his machine gun over our heads. Terrified, Prit, Broto, and I threw ourselves to the ground; lead flew just inches over our heads like buzzing flies. Only Tank and the sergeant remained standing, unflinching. When I dared to look up, the Argentine was glaring down at us, his eyes bright with anger.

"Sorry, folks, we don't have time to air our dirty laundry. The Undead are headed this way and we're getting the hell outta here!" His face red with rage, Marcelo waved Pauli into the tank. As she climbed aboard, she looked away for a split second.

That was enough for Tank.

The German pulled a small pistol out of his boot and shot the lame soldier as he struggled up the side of the tank. The soldier flew backward and crashed to the ground. A red stain spread across on his chest. With the measured precision of a professional gunman, Tank didn't miss a beat. He turned to Marcelo and fired twice. The first bullet hit the Argentine's arm and he let out a scream of pain; the second bullet just barely missed his head. He took cover behind the metal plate that shielded the turret. Tank advanced steadily, still firing, trying to climb into the vehicle, his bullets crashing against the metal shield.

Just then, Pauli popped out of the hatch like a jack-in-the-box, her face contorted with hate, and fired four bullets into the German commander's chest.

For a second, Tank gasped like a fish out of water. He locked eyes with Pauli, just inches from her face. He fell to the ground, with a look of disbelief that he, Kurt Tank, the great survivor, had been gunned down—by one of his own soldiers.

Other shots rang out on our left. Marcelo, his right arm bleeding, opened fire on the sergeant, who was clawing up the hatch of the tank. The Argentine's bullets shook the sergeant like a rag doll and he collapsed in the dust next to the German.

For a split second, the silence was so thick I thought I'd drown. I watched with horror as Marcelo aimed his MG3 at us. Death danced in his eyes.

We're dead. It's over.

"Hold your fire!" Pauli screamed. "Don't shoot, Marcelo! Wait a fucking minute!"

The Argentine's expression didn't change. We didn't dare move a muscle, as we lay there, unarmed and defenseless. At that distance, his MG3 would cut us in two before we made the slightest movement. Marcelo finally exhaled and relaxed his trigger finger. I nearly died of relief.

"Listen carefully! You civilians shouldn't be caught in the middle of all this!" Pauli said, standing very erect in the hatch. "But these are difficult times in the struggle for freedom and the future of the human race. They require sacrifices from everyone. Including you."

This is amazing! She's giving a fucking speech! From Prit's expression, I knew he was thinking the same thing, but we were smart enough to keep our mouths shut.

"It's time to take a stand! Illegitimate republic or legitimate government? Are you with us or against us? The Airbus at Cuatro Vientos Airport should be in the hands of loyalists by now. If you support the true prime minister of Spain and King Froilan, there's a place for you on that plane. Otherwise, you're on your own!"

I couldn't believe it. I'd heard about the political tensions on the islands, but I never dreamed I'd get caught in the middle of a civil war. I wasn't even clear which side was right and which was wrong—or if there was a right or a wrong side.

Pauli was waiting for an answer, so I stood up and said, "My wife's in Tenerife and so's my friend, Sister Cecilia, who's seriously ill. Those medicines could mean the difference between life and death for her. I can't abandon them. I've gotta get back to them. I'm not going to Gran Canaria."

"What about you, *Pretyinko*? That terrorist government means to throw you in jail. Here's your chance to be free and serve the representatives of the people."

"It's *Pritchenko*, ma'am," the Ukrainian replied, regally. "True, they want to put me in jail. But both islands're full of spies. In Tenerife, if they found out we'd collaborated with you, they'd make our friends pay. What's worse, they'd say we ran away like cowards. Viktor Pritchenko has never run away, and I'm not going to start now."

The Slavic peasant's code of honor, I thought, looking down to hide a smile.

"Besides," Prit said, throwing his arm over my shoulder, his terrifying, blue eyes boring into Pauli. "I never leave a friend behind. If he stays, I stay. We're a team. Comrades, him and me. That's how it's been and how it'll always be. *Kapish*?"

Pauli studied us for a moment with both contempt and amazement. She shook off her thoughts, then turned to Broto, standing next to us, his hair caked with dirt and dust.

"What about you, Broto? Are you coming or staying?"

David turned and studied us for a few seconds. Then he swallowed, coughed loudly, and bent down to pick up Tank's pistol, which was lying on the ground at his feet.

"Don't get me wrong, you've been fucking great to me. You really helped me out. But all that's waiting for me in Tenerife is a jail cell. On Gran Canaria, I got nothing to lose and everything to gain. I'm going with them. Sorry, pals."

"Okay, kid. No hard feelings," Prit said, disappointment in his voice.

"Enough with the speeches!" Marcelo's voice boomed. "Let's go! You two, hand your backpacks to Broto. Get a move on, tenderfoot."

We did as we were told, and Broto loaded our backpacks into the hatch. Marcelo kept his MG3 trained on us and didn't take his eye off us.

"Hold on, Marcelo!" Pauli blurted out. She jumped off the Centaur and raced over to the other tank sitting just a few feet away. She raised the hood, leaned over the engine, took out her knife. She cut out a bunch of wires, then stuck them in her pocket.

"Nothing personal. We don't want you following us . . . not for a while anyway."

"This is cold-blooded murder," I stammered. "Without that tank, we're dead. You know that as well as we do."

"Not true," she replied, as she slipped back into the Centaur. "I'm sure somewhere in this shit hole there're spare battery cables. But by the time you get that heap fixed—*if* you get it fixed—we'll be flying toward Gran Canaria."

"We don't have any weapons!" Prit protested.

"Not my problem. You made your choice," Pauli recited in a singsong tone. "Hey! Don't say I never gave you anything." With that, she threw the Ukrainian's combat knife at his feet, then closed the hatch and drove away in a cloud of black smoke. We watched as it disappeared around the corner. The sound of its engine rang in our ears over the deathly silence of Madrid.

4 5

MADRID

A fine rain started to fall as the Centaur disappeared in the distance. The pinging grew louder as big raindrops hit the dusty pavement, but I didn't notice. We were alone, unarmed, with no transportation, in a huge, deserted city infested with Undead. A despairing moan escaped my throat.

"Cheer up," the Ukrainian said, patting me on the back. "It could be worse."

"Oh yeah? How? How could it be worse?"

"Calm down," Prit said as he picked up his knife. "We've gotten out of tighter spots, right? Don't worry. We'll get out of this mess, too. All we gotta do is start that thing. Now, think. Where can we get some battery cables before things get ugly around here?"

Just then I heard a groan behind me that made my hair stand on end. I braced myself, looking around for the Undead, but there were none in sight. I heard the moan again. Confused, I looked down and saw the sergeant's hand move feebly.

"Prit! He's alive!"

He had four bullet holes in his chest, but he was still alive. When I grabbed his hand, he looked up at me. He had a hard time focusing on my face and when he tried to speak, all that came out of his mouth was bloody foam.

"Take it easy, friend," I said. His nametag read *Jonás Fernández.* "Listen Sergeant, keep your eyes on me, okay? Come on! Stay with me, Jonás. Prit'll get the Centaur started, then we'll get the hell outta here."

"Shit!" Prit bellowed in a fury. "That bitch ripped out the battery cables! Even if we find a replacement, I can't splice it without tools. This heap won't start without a battery! Son of a bitch!"

The blood drained from my face. The Undead could show up at any moment.

"Prit." I pushed a lock of rain-soaked hair out of my face and tried to keep the fear out of my voice. "This man'll die unless he gets medical attention right away and we're not going to be much better off if you don't think of something, dammit!"

"There's nothing we can do!" Prit said, pounding his fist on the side of the Centaur. "Without a battery we're dead!"

The Ukrainian straightened up and stared at me. "We've got to think of a way out, fast! Maybe if we take that wide street . . . La Castellana. Or maybe the subway tunnels." The Ukrainian's mind was racing.

"Prit." I pointed to the wounded sergeant. "What the fuck do we do with him?"

As an answer, Prit patted his knife. We couldn't take him with us if we had to make a run for it, but we couldn't leave him either. Helpless. A tasty snack for those bastards.

I took a deep breath, trying to muster up my courage. I could justify shooting an Undead monster but not taking a human life.

"Prit . . ." I wasn't sure how to finish the sentence. Just then Sergeant Fernández weakly lifted his arm, trying to get our attention.

"Back . . . back . . . up . . ." Then he choked as a fountain of dark red blood gushed out the corner of his mouth.

"Sergeant, take it easy." I loosened his flak jacket to make him more comfortable. "We'll get some backup, don't worry."

"Back-up . . . you idiot . . ." Impatience flashed in the sergeant's eyes as he coughed up red phlegm. "The . . . back-up . . . battery . . ."

"Back-up battery?" Prit pounced on his words. "Where is it?"

"In . . . the . . . turret." Rain mixed with the blood pooled around the sergeant. "Same terminals . . . and . . . voltage."

Before he finished talking, Prit had already scrambled up the Centaur like a monkey and slipped inside the turret. As the Ukrainian tinkered around inside, I lifted the sergeant's head so he could breathe better. I didn't know what else to do. Even if I'd had some medical training, I was pretty sure Jonás was beyond hope. He must've known that too, as he stoically endured the pain that had to be tearing him up.

"Here it is!" Pritchenko stuck his head out the turret, triumphantly cradling a rectangular box. "Just give me a couple of minutes and it'll be ready!"

We didn't have much time. Around the corner of the parking lot appeared three staggering Undead.

"PRIT!" I yelled at the top of my lungs. "Hurry! We've gotta go NOW!"

I threw an arm around Sergeant Fernández's shoulder and eased him as gently as I could through the Centaur's hatch. Fortunately Sergeant Jonás Fernández, veteran of the Tercio Don Juan de Austria Regiment of the Spanish Legion, was feeling no pain; he'd passed out. Over my shoulder, I saw that the Undead had advanced half the distance between us and them. In a burst of bravery, I ran to the three backpacks we'd abandoned under the window back at the tower. The Undead saw me and started walking in my direction. I grabbed two of the backpacks and dragged them along the pavement. As I staggered toward the tank, I threw a wary glance over my shoulder. Those things were already about a hundred yards from us.

"Prit! Get that damn thing started! They're right on our ass!" I shouted as I tossed the packs inside the tank.

"Almost . . . got it . . ." Sweat was pouring off the Ukrainian. His hands moved at lightning speed inside the belly of the engine. "All set! Get in! Get in!"

We scrambled into the Centaur and sealed the hatches overhead. Just in time. As we settled into the front seats, the Undead were roaring and beating on the sides of the armored tank.

"Start it, for God's sake!" I yelled at Prit.

"Whadda you mean?" He looked at me as if I'd lost my mind. "I don't know how to start this thing!"

"What do you mean you don't know how?" My eyes grew wide. "You're the damned pilot!"

"*Helicopter* pilot!" Prit replied angrily. "In the air force, we didn't have anything like this box on wheels! I thought you knew how to drive this thing!"

"Me?" It was my turn to be astonished. "Prit, I've never been in a tank in my life! I didn't even serve in the army. I was a lawyer, dammit!"

"Tell that to our friends outside! Do you or don't you know how to start this thing?"

"No! Of course not!" Suddenly, a flash of insight struck me with force. "Wait! The sergeant must know! Hey! Jonás! Wake up! Come on, Sergeant, open your eyes! We need you!"

Sergeant Fernández took a while to come around. His breathing had become spasmodic. From time to time, he vomited blood, which mingled with the blood coming out the holes in his chest. It was a wonder he was still alive.

In a wheezing, shaky voice, he told Prit how to start the tank. The ignition system was very durable and it still worked after over a year out in the open. But it was also painfully complicated. Prit got the ignition sequence wrong twice and had to start over. Meanwhile, dozens of Undead had gathered around the Centaur. Some even had climbed up on it and were walking above us, trying to get in. Even though the tank weighed several tons, it shook with all the Undead pounding on it. The noise was deafening. If we couldn't start the engine, we'd be trapped in there until we died of hunger and thirst. That was a chilling thought.

With a grinding screech, Prit finally got the tank in first gear and the engine coughed to life for the first time in a year. The Centaur lurched forward and stalled.

"Start it again! For God's sake!" As soon as those words left my mouth, I started laughing hysterically, despite the seriousness of the situation. I couldn't stop myself.

"What the hell's wrong with you?" Prit looked at me as if I'd gone mad. "Think this is funny?"

He tried a second time. The Centaur bucked a couple of times, but didn't stall. With a triumphant gesture, he looked at me and wiped the sweat out of his eyes. He gave it some gas and the powerful diesel engine roared.

"Purrs like a kitten!" he said, satisfied, his eyes glued to the display panel. "Now, let's get out of here!"

"We've got to get to Cuatro Vientos before they do. And they've got a head start."

That wasn't the only problem. The Centaur's gas gauge was on reserve. I didn't have a clue what obstacles we'd encounter in Madrid. I wasn't even sure I could find my way to the airport.

"Get us the fuck out of here!"

Prit accelerated and the Centaur inched ahead, pushing against the mass of Undead in its way. After a few agonizing feet—and some crushed bodies—Prit finally got the hang of the controls and drove us out of the parking lot.

The Ukrainian and I looked at each other and high-fived. Our race against the clock had begun.

4 6

MADRID

"Prit, look out!"

The Centaur swerved and almost turned on its side as we dodged a pile of garbage containers in the middle of the street. With a groan, the vehicle righted itself and we continued down the center of the street as fast as we could. But after driving down La Castellana for a nerve-racking half hour, we had to face the fact that it'd take a long time to get out of Madrid.

That street was ten-lanes wide, so we had plenty of room to dodge the Undead along the way. Now and then, we had to zigzag around a car wreck or an abandoned checkpoint but otherwise, the road was clear. Side streets were cut off by mountains of cars that had served as barricades. Some of those piles had fallen over or had been pulled down by the Undead. Thousands of beasts were ambling down the street, like drunken pedestrians. Prit could drive around them, but their numbers were growing.

"Whadda ya think those barricades were for?" the Ukrainian asked, his eyes glued to the road.

"Looks like they tried to secure a corridor that connected with roads outside the city," I said, pressing my eyes against the periscope. "That would've given them a pretty good escape route."

When the Ukrainian swerved, my chin came down hard on the edge of the periscope. I cursed under my breath, as I got a taste of my own salty blood.

"So, how come almost no one survived?"

"No idea. Their escape route must've been cut off farther down the line."

"So, how're *we* gonna get out?"

"I don't know. Let's cross that bridge when we come to it." I was lost in thought as we drove under the Gate of Europe, the twin leaning towers the locals called Torres KIO. One of those twenty-six-floor towers had burned to the ground. It was just a pile of twisted metal rising in the air like a rotten tooth. The Centaur shook like a cocktail shaker as Prit drove over scattered debris from those towers.

I got more and more uneasy as we moved through the heart of that dead city. La Castellana, usually full of traffic, was empty except for wrecks here and there. A thick layer of dust, debris, and ash covered the pavement. Trees had sprouted up, cracking the pavement. But what really got me down was the silence. The only sound was the growl of the tank's diesel engine. The Centaur inched past several office buildings; their windows were broken out and looked like dark eyes glaring down at us. My heart raced wildly when I spotted what I thought was a group of friends gathered in the doorway of a restaurant. When we got closer, we saw it was a handful of Undead. They were coming out of the woodwork, drawn by the noise of the passing Centaur.

After a few minutes, we reached the Plaza de Cibeles—its marble statues and fountains had been a symbol of Madrid. Someone had broken off the head of the statue of the goddess Cibeles as she sat perched in her carriage. Across the goddess's breast, a trembling hand had scrawled in red paint ISAIAH 34-35, referring to the passage "for the Lord's anger is against all the nations and his wrath against all their hordes . . ." The bowl of the fountain was filled to the brim with skeletons dressed in rags. Some very deranged person had neatly lined up dozens of skulls along the rim of the fountain. As we drove past, I felt the lifeless eyes of all those skulls, with their menacing smiles, following us.

When we came to the traffic circle at Plaza de Atocha, Prit braked hard, almost knocking me to the floor.

"What the fuck! Why'd you brake?"

"Look up ahead. We can't go that way."

Plaza de Atocha, with its fountains, train station, and wide streets, was once the hub of Madrid. It no longer existed. One of the buildings had been blown up and its debris blocked most of the road. Added to the rubble was a wide trench, ten or twenty feet wide, full of stagnant water. Completing the scene were several overturned eighteen-wheelers that formed an impenetrable wall, splitting that hub in two.

"End of the line," muttered the Ukrainian. "Now whadda we do?"

"Back up," I mumbled. "Let's retrace our path and get on the M-30. Maybe we'll make it farther on that highway. If that doesn't work, we can take side streets and bypass this area entirely."

Even I didn't believe what I was saying. On a boulevard as wide as La Castellana, the Centaur had a chance of getting through, but on the narrow back streets, filled with wrecked cars and collapsed buildings, we'd get stuck in a heartbeat. Yet what other choice did we have?

Prit circled wide and headed in the opposite direction. In that neighborhood, the Paseo de la Castellana merged with the narrow, tree-lined Paseo del Prado. Prit had to maneuver the Centaur between downed trees anytime a group of Undead forced him to change lanes. I couldn't say for sure how many of those monsters surrounded us, but it was way more than a couple of thousand. If the Centaur got stuck, we were goners.

My eyes were burning as I strained to look into the periscope. A bead of sweat slid down my forehead, so I pulled away to dry it off, then pressed against the rubber again. Out the corner of my eye, I caught a glimpse of the sun reflecting off something shiny. I turned the periscope to the right and yelled, "Stop, Prit!"

"What's the matter?" Ukrainian asked, alarmed.

"I saw something on that roof, over to the right." Prit craned his neck to look where I was pointing.

We were stopped in front of the main entrance to the Prado Museum. Through the trees, I'd gotten a glimpse of the cupola on top of that enormous building. Sitting on the roof, directly in front of that cupola, something with a Plexiglas windshield glinted in the sunlight. If the clouds hadn't parted just then, we'd have driven right past it.

"Whadda you think it is?" I asked trying to control the emotion in my voice.

"I'd bet my life it's the cockpit of a helicopter," the Ukrainian said, after a few seconds. "It's small, just a bubble cockpit, but hell, who cares? It's a helicopter."

My heart was beating so hard I thought it would fly out of my chest. If we could get that bird in the air, we'd have a chance to escape this hellhole.

"Perched up there, she seems to be in one piece," said Prit, peering into the lens. "But until we go up there, we won't know if she'll fly."

"Let's get in the building. We can knock the door down with the Centaur and then find the stairs to the roof."

Prit thought it over and said, "We'll barely fit between the columns on the portico, but I don't see any other option. Okay. Buckle up and hold on tight to Sarge. This is gonna shake a lot!"

Prit gunned the engine, steered the Centaur up the sidewalk with a bounce, and drove toward the door of the Prado at full speed. When we were just a couple of feet away, I realized that the space between the columns was way too narrow, but it was too late to change course. The tank's sides scraped against the columns with a horrible screech. The window on the right collapsed with an unearthly crash. When we rammed the door of the Prado Museum, chunks of granite the size of a washing machine had glanced off the shield on the turret, smashing it to bits.

For a few seconds, all you could hear was the patter of stones falling on the Centaur's roof. I felt like someone had yanked my guts out my mouth and then crammed them back in. My safety harness had held me against the seat, but under my wetsuit, I had one helluva bruise on my left shoulder.

"You okay?" Pritchenko's reassuringly calm voice came from down at my feet. The Ukrainian had unbuckled his safety harness and crawled toward the control panel.

"Just great. You?"

"I'm in one piece. Let's get outta here before any Undead figure out we're here."

I raised the hatch very carefully and stuck my head out. The front half of the tank was wedged inside the museum lobby. The back half was outside, buried under a huge pile of rubble and the toppled columns.

A chunk of the portico, the size of a small car, was lying next to the Centaur. If that piece of granite had fallen on us, the tank's armor wouldn't have saved us. We'd have been crushed to death.

The museum was cool, dark, and, most importantly, empty. There was no sign of survivors and not a fucking Undead in sight. That didn't mean there weren't any wandering around inside the building, but I'd bet my last cigarette no one—human or nonhuman—was in the Prado. The palatial building, with its thick stone walls and barred doors, was like a fortress. Prit and I were probably its first visitors since the quarantine was imposed.

I was relieved to see that the debris and the Centaur's chassis blocked the front door and would keep the Undead from getting in. I threw an arm around Sergeant Fernández's shoulders and lifted him up.

"Come on, Sergeant, hold on just a little longer. There's a helicopter on the roof and we're getting out of here."

"Save your breath," Prit said quietly, as he opened one of the sergeant's eyelids and looked at his pupil. "He's dead."

I gently settled the sergeant's body into the driver's seat. I remembered how he'd praised the Centaur in such glowing terms just minutes before Marcelo shot him. I had to admit that that tank was as superb as he'd said—and it had saved our lives. Now, that Centaur would be his coffin. I buttoned the collar of his blood-soaked jacket and wiped the dirt off his face. Sergeant Jonás Fernández had been very brave and he deserved a more dignified send-off.

I took one last look at the sergeant's body, then dragged one of the heavy backpacks out of the Centaur. Holding the other pack, Prit stood in front of the tank, a few feet from deserted ticket windows and piles of dust-covered brochures and museum guides, taking stock of the building.

"It's a shame about this place," Prit said pensively. "One day a fire'll burn half the city to the ground and no one'll be around to put it out. Everything in here will turn to ashes. It's a damn shame."

I stood there, silent for a moment. Then, on a whim, I sprinted into the building. Prit followed on my heels, confused.

"Where're you going? The stairs to the roof are the other way!"

"Just a second. Hand me your knife."

"My knife? Sure. But why?"

"I'll only be a minute, I promise." I grabbed Prit's knife.

My thoughts were racing. We could never save all those paintings, but at least we could take a couple. Out of that museum's vast collection, which ones should I take?

We came to the seventeenth-century galleries. The figures in Diego Velázquez's masterpiece, *Las Meninas*, looked down on us sadly from the wall as if they'd guessed that, someday soon, they'd be engulfed in flames. My heart fell when it occurred to me that those paintings were too big to carry, even if I took them out of their frames. Then, my eyes fell on a small painting in one corner.

It depicted a garden filled with cypresses. The plaque read MEDICI GARDENS IN ROME and below that, the artist's name, Diego Velázquez. In the background was an elegant white marble bridge with an arch in the middle, which had been carelessly boarded up. In a niche to the right, the statue of a Greek god pensively looked out at the viewer. In the foreground, some well-dressed men carried on a relaxed conversation. In his genius, the painter had captured a calm, quiet moment on a hot summer afternoon. Surrounded by majestic portraits of kings and queens who died centuries ago, that little painting stood out. It had more strength and life than the rest of the paintings in that room.

I grabbed the painting off the wall and laid it face down on a bench. Normally, that would've instantly triggered an alarm; a half-dozen armed guards would've surrounded me before I could draw a breath. Now, there was only silence as I used Prit's knife to pop out the staples that held the canvas in the frame. I carefully rolled the painting into a tube about forty inches long and only as wide as my index finger and stuck it into the empty sheath strapped to my thigh. Then I handed Prit his knife.

"Why'd you do that?" the Ukrainian asked.

"I had to. Those drugs in our backpacks are important, but this"—I helplessly pointed to the paintings around us—"this is just as important. It's our heritage, our legacy, the sum of who we are. When this is gone, in a few months or years, a part of us will be lost forever. Civilization won't shine quite as bright. We can't take all of those paintings, Prit, but we can save one."

"Okay," sighed the Ukrainian, dragging me by the arm toward the stairs. "But if we don't hurry, we'll share the fate of those paintings."

I gazed at the famous paintings one last time. Astride his rearing horse, Charles V bid us farewell with a cynical look on his face, as if he knew we were the last to walk through that room.

4 7

MADRID

We headed up the stairs tucked behind the guard booth. It was a narrow, very dark space; the only light filtered through a dirt-covered skylight. We eased up those stairs with Prit in the lead, knife in hand.

It took both of us to push open the bulletproof glass and steel door at the top. When we walked out onto the roof, we got a real shock. As far as the eye could see, tens of thousands of Undead surrounded the museum. I took a step back, my head spinning.

"My God . . . look at all of 'em!"

A chorus of groans rose when the crowd saw us head for the helicopter. We knew they couldn't reach us up there, but that sound set our teeth on edge.

We rushed around checking out the helicopter. It was painted white with no markings except for the registration number on its tail. That told us nothing about its owner or why or when he landed there, but there was no time to investigate. If he was dead, he didn't need it. If he was alive, well . . . he shouldn't have left the keys in the ignition.

Prit gave the bird a thorough going-over. "The battery's charged up. And it has about a quarter of a tank of fuel. That pilot was a really careful guy. Cross your fingers, amigo. If the engine starts, we'll be out of here in a couple of minutes."

The engine let out a yowl and the helicopter's blades slowly came to life. Compared to the Sokol or the SuperPuma, it looked very fragile, but Prit seemed satisfied with it. As he pushed the throttle, the blades picked up speed and we rose into the air.

"You did it, Prit! You did it! We're flying again! Where's your damn fatalism now?"

"Gone for good, I hope," was all the Ukrainian said, but a big smile showed under his mustache. "Gone for good. Now, if you don't mind, I've got a helicopter to fly."

With a gentle flick of my friend's wrist, the helicopter lifted into the air. We were finally on our way to Cuatro Vientos Airport.

The ruined city grew smaller and smaller behind us, until it finally disappeared. And then, there was silence again.

4 8

MADRID

The Airbus was resting at one end of the runway, its burnished metal glowing in the setting. We flew the helicopter over the plane a couple of times, but no one stuck his head out. If it weren't for the shiny fuselage, you'd have thought it'd been abandoned like all the other vehicles scattered across that runway.

"Look over there." Prit banked so I could see where he was pointing.

At the end of the runway was a pile of twisted metal that was still smoldering.

"It's one of the Buchones! Think the Froilists shot it down?" I shouted.

"Don't think so. The pilot probably crashed as he tried to land. Those birds weren't easy to handle, even in their heyday. Imagine all the things that could've failed after they'd sat in a museum for fifty years."

"I don't think the pilot survived," I muttered, grimly, staring at the burning pyre.

"Me, neither. But the important thing is not who's *dead* but who's *alive* down there."

With a final turn the helicopter started to descend. When we landed, Prit powered the engine down, but he didn't turn it off. If we had to make a break for it, it'd be better if the engine were running.

I got out and walked cautiously up to the Airbus. The interior lights were on and the giant airliner engines were running, as if they might take off any moment.

The door flew open and a nervous soldier pointed a rifle at us. "Halt! Who goes there?"

"Friends!" I shouted.

"Friends!" thundered the soldier. "Whose friends?"

From the sound of the guy's voice, I guessed he was really on edge, not a good thing when someone's pointing a gun at you. Throughout history, thousands of people have been killed by someone with a jumpy trigger finger, so I gave my answer some careful thought. There were two options—only one was correct.

"The republic!" I shouted, betting it all. "Friends of the republic!"

I held my breath, waiting to see if my bet paid off. If the Froilists had infiltrated the team in the plane, I expected a hail of bullets and death in the middle of the Cuatro Vientos runway. If Republicans were on board, we had a chance.

I saw the soldier relax and lower his gun. I nearly collapsed in the middle of the runway from the adrenaline rush. Heads or tails—and it came up heads. Again.

"Where's the rest of the team? Where's the commander!" the soldier shouted.

I could see the guy better now. He was very young, little more than a teenager. "We've got a group of Froilist infiltrators in here!"

"We know," I said wearily, as I picked up one of the bags Prit had dragged out of the helicopter. "We're the only ones left. Everybody else is dead, including Tank."

"They're all dead?" The boy nearly choked in fear. "Tank, too?"

"That's right," Pritchenko added. "Three heavily armed Froilists are headed this way in a tank with a really big gun. It's not a good idea to hang around."

"That's up to the pilot, I guess," the soldier replied with a shrug.

We quickly climbed onboard. Three bodies lay on the floor, covered with bloodstained blankets. A clenched fist stuck out from under one of the blankets.

"There were three of them?" Prit asked.

"Just two." The soldier shook his head. "The third guy's Ensign Barrios. He got one of them before they killed him."

A middle-aged lieutenant came out of the cockpit. Judging from his uniform, I guessed he was one of the pilots. We shook hands warmly.

"Be glad you got here when you did! An hour later and we would've left without you! We've been trying to get Tank on the radio for hours, but nobody answered. When those bastards tried to hijack the plane, I guessed the same thing had happened to the team on the ground."

"More or less," I said, remembering that the radio operator had plunged down the stairs. "Only in our case, the Froilists took over. They'll be here any minute. They're in a tank with a cannon that could blow this plane to pieces, Lieutenant."

"What're we waiting for?" The pilot hurried to the cockpit. "You can fill us in later. Now, let's get outta here!"

Exhausted, I fell into a seat, while the two surviving soldiers and the pilot closed the Airbus' door. Prit, buzzed on methamphetamines, slipped into the copilot's seat. His predecessor was smoldering in the wreckage of the Buchon. He declared loudly enough for everyone to hear that he wasn't going to ride back in the cabin.

A couple of minutes later, the Airbus rolled slowly down the runway. Its wing cast a brief shadow over hundreds of thousands of enraged Undead pressed against the other side of the fence. As the pilot made the final checks, I glanced out the windows, trying to make out the silhouette of the other Centaur coming down the road, but all I saw was an endless tide of Undead.

Discovering that the plane had left without them would probably be a death sentence for Marcelo, Pauli, and Broto. In the middle of nowhere, almost out of ammunition and provisions, their chances were slim. I felt bad for Broto, but he'd made his choice. Heads or tails. And he chose tails.

At least he has the bullet Marcelo gave him. Hope he has the guts to use it.

The Airbus' engines roared when the pilot gave it some gas. Amid a symphony of groans and creaks, the plane accelerated down the runway, shaking like crazy, then miraculously rose into the air, clearing the fence only by about two feet.

After ten minutes, the plane leveled off at five thousand feet and began the two-hour trip back to Tenerife. Too hopped up on speed, I couldn't sleep. I was elated to be alive and heading home. My mind wandered, thinking about the heroes' welcome we'd get. Prit had cleared his name, we had two backpacks with enough drugs to supply a pharmacy, and I had a beautiful girl waiting for me. Life was good.

I patted the Velázquez painting I'd rescued from the Prado Museum, picturing Lucia's astonished face when I gave her that painting to hang on our living room wall. Satisfied, I smiled and curled up in my seat. She'd be thrilled.

4 9

TENERIFE

"Hey! What the hell's going on down there?" asked the pimple-faced, young soldier as our plane made its approach into Tenerife North Airport.

The flight had gone smoothly. We'd had nice, early summer weather all the way. Exhausted but smiling, Prit and I slapped each other on the back as the plane came to a stop. But then that question got our attention.

"What's happening?" I asked as I looked out the window.

No one answered. Everyone was too engrossed in the scene below. The airport looked like an anthill some naughty little boy had kicked over. A long convoy of military trucks filed out of the base; packed like sardines into each truck were dozens of grim-faced soldiers rushing here and there, armed to the teeth.

"That doesn't look good," Prit whispered to me. He looked worried as he watched out the window.

"Maybe it's a drill or maneuvers," I said, trying to be nonchalant.

"I don't think that's it," said the Ukrainian. "Look at all those trucks. Given the fuel shortage, moving that many vehicles is a drain on supplies. No, this must be something big. Really big."

We didn't have to wonder for long. A set of stairs were rolled up to the Airbus and then the doors flew opened. Before we could deplane, a group of heavily armed soldiers covered in hazmat suits entered the cabin.

My first thought was, *Dammit, not again!* But then I calmed down. The soldiers seemed friendly, not hostile. After carefully checking out everyone onboard to make sure we weren't a bunch of slobbering Undead, they lowered their weapons and took off their helmets. Everyone relaxed.

"Welcome back, boys," the commanding officer said, wiping his forehead with the back of his hand. "You picked a fine time to come back. It's hot as hell and we're on high alert."

"What the hell's going on?" asked Prit.

"We have reports that Froilists have attacked Tenerife Hospital. The situation seems to be under control, but apparently there're dozens of dead."

"Prit!" I grabbed his arm. "The hospital! Lucia and Sister Cecilia!"

"What happened exactly?" asked the Ukrainian, as he motioned for me to calm down. "How many casualties?"

"Nobody's sure," said the officer, taken aback by Prit's military-style interrogation. "Some think their target was the hospital's lab, but I think they wanted to rob the pharmacy. Drugs are worth a fortune these days."

He cast a greedy glance at the bulging backpacks lying in the aisle.

"What happened? You brought back just those two backpacks? Where's that old SOB, Tank?"

Nobody said a word. The officer's expression changed to disbelief.

"Tank? Dead?" He stammered, shaking his head. "What about the rest of the team? So it's just you guys? Fuck! What the hell happened out there?"

"Froilists," Prit said quietly. "Same as here."

"Shit!" The officer pounded his fist on the plane's bulkhead. "This fucking civil war's going to finish off the few of us those Undead didn't get. Hell! We don't need an infection to exterminate the human race—we'll do it ourselves!"

I leaned in close, as his men escorted the rest of Tank's team off the plane. "Sir, we've got to get home as soon as possible. My girlfriend works at the hospital and we have a friend being treated there. We need to know ... "

"There's a procedure we've got to follow," said the officer, bluntly. "Seven day quarantine for the entire team. You were informed of that before you left."

I tried to contain my impatience. I couldn't wait seven days. Or even an hour. Something was terribly wrong. I could feel it. I needed to find Lucia and Sister Cecilia right away.

"Listen, officer," I said, pulling him aside, "I just need an hour to make sure she's okay. One lousy hour. I'll be back before anyone misses me. Swear to God."

"You know I can't do that. We'd both get in big trouble if anyone found out."

"No one'll find out, I swear," I said as I searched my pockets.

I finally found what I was looking for—a half-dozen boxes of antibiotics I'd stuffed in my pocket back at the supply room. That little stash was worth a fortune in Tenerife. The officer's eyes grew wide when he saw what I was offering him. I'd planned to sell it on the black market, but getting out of there was an emergency.

"One hour, not a minute more," the officer muttered, as he slipped the boxes in his pockets. "If you're not back in an hour, I'll report that you two escaped. Then the problem will be on your shoulders. They'll shoot to kill, you know."

"I'll take that chance." I grabbed a Glock and stuck it in my belt.

"We'll both take that chance," Prit said, grabbing one of the HKs.

"Thanks, Prit, but you don't have to come. This is my concern. I've got a bad feeling Lucia needs me now, not in a week. I hope I'm wrong because if they pick us up out there, we'll be in deep shit. God knows you've got enough problems of your own."

"Cut the crap! I'm going with you and that's that. So, let's move. We've only got an hour to get there and back."

I gave the Ukrainian a grateful look and resisted the urge to hug him. What a friend!

We rushed out of the plane as the officer trotted toward the quarantine area in the terminal. I had no idea how he'd justify our absence, but I was sure he had the situation under control, at least for that hour. People like him always manage somehow.

After five minutes of furious negotiation (and trading two more boxes of antibiotics, which quickly disappeared into the right pockets), Prit and I were perched on a pile of scrap metal in the back of an asthmatic truck headed for Tenerife, its driver terribly pleased with his unexpected fortune.

The trip took forever. The closer we got to town, the stronger my hunch got. We passed through all the extra checkpoints without a hitch. At one, the officer in charge told us they were tracking a woman, a Froilist spy who'd taken part in the assault on the hospital, but gave no details.

"Whadda you think, Prit?"

My friend suddenly looked tired. "I don't like this one bit. I hope we find Lucia soon. In case you hadn't noticed, those people are paranoid and armed to the teeth. Out of the blue, some nut job could lose it and start shooting. Then we'd be in big trouble."

"You're right. I hope Lucia's someplace safe."

Five minutes later the truck came to a more heavily manned checkpoint. Soldiers and the police had parked a couple of tanks sideways and set up a machine gun nest.

The truck driver talked briefly with the officer in charge. "Here's where you get out. The entire area within a thousand feet of the hospital has been evacuated and no one can go through."

"Why? What the hell happened?" I asked as we climbed out of the truck.

"Not sure," said the driver, looking really scared. "Apparently the Froilists attacked a medical lab. They might've released some kind of germ. Didn't those people learn anything from what TSJ did? Only an idiot would rob a lab, for God's sake."

Muttering under his breath, the driver lit a cigarette, his hands shaking. On the seat of his truck, he set a poster that the officer at the checkpoint had given him. With a terrible sense of dread, I reached over and picked it up.

It was a blurry photocopy of an ID. Below the picture, in bold letters, was the word *WANTED*. It warned anyone who saw the woman in the picture not to go near her and to contact the military.

I handed the poster to Prit, without saying a word. A cold sweat ran down my back as a sense of doom came over me.

The woman in the poster was Lucia.

5 0

I have no idea how we got through that checkpoint. My mind had shut down, so it was all a blur.

Lucia, a Froilist spy. That was impossible, for God's sake! My girl-friend couldn't have cared less about politics. Hell, she didn't even know all the details of the problem. If she'd gotten involved, wouldn't she have told me? All those ideas whirled through my mind.

"Hey! Wake up!" Prit snapped his fingers in front of my eyes. "I get it—you're overwhelmed, but if you really want to help Lucia and Sister Cecilia, you'd better get it together. Those two need us to be at the top of our game. Agreed?"

I took a deep breath. "Of course, dammit! What're we gonna do?"

"First, find Lucia. Then clear things up, if we can."

"How do you suggest we find her in all this chaos?" I said, pointing to the riot troops that just drove up. "Half the island's looking for her and the other half thinks the fucking Froilists are invading."

"Let's start at the most logical place—our home."

We didn't have much choice, so I agreed. At first the truck driver flatly refused to take us to our home in the hotel. After a brief talk with Prit away from prying eyes, he became more cooperative. I'd guess the nick on his neck from Prit's knife had something to do with his sudden change of attitude.

I was not surprised to find a URO parked outside our building. A couple of soldiers lounged against the hood, while another soldier was sitting in the driver's seat, reading a well-thumbed girly magazine.

"They're on the lookout for her," I whispered to the Ukrainian. "Lucia wouldn't come here with those guys hanging around."

"Well, they're sure not going to find her sitting on the couch reading Tolstoy, idiot," Prit said, as he got out of the truck. "Maybe we can find something in there to clear things up."

The soldiers barely glanced at us as we entered the building. They were looking for a seventeen-year-old brunette, not a tall, skinny guy with a pained look on his face or a short guy with a blond mustache.

As we walked through the doorway, the door flew open and someone stuck her head outside. Just in time, I grabbed Pritchenko's shirt and dragged him behind a dusty flowerpot with a plant big enough to hide behind. The open door cast a rectangle of light along with the smell of cooked cabbage.

I recognized the block leader, an old gossip I'd always distrusted. The woman squinted as she scanned the dark lobby. Most of the light bulbs had burned out months ago and no one had replaced them.

"Who's there?" she chirped.

Prit and I held our breath. If that snitch saw us, she'd raise the alarm and we'd have to explain ourselves to the guards stationed in front.

After a tense moment, that old biddy turned, muttered something under her breath, and went back into her lair.

We made it through the lobby and to the stairs without crossing paths with our neighbors. The soldiers at the front door must've scared everyone off, as we didn't see a soul on the stairs that were usually crowded.

When we reached our floor, I wasn't surprised to find the front door broken down. They'd given our home a thorough going-over. It looked like a tornado had hit it. Nothing was spared. They'd even ripped up the mattresses and cushions, searching for God-knows-what. My heart sank. If Lucia had left us a clue, they'd have found it.

Out of the corner of my eye, I saw something rush through the door. Instinctively, I drew my pistol, but then I heard a pitiful meow coming from an orange blur.

"Lucullus!" I shouted as my cat bounded over to me. When I picked him up, I could tell he'd put on some weight. I scratched his belly and he purred ecstatically.

Lucullus shot me an angry look when I stopped petting him. I looked closely at his collar. All his life, he'd worn a black flea collar. Now strapped around his neck was a strip of red leather I knew well. It wasn't a collar; it was a bracelet I'd given Lucia.

My hands shook as I unfastened the bracelet and turned it over, with Pritchenko peering over my shoulder. Just one word was written on the back in Lucia's handwriting, a word only Prit and I would understand: *Corinth*.

5 1

It took us nearly two hours to reach the port of Tenerife. We had to do some tricky maneuvers to get out of the building without anyone seeing us, and to give the checkpoints a wide berth.

"It's just a matter of time till someone links us to Lucia and starts circulating our photos, too," Prit said.

I agreed. Plus, the hour the officer at the airport had granted us had long since expired. Prit and I were now deserters and fugitives. It wasn't the triumphant welcome I'd pictured, but at least we were alive—and free.

By the time we reached the docks, we'd come up with a plan. We guessed that Lucia had hidden out in one of the boats anchored there. Only we knew about the *Corinth*, the boat I'd sailed to Vigo where I met Prit. Lucia's cryptic message had to mean she was hiding on a sailboat . . . but which one? Surely she'd left us another clue, one that wasn't too obvious.

When we reached the docks, our spirits fell. There were hundreds of sailboats anchored among dozens of rusting freighters and warships. Thousands of refugees had trickled in on those boats. When fuel became scarce, the government organized a fishing fleet that went out every morning to feed the hungry masses packed on Tenerife.

For a boat lover like me, it was painful to see those thoroughbreds of the wind buried in nets, fishing gear, and traps. But people had to eat. No matter how hard I looked, I couldn't spot a boat like the *Corinth* under all that gear.

"What now? Which one's she in?" Prit nervously asked. From our hiding spot between containers stacked on the pier, we watched dock workers head to work.

"If I knew, we wouldn't be standing around wasting time," I snapped. I struggled to hold on to Lucullus, who kept trying to launch himself out of my arms. My mind raced as my eyes searched for a sign. None of those boats reminded me of the *Corinth*.

I was about to give up when I spotted a small sailboat anchored at the end of the pier. I blinked several times to make sure my eyes weren't playing tricks on me. Then I smiled. Flying from the top of her mast like a flag was a faded, old wetsuit.

5 2

The *Crocodile II* was an old twenty-four-foot sailboat. Once upon a time, she must have been a real gem, but when Prit and I rowed up in a dinghy, it was clear that she was pretty run down. You could tell from her teak decking and elegant steel fittings that her original owner had really lavished her with love, but all those months used as a fishing boat in less careful hands had taken its toll.

The rigging was a mess and damp lines were strewn around the deck. The bow was almost buried under a thick layer of nets— all shapes and sizes—that smelled of rotting fish. If Lucia had taken refuge there, it was an excellent choice. No one would've boarded that floating trash heap.

We rowed alongside the *Crocodile II* and climbed aboard. The deck was in complete disrepair. The front half of the cabin had been transformed into a hold for their catch. Peering in the cabin door, all I could see were white plastic crates stacked every which way and a filthy mattress tossed on the deck.

"No one's here," Prit said despondently. "I don't think . . . "

Before he could finish, Lucullus jumped aboard the *Crocodile II* and took off like a shot between the crates. There was a muffled yelp of surprise and suddenly, a hand I knew so well pushed aside a stack of crates.

Standing before us, petting a contented Lucullus, looking at us through tears of relief was Lucia.

I grabbed her hands. Not saying a word, she squeezed mine as tight as she could. We stood there, speechless, until Prit coughed to get our attention.

"Sorry to interrupt this reunion, but we've got a lot to do. They're looking for us and we don't know how Sister Cecilia is. Maybe we should—"

"Oh, Prit," Lucia dropped my hands and hugged the Ukrainian. Her pained voice broke and she started to cry. "Prit, I'm so sorry. They killed her right in front of me. It was horrible."

"Calm down. Calm down," Pritchenko managed to say, as he gave her a clumsy pat on the back. The Ukrainian was as pale as a ghost, his eyes like two black marbles. I knew my friend, and whoever killed the nun had earned a mortal enemy.

Lucia pulled away from Prit and leaned on me, sobbing, as she described the nightmare she'd lived through over the past two days, from the time she entered the hospital until she took refuge in that boat.

"How'd you know no one would find you on this boat? What about her crew?" I asked as I held her tight.

"They were admitted to the hospital for botulism. They ate some rancid canned food," Lucia managed to say between sobs. "They were patients on my wing. I knew no one would come around for at least fifteen days."

"What if we hadn't found you? What would you've done?"

Lucia stopped crying. A sad smile lit up her face and she gave me a long kiss. "I was sure you'd come," she said, calmly looking me in my eye. "I never doubted you for a minute. Nothing in the world—not human or Undead—can stop you."

I hugged her tight. I'd never let any harm come to her.

I turned to Prit, who was sitting on the cabin stairs, crestfallen, his arms folded. Not only had he lost his best friend, he'd been robbed of the chance to get revenge. I knelt beside him. "Prit, don't fall apart now. We need you, old friend. We're comrades-in-arms, remember?"

The Ukrainian raised his glassy eyes. I saw a spark of life in the back of his eyes. "*Fatalism*," he said, with a bitter smile.

"*Fatalism*," I answered, returning his smile. "But I promise we'll make sure that changes very soon."

5 3

Five hours later, as the sun was coming up, the Tenerife fishing fleet set sail for the traps they'd set a few nautical miles away. From the shore, the sight of hundreds of sailboats spreading their sails on a dimly lit sea was unforgettable.

A veteran sailor might've noticed that the rigging of one of the boats was pulled tight on the leeward side, as if she were in a race. Her crew was scurrying around on deck, tying down loose ends.

Two hours later, when the boats reached the fishing ground, the same sailboat didn't cast her nets like all the rest. Instead, the crew let out the spinnaker in the morning breeze and set sail for Gran Canaria. No one in the fleet noticed as the boat pulled away.

She grew smaller and smaller on the horizon.

And finally disappeared.

5 4

SOMEWHERE TWO MILES OFF
THE COAST OF SENEGAL

Twelve-year-old Marcel Mbalo and his fourteen-year-old cousin, Yayah, had gone out on their fishing boat very early that morning to catch the trade winds at dawn. Although their long, dug-out canoe had an old noisy outboard motor, his uncle had forbidden them to use it unless it was an emergency, since the village had almost no gas left. So Yayah and Marcel had to paddle hard every morning to get past the surf at the beach and then let out the sails to reach their fishing ground.

Marcel thought it was an exciting life. A year ago, the men of the village would never have allowed two children to fish alone in one of their beautiful boats, but now there was no alternative. Most of the men had been forced to serve in the army when the demons from hell had taken possession of the souls of the living. None of those men had returned, so there were hardly any working-age adults left in the village.

The few who remained kept watch night and day at the small bridge over the marshes, the only access to N'Gor peninsula, where the village was located. Marcel's uncle said that being so isolated was a blessing from Allah, but Marcel and Yayah didn't understand what the advantages were, living in such a remote place, hundreds of miles from the nearest town. There were about two hundred men, women, and children in their village. They lived off those fish and the crops they grew outside of town. No one went hungry, but they couldn't afford any luxuries. At night, they all slept in the old school, which everyone thought was fun.

Yayah manned the tiller, while Marcel tightened the boat's small triangular sail that propelled their canoe. His mind was wandering over the horizon when he spotted a white dot in the distance. That white dot turned out to be a sailboat approaching fast.

Marcel pointed out the sailboat to Yayah. Under those circumstances, an older, more cautious man would've sailed away from any stranger, but Marcel and Yayah were just teenagers with no sense of danger. Their curiosity got the better of them and they let their canoe drift toward the boat.

When they were about three hundred feet from the sailboat, Marcel unconsciously reached for his *gri-gris*, the amulet that hung around his neck to ward off demons. That boat scared him.

The vessel looked like it had been through a ferocious storm. The mast was broken in half and its cockpit was flooded with seawater. With no one to control it, the rudder rolled freely, driven by the wind. There wasn't a soul onboard.

Marcel called out a few times, but no one came on deck. When Yayah brought the canoe alongside the sailboat, Marcel jumped aboard, clutching the machete he used to cut the heads off fish.

The little fisherman immediately wanted to turn and run away from that ruined, sinister boat, but his older cousin was watching. If he let on that he was afraid, he'd have to endure the taunts of the other children in the village. He took a deep breath and pushed open the cabin door.

The cabin looked deserted. A black assault rifle lay on the table next to a large knife. Marcel trod carefully across a carpet of broken glass. Spread out on one of the seats was a painting that caught his attention. It was a garden landscape with a statue and some white men talking in the foreground. Marcel thought the painting was ugly, so he tossed it onto the floor, where it floated face down in seawater.

After checking out every inch of the deserted cabin, he picked up the assault rifle and knife and started out. Satisfied with his haul, picturing Yayah's face when he saw all that loot, he took one last look inside the abandoned boat.

In a corner, hanging from a hook attached to the ceiling was an old wetsuit, watching him, swaying to the rhythm of the waves.

TELL THE WORLD THIS BOOK WAS

GOOD	BAD	SO-SO

ACKNOWLEDGMENTS

It is very hard to mention, in just a few lines, everyone who has been part of this adventure called *Apocalypse Z*. So many people helped make this possible.

First my wife and family, for their endless patience, love, and understanding in those moments when I ran aground on the reefs of bewilderment.

Of course, Juan Gómez-Jurado, my friend and fellow writer who opened doors, guided me through the rough parts, and illuminated paths that would have otherwise remained hidden to me. I know I can never repay my debt to him. He has been my Pritchenko (but without the mustache).

Of course, Emilia Lope, at Random House Mondadori, not only for her caring, patience, and understanding, but also for believing in this project and supporting it. Emilia: You're fantastic and without you this would not have been possible.

And the hundreds of thousands of readers on the Internet who always conveyed their warm support and encouragement and who watched this story grow, step by step, from a blog to a short story published in an obscure Internet website into a series of books. Reader: You now have the second volume in your hands. This book, like the previous one, is as much yours as mine.

ABOUT THE AUTHOR

An international bestselling author, Manel Loureiro was born in Pontevedra, Spain, and studied law at Universidad de Santiago de Compostela. After graduation, he worked in television, both on-screen (appearing on Television de Galicia) and behind the scenes as a writer. *Apocalypse Z: The Beginning of the End*, his first novel, began as a popular blog before its publication, eventually becoming a best seller in several countries, including Spain, Italy, Brazil, and the United States. Called "the Spanish Stephen King" by *La Voz de Galicia*, Manel has written three novels in the Apocalypse Z series. He currently resides in Pontevedra, Spain, where, in addition to writing, he is still a practicing lawyer.

ABOUT THE TRANSLATOR

Pamela Carmell received a Translation Award from the National Endowment for the Arts to translate *Oppiano Licario* by José Lezama Lima. Her publications include Matilde Asensi's *The Last Cato* (HarperCollins), Belkis Cuza Malé's *Woman on the Front Lines* (sponsored by the Witter Bynner Foundation for Poetry), Antonio Larreta's *The Last Portrait of the Duchess of Alba* (a Book-of-the-Month Club selection), and the short-story collection, *Cuba on the Edge*. Her translations of poetry by Nancy Morejón is forthcoming from Cubanabooks. She is also published widely in literary magazines and anthologies.